# 吉祥子：孟加拉民间故事集

## FOLK-TALES OF BENGAL

[印] 戴博诃利 著

许地山 译

时代文艺出版社

图书在版编目（CIP）数据

吉祥子：孟加拉民间故事集/(印)戴博诃利 著；许地山 译.
—长春：时代文艺出版社，2012.8（2021.5重印）

ISBN 978-7-5387-4105-6

I. ①吉… Ⅱ. ①戴…②许… Ⅲ. ①民间故事－作品集－孟加拉国 Ⅳ. ①I354.73

中国版本图书馆CIP数据核字（2012）第151381号


出 品 人　陈　琛
责任编辑　付　娜
装帧设计　孙　俪
排版制作　隋淑凤

# 吉祥子：孟加拉民间故事集

[印] 戴博诃利 著　　许地山 译

出版发行 / 时代文艺出版社
地址 / 长春市福祉大路5788号　龙腾国际大厦A座15层　邮编 / 130118
总编办 / 0431-81629751　发行部 / 0431-81629755
官方微博 / weibo.com / tlapress　天猫旗舰店 / sdwycbsgf.tmall.com
印刷 / 保定市铭泰达印刷有限公司
开本 / 640×980毫米　1 / 20　字数 / 171千字　印张 / 15.5
版次 / 2012年9月第1版　印次 / 2021年5月第2次印刷　定价 / 49.80元

# 出版说明

　　本书是印度作家戴博诃利1833年创作的东印度民间故事的集子"Folk-Tales of Bengal"，许地山翻译为《孟加拉民间故事》。原书为单册本，本次出版按照新的编排方式，拆分为两集。为了纪念许地山先生，本书仍然保留其《孟加拉民间故事》的译法，将第一集改为《吉祥子：孟加拉民间故事集》，第二集改为《新月王子：孟加拉民间故事集》。

　　许地山在宗教学、印度哲学、梵文、人类学、民俗学等方面的造诣颇深，而且他十分崇敬印度的"诗圣"泰戈尔，所以他对印度的宗教、哲学、民俗和文学也格外感兴趣，为此他还翻译了一大批印度文学著作，其中就包括这本具有"传播民俗学"价值的《孟加拉民间故事》。其实，许地山翻译这本书，不只是为了学术目的，更重要的是为了满足"爱读故事的芝子"。许地山和妻子周俟松（字芝子）的感情是令人羡慕的，周俟松爱看故事，许地山就专门为心爱的妻子翻译了此书。许地山曾对周俟松说："泰戈尔是我的知音长者，你是我知音的妻子，我是很幸福的，得一知音可以无恨矣。"两人的共同生活虽然只有12年，却胜似百年。

本书选择的是20世纪英国最杰出的插图画家之一——沃里克·戈布尔（Warwick Goble）的插图，他对东方绘画情有独钟，他的绘画技法也深受东方绘画的影响，所以他创作的东方民间故事插图更富有东方的异域特色，更能体现其民族风情，其唯美艳丽的画风与本书浪漫积极的基调也非常契合。

本书是1929年商务印书馆初版之后的首次简体中文彩图本出版，并且首次采用了中文和英语的双语版本，以满足读者的不同阅读口味，为读者尽心呈现绝美的阅读和视觉的盛宴。

# 译　序

　　戴博诃利（Lal Behari Day）的《孟加拉民间故事》（Folk-Tales of Bengal）出版于一八八三年，是东印度民间故事的小集子。著者的自序中说他在一个小村里，每夜听村里最擅于说故事的女人讲故事。人家叫她做三菩的母亲。著者从小时便听了许多，可是多半都忘记了。这集子是因为他朋友的请求而采集的。他从一个孟加拉女人那里听得了不少，这集子的大部分就是从她所说的记下来。集中还有两段是从一个老婆罗门人那里听来的；三段是从一个理发匠那里听来的；两段是从著者的仆人那里听来的；还有几段是另一位婆罗门人为他讲的。著者听了不少别的故事，他以为都是同一故事的另样讲法，所以没有采集进来。这集子只有二十二段故事，据著者说，很可以代表孟加拉村中的老婆子历来对孩子们所讲的故事。

正统的孟加拉讲故事的村婆子，到讲完一段故事以后，必要念一段小歌。歌词是：

我的故事说到这里算完了，

那提耶也枯萎了。

那提耶呵，你为什么枯萎呢？

你的牛为什么要我用草来喂它？

牛呵，你为什么要人喂？

你的牧者为什么不看护我？

牧者呵，你为什么不去看牛？

你的儿媳妇为什么不把米给我？

儿媳妇呵，你为什么不给米呢？

我的孩子为什么哭呢？

孩子呵，你为什么哭呢？

蚂蚁为什么要咬我呢？

蚂蚁呵，你为什么要咬人呢？

喀！喀！喀！

为什么每讲完一段必要念这一段，我们不知道，即如歌中词句的关系和意义也很难解释。著者以为这也许是说故事的在说完之后，故意念出这一段无意义的言词，为的是使听的孩子们感到一点兴趣。

　　这译本是依一九一二年麦美伦公司的本子译的。我并没有逐字逐句直译，只把各故事的意思率直地写出来。至于原文的词句，在译文中时有增减，因为翻译民间故事只求其内容明了就可以，不必如其余文章要逐字斟酌。我译述这二十二段故事的动机，一来是因为我对"民俗学"（Folk-Lore）的研究很有兴趣，觉得中国有许多民间故事是从印度辗转流入的，多译些印度的故事，对于研究中国民俗学必定很有帮助；二来是因为今年春间芝子问我要小说看，我自己许久没动笔了，一时也写不了许多，不如就用两三个月的工夫译述一二十段故事来给她看，更能使她满足。

　　民俗学者认为民间故事是重要的研究材料。凡未有文字，或有文字而不甚通行的民族，他们的理智的奋勉大体有四种是从嘴里说出来的。这四种便是故事、歌谣、格言（谚语）和谜语。这些都是人类对于民间故事的推理、记忆、想象等，最早的奋勉，所以不能把它们忽略掉。

故事是从往代传说下来的。一件事情，经十个人说过，在古时候就可以变成一段故事，所以说"十口为古"。故事便是"古"，讲故事便是"讲古"，故事的体例，最普遍的便是起首必要说，"从前有……（什么什么）"，或"古时……（怎样怎样）"。如果把古事分起类来，大体可以分为神话、传说、野乘三种。神话（Myths）是"解释的故事"，就是说无论故事的内容多么离奇难信，说的和听的人对于它们都没有深切的信仰，不过用来说明宇宙、生死等等现象，人兽、男女等等分别，礼仪、风俗等等源流而已。传说（Legends）是"叙述的故事"，它并不一定要解释一种事物的由来，只要叙述某种事物的经过。无论它的内容怎样，说的和听的对于它都信为实事，如关于一个民族的移植、某城的建设、某战争的情形，都是属于这一类。它与神话还有显然不同之处，就是前者的主人多半不是人类，后者每为历史的人物。自然，传说中的历史的人物，不必是真正历史，所说某时代有某人，也许在那个时代并没有那人，或者那人的生时，远在所说时代的前后也可以附会上去。凡传说都是说明某个大人物或英雄曾经做过的事迹，我们可以约略分它为两类，一类是英雄故事（Hero-Tales），一类是英雄行传（Sagas）。英雄故事只说某时代有一个英雄怎样出世，对于他或她所做的事并无详细的记载。英雄行传就不然，它的内容是细述一个英雄一生的事业和品性。那位英雄或者是一个历史上的人物，说的人将许多功绩和伟业加在他身上。学者虽然这样分，但英雄故事和英雄行传的分别到底是不甚明了的。术语上的"野乘"是用德文的"M-rchen"："它包括童话（Nursery-Tales）、神仙故事（Fairy-Tales）及民间故事或野语（Folk-Tales）三种。"它与英雄故事及英雄行传不同之处在于，第一点，它不像传说那么认真，故事的主人常是没有名字的，说者只说"从前有一个人……（怎样怎样）"或"往时有一个王……（如此如彼）"，对于那个人、那个王的名字可以不必提起；第二点，它是不记故事发生的时间与空间的；第三点，它的内容是有一定的格式和计划的，人一听了头一两段，几乎就可以知道结局是怎样的。传说中的故事，必有人名、时间、地点，并且没有一定的体例，事情到什么光景就说到什么光景。

从古代遗留下来的故事，学者分它们为认真说与游戏说两大类，神话和传说属于前一类，野语是属于后一类的。在下级文化的民族中，就不这样看，他们以神话和传说为神圣，为一族生活的历史源流，有时禁止说故事的人随意叙说。所以在他们当中，凡认真说的故事都是神圣的故事，甚至有时只在冠礼时长老为成年人述说，外人或常人是不容听见的。至于他们在打猎或耕作以后在村中对妇孺说的故事只为娱乐，不必视为神圣，所以相对于神圣的故事而言，我们可以名它做庸俗的故事。

庸俗的故事，即是野语，在文化的各时期都可以产生出来。它虽然是为娱乐而说，可是那率直的内容很有历史的价值存在。我们从它可以看出一个时代的社会风尚、思想和习惯。它是一段一段的人间社会史。研究民间故事的分布和类别，在社会人类学中是一门很重要的学问。因为那些故事的内容与体例不但是受过环境的陶冶，并且带着很浓厚的民族色彩。在各民族中，有些专会说解释的故事，有些专会说训诫或道德的故事，有些专会说神异的故事，彼此一经接触，便很容易互相传说，互相采用，用各族的环境和情形来修改那些外来的故事，使成为己有。民族间的接触不必尽采用彼此的风俗习惯，可是彼此的野乘很容易受同化。野乘常比神话和传说短，并且注重道德的教训，常寓一种训诫，所以这类故事常缩短为寓言（Fables）。寓言常以兽类的品性抽象地说明人类的道德关系，其中每含有滑稽成分，使听者发噱。为方便起见，学者另分野乘为禽语（Beast-Tales）、谐语（Drolls）、集语（Cumulative Tales）及喻言（Apologues）四种。在禽语中的主人是会说人话的禽兽。这种故事多见于初期的文化民族中。在各民族的禽兽中，所选的主人、禽兽各有不同，大抵是与当地当时的生活环境多有接触的动物。初人并没有觉得动物种类的不同，所以在故事中，象也可以同家鼠说话，公鸡可以请狐狸来做宾客，诸如此类，都可以看出他们的识别力还不很强。可是从另一方面说这种禽语很可以看出初民理智活动的表现方法。谐语是以诙谐为主的。故事的内容每以愚人为主人，述说他们的可笑行为。集语的内容和别的故事一样，不同的只在体例。它常在叙述一段故事将达到极盛点的时候，必要复述全段的故事一遍再往下说。喻言都是道德的故事，借譬喻来说明一条道理的，所以它与格言很相近。喻言与寓言有点不同。前者多注重道德的教训，后者多注重真理的发明。在低级文化的民族中常引这种喻言为法律上的事例，在法庭上可以引来判断案件。野乘的种类大体是如此，今为明了起见，特把前此所述的列出一个表来。

我们有了这个表，便知道这本书所载的故事是属于哪一类的。禽语的例如《豺媒》，谐语如《二窃贼》，喻言如《三王子》、《阿芙蓉》等是。

孟加拉民间故事的体例，在这本书中也可以看出它们有禽语、谐语、集语、喻言四种成分，不过很不单纯，不容易类别出来。故事的主人多半是王、王子和婆罗门人。从内容方面说，每是王、王子，或婆罗门人遇见罗刹或其他鬼灵，或在罗刹国把一个王女救出来，多半是因结婚关系而生种种悲欢离合的事。做坏事的人常要被活埋掉。在这二十二段故事中，除了《二窃贼》及《阿芙蓉》以外，多半的结局是团圆的，美满的。

在这本故事里有许多段是讲罗刹的。罗刹与药叉或夜叉有点不同。夜叉（Yaksa)是一种半神的灵体，住在空中，不常伤害人畜。罗刹（Rakshasa）男声作罗刹娑，女声作罗叉私（Rakshasi）。"罗刹"此言"暴恶"，"可畏"，"伤害者"，"能瞰鬼"等。佛教的译家将这名字与夜叉相混，但在印度文学中这两种鬼怪的性质显有不同的地方。罗刹本是古代印度的土人，有些书籍载他们是，黑身，赤发，绿眼的种族。在印度亚利安人初入印度的时候，这种人盘踞着南方的森林使北印度与德干（Deccan）隔绝。他们是印度亚利安人的劲敌，所以在《吠陀》里说他们是地行鬼，是人类的仇家。《摩诃婆罗多》书中说他们的性质是凶恶的，他们的身体呈黄褐色，具有坚利的牙齿，常染血污。他们的头发是一团一团组起来的。他们的腿很长，有五只脚。他们的指头都是向后长的。他们的咽喉作蓝色，腹部很大，声音凶恶，容易发怒，喜欢挂铃铛在身上。他们最注重的事情便是求食。平常他们所吃的东西是人家打过喷嚏不能再吃的食物，有虫或虫咬过的东西，人所遗下来的东西，和被眼泪渗染过的东西。他们一受胎，当天就可以生产。他们可以随意改变他们的形状。他们在早晨最有力量，在破晓及黄昏时最能施行他们的欺骗伎俩。

在民间故事中，罗刹常变形为人类及其他生物。他们的呼吸如风。身手可以伸长到十由旬（约八十英里，参看本书《骨原》）。他们从嗅觉知道一个地方有没有人类。平常的人不能杀他们，如果把他们的头砍掉，从脖子上立刻可以再长一个出来。他们的国土常是很丰裕的，地点常在海洋的对岸。这大概是因为锡兰岛往时也被看为罗刹所住的缘故。罗刹女也和罗刹男一样喜欢吃人。她常化成美丽的少女在路边迷惑人，有时占据城市强迫官民献人畜为她的食品。她们有时与人类结婚，生子和人一样。

今日的印度人，信罗刹是住在树上的，如果人在夜间经过树下冲犯了他们就要得呕吐及不消化的病。他们最贪食，常迷惑行人。如果人在吃东西的时候，灯火忽然灭了，这时的食物每为罗刹抢去，所以得赶快用手把吃的遮住。人如遇见他们，时常被他们吃掉，幸亏他们是很愚拙的，如尊称他们为"叔叔"或"姑母"等，他们就很喜欢，现出亲切的行为，不加伤害。印度现在还有些人信恶性的异教徒死后会变罗刹。在孟加拉地方，这类的罗刹名叫"曼多"（Māmdo），大概是从阿拉伯语"曼督"（Mamdūh），意为"崇敬""超越"，而来。

这本故事常说到天马（Pakshiraj），依原文当译为"鸟王"。这种马是有翅膀能够在空中飞行的。它在地上走得非常快，一日之中可以跑几万里。

印度的民间故事常说到王和婆罗门人。但他们的"王"并不都是统治者，凡拥有土地的富户也可以被称为王或罗阇，所以《豺媒》里的织匠也可以因富有而自称为王。王所领的地段只限于他所属所知道的，因此，印度古代许多王都不是真正的国王，"王"不过是一个徽号而已。

此外还有许多事实从野乘学的观点看来是很有趣味的。所以这书的译述多偏重于学术方面，至于译语的增减和文辞修饰只求达意，工拙在所不计。

　　　　　　　　　　　　　　　　许地山

　　　　十七年六月六日　海甸朗润园

　　　　　赠与爱读故事的芝子

# 目　录
## CONTENTS

一
死
新
郎

从前有一位王，他有两位王妃，一位名叫憎，一位名叫爱。两位王妃都没有子息。有一天，一个乞士行到宫门来求布施。爱妃便捧了一掬米到门口要将它施舍给乞士。那乞士于是问她有没有子息。爱妃回答没有，那乞士便不受她的布施，因为从没有儿孙福分的女人手中所得的东西都是不洁净的。那乞士因为感谢她的诚意，便给她一种生育的良药。爱妃自然表示十分喜欢要领受他的秘方。他将药材递给她，又教了它的用法，说："你用这秘方的时候，可以和着石榴花汁咽下去。如果你照这法子办，在相当的时间，你必定能够得着一个儿子。你那个儿子必定要长得很美丽，他的颜色要像石榴花一样，所以你应当为他起名字叫达林鸠摩罗，意思就是"石榴童子"。因为那时必定有人要谋害你的儿子，所以我也应当告诉你，那孩子的生命要寄在你宫前那个水池里一只大的波尔鱼的身体里头。在那条鱼的心里有一个小木匣，匣里头藏着一条金项串。那条金项串便是你儿子的生命。再见吧。"

过了一个多月以后，宫里的人彼此都私下议论，说爱妃将要有一个儿子了。王听见了，自然非常欢喜。他想着他将要生出一个王子来承继王位，使他有威力的王统不至于断绝。他这样愉快的心情是他一生所未曾有过的。王子将要生出来的时候，照例举行庆祝的赛会，人民也尽量地表示他们的欢悦，大声欢呼吉祥的话。等到十

爱妃捧了一把米到门口要将它施舍给乞士

个月满了，爱妃果然生了一个非常美丽的儿子。王头一次看见他的婴孩，他的心就充满了无量的愉快。这新生的王子行初饭礼时，王又为人民开了一个极热闹的赛会，全国的人民个个都为这事欢乐。

过了几年，石榴童子长大了。他是一个很好的孩子。他对于各种游戏都很熟练，尤其是喜欢与鸽子玩。他的鸽子常常飞到姨母憎妃的宫里，因此，他也常常到她那里。第一次飞到她屋里的时候，她便将那些鸽子送回给他。但是第二次飞来的时候，她就带着厌恶的颜色，仍然送回给他。因为憎妃见石榴童子的鸽子时常喜欢飞到她的屋里来，她就想利用这个机会去实现她的自私心。她本来就很怨恨这王子，因为王自从王子生了以后，就一天一天地疏远了她，将宠爱都加在爱妃身上。她不晓得从哪里听见爱妃受了乞士的秘方，那乞士并且告诉她孩子生命的秘密，等等情形。她听见孩子的生命是藏在一种东西里头，可是不晓得是什么。她于是想从孩子这方面探求这个秘密。有一次，鸽子又飞到她屋里来了，她这次不把鸽子送回给石榴童子，但对孩子说："除非你能告诉我这件事，我必不把鸽子给回你。"

石榴童子说："嬷嬷，什么事？"

憎妃说："我的宝贝，没有什么特别的事情，我只要知道你的生命存在哪里。"

石榴童子说："嬷嬷，那是什么意思？我的生命除了存在我身里以外，还能在别的地方么？"

憎妃说："好孩子，不，那不是我的意思。从前有一位乞士对你母亲说你的生命是系在一件东西上头的，我愿意知道那件是什么东西。"

石榴童子说："嬷嬷，我从来不曾听过有那样东西。"

憎妃说："如果你应许我去问你母亲，看你的生命存放在什么东西里头，回来再告诉我你母亲所说的，我就把鸽子给回你，不然，我就不给。"

石榴童子说："好，好，我去问，回来再告诉你。现在请你把鸽子给回我吧。"

憎妃说："你如再应许我一件事，我就立刻给回你。你应许我不要告诉你母亲，说是我叫你来问的。"

石榴童子说："我应许你。"

憎妃将鸽子尽数给回石榴童子，可是小孩子因为过于喜欢的原故，把他姨母要他去问的话，一概都忘记了。第二天，鸽子又飞到憎妃的屋里来。石榴童子再到她那里。憎妃一定要他立刻去问，不然就不给回他。石榴童子应许当天就去问来回报给她知道。她于是又将鸽子还他。玩了一会儿，石榴童子跑去问他母亲说："母亲，请告诉我，我的生命藏在什么东西里头？"母亲听见这个问题，便很惊讶地问："好孩子，你的意思是什么？"孩子随着回答说："是的，母亲，我曾听人家说有位神圣的乞士告诉你，我的生命是放在一件东西里头的。请你告诉我那是件什么东西。"母亲诚恳地对他说："我的掌中珠，我的心肝，我的小宝贝，我的金月亮，不要问那不吉利的话。愿我的怨家的嘴被灰塞住，愿我的石榴长命。"可是孩子一定要他母亲告诉他这个秘密。他说若是不告诉他，他就不吃不喝了。爱妃因为受她儿子的强迫，在一个不吉利的时间把他生命的秘密说出来。因为命运该如此，第二天，鸽子又飞到憎妃的屋里了，石榴童子跟着过去要，憎妃便用甜话哄着孩子把他生命的秘密说出来。

自从憎妃知道石榴童子生命的秘密以后，她就立刻实行她的毒计。她叫她的婢女为她取些苎麻的干梗来。那些梗子很脆，如果用力压它们，就发出怪响，好像人体里的骨节坼裂的声音一样。憎妃把麻梗放在她自己的床底下，躺在上头装作病得很厉害的模样。王虽然不爱她，因为她病，也得尽本分去看她。憎妃故意要王听见她骨节的爆响，将身体在床上翻来覆去，把麻梗压得一阵怪响。王以为憎妃真病得很厉害，就命令他最高明的御医来医治她。不幸，那御医又是与憎妃同谋的。他对王说，只有一种药材能治王妃的病，就是宫前那个水池里头那一条大的波尔鱼。从它肚里可以得着一点东西来做药材。于是王便命御渔人把波尔鱼网上来。渔人撒了一次网便把鱼打上来了。在打鱼的时候，石榴童子正和别的孩子在离池子不远的地方游戏。在波尔鱼被网住时，石榴童子立刻不舒服起来。等到鱼被放在地上的时候，石榴童子也晕倒在地，他的呼吸急促，好像将要死的样子。宫人立刻把他送到他母亲那里。王听见儿子忽然病起来，也非常惊讶。御医命将那鱼送到憎妃宫里去。那鱼用鳍在地上拍来拍去的时候，石榴童子在他母亲的屋里也辗转得很凶。等到那鱼被剖开，果然在肚里头找出一个小木匣，匣里藏着一条金项串。憎妃把金项串套在自己的脖上，同时石榴童子死在他母亲的房里。

当王子的凶信到达王宫，王非常伤心，好像自己沉在悲哀的海洋里一样，虽然他听见憎妃的病已经痊愈了，但他的悲哀也不少减。他恸哭他的石榴童子，致使他的侍从恐怕他的精神要愈加紊乱。王不许人把孩子的尸体埋葬，也不许焚毁。他总不明白他的儿子是怎样死的，因为他一点病也没有，死得似乎太唐突。王命人把尸体安置在城外一所御苑里头。又命令将应用的东西都搬到那里去，好像那死的王子有时会用到一样。王命人把苑门不论日夜常时锁着，除非石榴的密友，宰相的公子以外，别人都不许进去。苑门的钥匙就在公子的手里，由他管着。他每次可以开门进去待一日一夜。

爱妃因为失去她的爱子，自然非常伤心，她也无心伺候王，所以王每夜都到憎妃那里去留宿。憎妃因为要避嫌疑，每夜当王在屋里的时候，必将金项串脱下来放在一边。命运所定的是那金项串如果挂在王妃的脖上，石榴童子便要现出死的状态；如果它被脱下，他也就复活过来。因为憎妃每夜把金项串脱下来，所以王子每夜必要复活。等到早晨，憎妃把它带在脖上，他又死过去。石榴童子在夜间复活时，因为王曾命将所有应用的东西放在苑里，所以他可以随意吃他所喜欢的东西。他每夜在苑中自在地游行和安详地休息。可是他的朋友每在日间来看他，所以时时看见他是一个僵硬的尸首。公子起首惊讶，因为他觉得每次进去看他，他的尸首都是和他头一次所见的一样，除掉颜色青白无生气以外，他看不出有什么败坏的现象，尸首的皮肉仍然很完好。对于这奇异的现象他想来想去，总不明白其中的缘故，于是决定要守着那尸首，看看有什么变动。他不但是白天来，有时晚间也来。他第一晚上来到苑里。就很惊讶地看见他死掉的朋友在花园里散步，起先他以为不过是他朋友的鬼魂，后来他摩触他，就觉得他的血肉都是活的。石榴童子把他死的因果告诉给他的朋友知道。他们都知道王子复活的现象是因为

008

王到憎妃屋里，妃子把金项串脱下来所致。他们明白了那条金项串是王子生命所寄托的。于是大家想着要用方法把它弄来。每夜他们必讨论这事，可是想不出一个靠得住的计谋。后来还是诸天用神异的方式把石榴童子救出来。

在我们现在所说的故事前几年，毘达多普路沙的妹子生了一个女儿。毘达多普路沙是司男女命运的神，他在婴儿生后六日，把一生的命运写在他们的额上。那亲切的母亲请问她的哥哥对于女儿的命运写了些什么在她额上。毘达多普路沙说她的女儿应当嫁给一个死新郎。她听见了这可悲的预言，对于女儿的前途便产生无限的伤感。她明知道求她哥哥改变他的意思是不可能的，因为他在婴儿额上写了什么就永不再更变。过几年，女孩长大了。她长得很美丽，可是她的母亲一见她就伤心。因为她的哥哥将她女儿的命运定得那么凶，所以女儿的美不能使她产生丝毫的快感。女儿到了可以婚嫁的年岁，她的母亲带她离开本国，为的是希望可以把女儿的凶运避过去。但是命运已经定了，不能轻易逃脱。她们母女二人经过许多地方，就到了停着石榴童子尸体的御苑门口。那时已经很晚了。女儿说她很渴，需要喝水。母亲便命女儿坐在苑门旁边，她自己便到村舍去求水。女儿那时，因为好奇的缘故，用手去推那苑门，门便自己开了。她走进去，看见一所很华丽的宫廷。她看完想从原路出

王子复活后就出去散步，在他走近门口的时候，他看见一个人形站在门边

去，可是那苑门又自己关上了。她最终不能出去。王子每夜是要复活的。他一活过来，就出园中散步。在他走近门口的时候，他看见一个人形站在门边。他走近看看，原来是一个很美丽的女郎。他问她是谁。她便将一切的事由告诉石榴童子，说她的舅父毘达多普路沙怎样把与死新郎结婚的字样写在她额上；她母亲怎样为她的凶运而不乐；她长大了，她母亲怎样带她离开本国，遍处游行；她在母亲求水的时候，怎样跑进这园子里来；一件一件都说出来。石榴童子听见她可怜的话，便对她说："我就是那位死新郎，你就与我结婚，同进屋里去吧。"女孩说："你现在站着与我说话，怎能说是死新郎呢？"王子答她说："你以后就会明白，现在且跟着我进去吧。"女孩于是跟着王子到屋里去。她已经一天没有吃过东西，王子便将所有的食物端来款待她。那位天神毘达多普路沙的妹子，女儿的母亲，到很晚才回到苑门旁边。她大声叫她的女儿，可是没有听见回答。她便走到各村舍去找寻她，但人人都对她说没有看见她的女儿。

毘达多普路沙的外甥女正在受王子款待的时候，石榴童子的朋友也如平常一样来到范里。他对于这美丽的少女十分惊异，一听见从她自己的口中说出从前的事迹就更加惊异。他们商定就在晚上举行婚礼。合婚的司祝是不成问题的，因为他们行的是干达婆婚礼，只要彼此互换华鬘就算了。新郎的朋友于是离开这对新人回到他自己的家里去。两位新人通宵诉说眷恋的情话，并没曾合着眼睡，一直到太阳从东方升起来。新妇睡了一会儿，醒来时，只见王子已成为一具僵冷的死尸，一点生气也没有。她对着这样的光景，我们自然容易理会她的惊讶和悲伤。她摇她的丈夫，向他的冷唇上印上热烈的吻，可惜她无论怎样做，也不能叫他复活过来。他躺在一边，僵硬得好像石像一样。因为受这悲惨的刺激，她捶胸，拊额，把头发弄散了，在苑里跑来跑去，几乎成为一个疯人。石榴童子的朋友日间是不来的，并且他明知道王子日间必定要成为僵尸，在这样的时间去看他的新妇，也是不合宜的。那一天在不幸的新妇心中简直是像一年。可是最长的日子也有尽期。当黑夜的影印在四围的山林和房舍的时候，她的死新郎又渐渐复苏，直到坐起来，拥抱着他那忧闷的妻子，与她一同吃喝。她的愉快又回复过来了。王子的朋友夜里也照常来。他们用通宵的工夫来行宴乐。时间过得很快，王子日死夜活和他的爱妻已同住了七八年，已经生了两个儿子，和石榴童子的模样一点也不差。

　　那时，王和两位王妃，乃至朝中一般的官吏都还不晓得石榴童子在夜里还是活着的。他们想着他已经死去很久了，他的尸首已经被焚毁了。可是石榴童子的爱妃很想见见她的姑嫜，因为她们一向未尝相会。她想她不必正式地去拜见她的姑嫜，只要远远地见她一面就够了。她又想着找一个机会把存在憎妃手里的金项串取回来，因为那与她丈夫的生命有连带的关系。她与她的丈夫和他的朋友商量好了，化装成一个女整容师。她和别的女整容师一样，携带一切应用的器具：如修指甲的刀剪；刮削油脂的镊子和小刀；一块"耶摩"，是烧过的砖，用来磨光脚底；一张"阿罗克达纸"，是用来染脚和脚趾的。她把一切的用具执在手里，带着两个孩子，跑到王宫门口。她对阉人说她是一个整容师，愿意入宫去伺候爱妃。于是阉人就领她到爱妃那里。妃子一见两个孩子，不由得想起她的爱子石榴童子。她为她失去的宝贝泪落不止，可是她想不到那两个孩子便是她的石榴所生的。她对那自以为是整容师的媳妇说，她毋须她的伺候，因为自从爱子死掉，她就无意于装饰，一切人间的虚荣她尽都捐弃，甚至连染红脚和脚趾那么平常的事情也不做了。她说，虽然她不要她来做整容师，可是很愿意时时见她和她的两个小孩子。这位女整容师于是又到憎妃那里去，说明要被她差使，为她服务。那王妃就命她为她修甲，削去脚上余剩的皮肉，又用阿罗克达纸为她染脚。憎妃很喜欢她的手艺娴熟，又爱她性情柔和，就命她依时入宫来伺候她。那女整容师一到憎妃宫里，就没有一刻不注意到戴在妃子脖上那条金项串上头。第二天，她再入宫里去，她预先教她的大孩子在她伺候王妃的时候放声大哭，非要等到那金项串落在他手里，否则就不要住声。第二天早晨，整容师果然带着她的孩子入到憎妃的宫里。正当她为妃子染脚的时候，孩子便大声哭起来，问他为什么哭，他就说要王妃脖上的金项串。憎妃说那可不能给，因为那是她最宝贵的首饰。可是孩子仍然大哭不止。为要哄他的缘故，王妃把金项串脱下来交到孩子手里。孩子于是不哭了。他把那条金项串缠在手上，就在一边玩耍着。整容师把工作做完，临要走时，王妃便问她要那条金项串回来。可是孩子死也不肯给，又放声大哭，好像非常凄惨的光景。在那时候，女整容师便求王妃说："求王后恩赐给他，容他把金项串暂时带回家去吧。等到他喝过奶睡觉的时候，我必定要取来奉还。他不到一个时辰就可以睡着了。"王妃看见一时必不能把项串从孩子手里夺回，而且她想着石榴童子已经死掉很久，现在不戴它也不要紧，所以就应许暂时给孩子带回去。

整容师一得着那项串，一气跑到苑里来，将它递到石榴童子身边，石榴童子立时复活了，他们欢喜极了。他们的朋友，宰相的儿子，叫他们第二天就进宫去见王和爱妃。第二天，宰相的儿子为他们预备一切的仪仗。一只佩着美丽毡毛的乘象上头坐着石榴童子，两个孩子骑着两只小马，一乘为新人预备的"阇都达罗舆"，用金线织的铺毯垫着，上头就坐着那位整容师。有人已经先到王宫里去奏报，说石榴童子不但复活，并且领着他的妃子和两个孩子要来参见他的父王和母后。王和爱妃起先哪里肯信，后来见成了事实，他们的愉快自然不用说，是不能形容的。憎妃那时才觉得从前自己所做的都不对，独自一个人在一边非常悲伤。石榴童子的乘象被一队乐工引着，一直来到宫门口。王和爱妃出来迎接他们丢了很久的爱子。他们的欢喜不用说是非常大。父母子媳相会后，彼此哭了一场。石榴童子又把他致死的缘故述说出来。于是王立刻愤怒非常，命人将憎妃带到面前，又命人把地掘开到可以容得一个人的广延。他于是命人将憎妃放进地穴，使她直立着，把用荆棘做的冠戴在她头上，然后活活地将她埋掉。


我的故事说到这里算完了，

那提耶也枯萎了。

那提耶呵，你为什么枯萎呢？

你的牛为什么要我用草来喂它？

牛呵，你为什么要人喂？

你的牧者为什么不看护我？

牧者呵，你为什么不去看牛？

你的儿媳妇为什么不把米给我？

儿媳妇呵，你为什么不给米呢？

我的孩子为什么哭呢？

孩子呵，你为什么哭呢？

蚂蚁为什么要咬我呢？

蚂蚁呵，你为什么要咬人呢？

喀！喀！喀！

二
骊
龙
珠

从前有一位王子和一位公子做好朋友。他们从小就同住在一个地方，起居，饮食，出入，乃至等等事情，都是一同去做。两人亲密的友谊不用说就可以理会出来。他们同过这样的生活已经好些年，后来彼此都想出国去看看国外的光景，又相约一同出去。他们俩一个是王子，一个是宰相的公子，虽然很富贵，却故意不带侍从的人与他们同行，各人只骑着马空身地走。那两匹马非常俊美，乃是有名的天马，所以人又叫它们做马王。王子和公子一同走了好几天，经过很辽阔的稻田，很繁盛的城市，和许多村落；经过没有水、没有树的沙漠；又经过稠密的树林，在里头常常遇见虎、熊和别的猛兽。有一晚上，他们走到一个地方，四围都看不见城市和村落。天色已渐渐黑暗了，他们又不认得道路，就找一棵很高的树把马拴在树下，两人攀上树，找了一根有很多叶子的横枝来做歇息的地方。那棵树旁边有一个很广大的池子。池里的水清净幽暗得像老鸦的眼睛一样。王子和公子在树上用各人的安身方法在那里歇着。他们决定要在那上头过一宿的工夫。他们常常彼此耳语，有时候就面对面地静默着很久，因为在那奇异的环境中，危险是很大的。他们睡了不久，眼睛却被一种不可思议的光明刺开了。

他们睁开眼睛四面地望，倾着耳朵听着周围，觉得池的中央发出一种激水的声音，有一只东西从那里浮上来。他们定睛一看，原来是一条非常大的龙，它的头部很大。那龙渐渐地泅到岸边，伸着舌，摇着头，到处发出微细的声音。最能使王子和公子注意的是它头上顶着一颗明净的摩尼宝珠。那珠的光直如千万颗大金刚钻合在一起一样。它的光明照耀满地和岸上四围的山林。那龙到岸上，就把珠从顶上摔到地下，自己到别处去找东西吃。树上的两位朋友都称赞那珠的光明，因为它把四周的风景照得清楚。他们以前并没见过这样的珠，可是曾听人家说过这样的珠的价值等于七个王的宝藏。他们的赞羡忽然变为恐怖和哀悲，因为那龙匐行到树下，把他们拴着的马一匹一匹吃掉。他们想着，不久他们必要变成龙的美馔。可是很幸运，那龙将马吃完以后，便从容地走到别处去。它走得很远了。公子心里便想，为何不把那颗宝珠捡起来？他曾听人说过，如果看见这样的珠，要得它时，必要先用牛粪或马粪盖着它。恰巧他们的马在树下遗下许多粪。于是他爬下来，把马粪堆在宝珠上头，直到把它全部掩蔽了，才爬回树上去。那条龙，在很远的地方觉得珠光忽然消失了，赶快跑到那里，不见了宝珠，就蟠来蟠去，显出很焦急和愤怒的样子。它蟠着那堆马粪，渐渐地失掉它的力量，垂着头就断了气。第二天一破晓，王子和公子都从树上下来，走到昨夜埋珠的地方，那龙已经死了很久。公子把马粪拨开，取出蒙着污秽的明珠与王子一同到水边去冲洗。直到粪秽洗净的时侯，宝珠的光明就恢复过来，与昨晚所见的一样。在水边的宝珠照耀得满池都很明朗。水底的鱼类，一条一条显露在二人的眼前。他们不但看见水里一切的动植物，并且因为珠的宝光透到水底，使他们出乎意外地看见那里有一所极庄严的宫阙。有冒险性的公子向王子说，不如大家没入水底去看看那到底是谁的宫阙。他们于是跃进水里。因为宝珠在公子手里的缘故，他们并不感觉困难或危险，不一会儿已降到宫门口。宫门是开着的。他们探头向里观望，看不见人，也看不见神灵。他们便胆大了一点，入了宫门，看见一所很华丽的花园，当中有一所很庄严的房子。园里的花木是王子和公子所不曾见过的。那里有各种玫瑰、茉莉、百耳花、摩里迦花、香王花、百合花、瞻婆迦花和一切发出妙香的花草。因为遍处是花，所以他们一到里头，真像在众香界一样。他们穿过许多花丛，享受了无量的香味与美色，到了一所四面围着高树的屋里。他们站在门口不敢进去，想着这必定是个仙境。他们看见各堵墙都是用纯金砌成的，到处都嵌着金刚钻及其他宝石，光耀四射，极其壮丽。他们并没看见人或别的东西，就迈步进到屋里。屋里的陈设也是他们一生所未见过的。他们走过一间一间的屋里，并没有看见什么人，好像到了一个荒芜的地方一样。最后，他们到了一间屋子，看见一个非常美丽的少女睡在一铺金床上头。她的美丽，很难形容，只觉得她的脸是由红白两种颜色混合而成。从她的模样看来，不过一个十六岁左右的少女。王子和公子将四只眼睛注视在她身上，正觉得非常愉快，少女的眼睛忽然睁开了。她很惊讶地望着他们，对他们说："唉，你们不幸的人，怎样跑到此地来？快走，快走！这是大力龙王的宫廷。那龙王把我的父母兄弟和一切的眷属都吃了，只剩下我一人是它留着的。快去逃命吧，不然，那龙王回来就要把你们放在它庞大的肚子里头。"公子知道那龙便是昨晚所见的，于是把它怎样死的情形告诉了她。他又告诉她他们怎样把龙珠夺过来，怎样因着珠光来到这里。她谢谢他们为她除掉那毒龙，请求他们住在宫里，不要使她一个独住着，怪孤零的。王子和公子都应许了她并要与她同住。王子钟爱了她那无瑕的美丽，不久便与她结婚。因为水底没有祭司，他们就彼此交换华鬘成礼。

王子自娶了他的爱妃，心里就非常愉快。妃子不但是容貌美丽，性情人品都极温存。虽然公子的妻子住在本国，没在公子身边，公子也因着王子的愉快，自己也愉快得很。他们一同过了些美满的生活。王子想着要带他的妃子回到本国去。两位朋友商量了，要公子先回国去见王，说明一切的际遇，请他遣派侍从、象、马等，来迎接这一对新人。这回又用得着那宝珠了。王子执着宝珠，拉着公子的手一同上浮到水面，为他送行后，又降到水底去和他的

妃子手里拿着宝珠离开宫殿，成功地上浮到岸上来

爱妻同住。在分离的时候，公子曾与王子约定时日，他把象、马和仆人领到水边的时候，王子必用宝球上来接他们下去。

　　自从公子回国以后，水底的夫妇每日过着他们的爱恋生活，不觉过了好些日子。有一天，王子于中餐后午睡的时候，妃子心想上岸去看看，就把宝珠执在手中，安然地将水分开，上浮到岸边来。岸上一个人也没有，所以没人知道她浮上来。在岸边有几级石阶，是为洗澡的人建筑的。妃子坐在石阶上洗她的身体，洗她的头发，在水中玩了一会儿，又在水边走了一周，然后回到水底的宫里去。她回去的时候，她的丈夫还在睡着。到王子醒过来时，她也没有把上岸的事告诉他。第二天午餐后，她又在王子午睡那时候，私下取了宝珠，浮在水面做第二次的游玩。那一次，没遇见什么人，她又安然地降到水底。因为两次的成功，使她的胆量更大，不久，她又要冒第三次的危险。这一次，正好罗阇的儿子出来打猎，在离水边不远的地方安下帐幕。这水池是在他父亲所统治的境界里头，所以他一直是这水池的小主人。当所有的侍从去预备午餐的时候，王子就在水边独自散步。那时岸边还有一个老婆子在那里捡柴。水底的妃子正当王子和老婆子在岸边的时候，从水里浮上来。她四围一望，看见岸上有一个男子和一个老妇人，不敢久留，又下沉回到水底的宫廷去。王子和拾柴的老婆子都看见她上来又下去。因为被她美丽的魔力所牵引，王子站在水边发呆了很久。他生来不曾见过这样美丽的女子。在他心中，她简直是一位天女。天女的形状，他曾在古书里体会过。古书里说天女有时也会眷恋世间，下来与世人相见，但这样的际遇是很稀罕的。他见那妃子的容貌不过是一瞬间的工夫，却已能使她的形象深印在他的心里，使他深为眷慕而不安。他站在水边，木立着望着水中央，直如一座石像。他站在那里，希望可以再见她一次。站了许久，连影儿也没有，王子因此就失了神。自从那时候，他想念那妃子渐渐地疯痴起来。他不说别的，只说："一会儿在这里，一会儿又走了！一会儿在这里，一会儿又走了！"他不愿意离开池边，后来被他的侍从们强挽着回宫去。有人去禀奏他的父王，说王子自从打猎回来，不晓得犯了什么病，整日呆呆地只说一句话。他也不同别人说话，只是自己对自己沉吟地说："一会儿在这里，一会儿又走了！一会儿在这里，一会儿又走了！"没有停过一分钟，他必这样说。罗阇自然不明白他儿子所说的话意。他也不晓得他儿子到底是为什么缘故犯了这病。"一会儿在这里，一会儿又走了！"在他的心中是一句难以解释的语言，就是他的侍从们也不明白。王把国中的名医都招来看他儿子的病症，可是没有一个人能把他治好。疯狂已是没有药可治了，何况他为爱而狂，世间哪里能找出医治爱病的药饵来？所有的医生一问王子的身心到底有什么不舒坦的地方，他不说别的，只回答说："一会儿在这里，一会儿又走了！"

王觉得国中的名医对于他儿子的病症是没有把握的，于是命人拿大鼓到四城去，大声号召说，若有人能够把王子的病治好，王必将公主许他为妻，并且使他管领全国土的一半。王的使者在四城敲了许久的大鼓，却没有人敢来摩触它。因为没有人知道王子的病根在哪里。最后，来了一个老婆子跑来摩触大鼓，说她不但知道王子的病根，并且能够医治他。这老婆子便是那天在池边捡柴的那个妇人。她有一个犯精神病的儿子名叫八奇珍，所以人家都叫她八奇母。使者听见八奇母说能把王子治好，就带领着她到王宫来。

王说："你就是那摩触征医大鼓的妇人么？你知道我儿子的病原么？"

八奇母说："是，由公义化身的大王，我知道他的病源，可是我现在暂时不说出来，要等到我把王子治好了才说。"

王说："这样，我怎能相信你有医治我儿子的本领呢？因为全国的名医都治不好他。"

八奇母说："大王，你现在可以不必相信，等到我把王子治好以后再看吧。许多老婆子所知的秘术是一切有智慧的人所不知道的。"

王说："很好，我就静看着你怎样医治他吧。你愿意在什么时候施行你的医术呢？"

八奇母说："现在还不能说准，可是必要立刻去预备，请大王遣派几位侍从来帮助我。"

王说："你要什么人帮助和什么东西应用呢？"

八奇母说："请求大王命人在城外王子得病的大池边搭一座草舍，我要在那里医治他。我自己在那里先住几天，然后回来。还请大王派些侍从驻守在离我所住的草舍三百尺远的地方，我或许要他们的帮助。"

王说："很好，就照这样办吧。我必定命人立刻到池边去搭一座草舍。此外你还需用什么呢？"

八奇母说："大王，在治病的设备上，我不需什么了。可是我要申明的是，大王将来对于征医时所应许的条件要逐条履行，就是将公主及国土的一半赐给那治愈王子的人。我是一个女人，不能与公主结婚，所以要求大王，如我把王子治好，可否由我的儿子八奇珍与公主结婚，并且承受王的领土的一半？"

王应许了她。用不了许久的工夫，池边的草舍已经搭好了。八奇母于是住在那里。在离草舍约三百尺的地方，也为侍从支起一个帐幕，王命他们住在那里，听候八奇母的差遣。老婆子对侍从们说，除了她以外无论谁都不许到池边去。

　　再讲到住在水底的妃子，因为那天浮上水面的时候，无意中看见一个男子和一个老婆子在水边，吓了一跳，再不敢冒第四次的险。妇人的好奇心常比男子大，妃子也和一般的女人一样，终没有把浮上水面的心情放弃掉，还是想再上去一次。有一天她的丈夫又午歇去了，她就跑到屋里把龙珠执在手里，出了宫门，一直浮上水面来。八奇母那时正在草舍里守着，她一听见水面有点动静就躲在篱笆后面悄悄看着。妃子看见四围没有人，便上了岸，坐在石阶上揩拭她的身体。八奇母立时从草舍出来，用一种很柔和的声音对妃子说："来吧，我的宝贝，美丽的王后，来我这里，我替你洗澡。"说着，她已到了妃子面前。妃子看见她不过是个女人，所以没有拒绝她。当老婆子给她洗头发的时候，看见她手里那颗宝珠，就说："请把那宝珠放在一边，等到洗完再拿着吧。"妃子把宝珠放在一边，老婆子便快快地把它偷过来，藏在自己的腰巾里头。老婆子晓得妃子没有了宝珠是不能逃脱的，就发出暗号命驻守的人出来把她捉住。

　　满城的人听见八奇母将住在池底的水仙捉到了，都为王子庆贺。城里的百姓都跑来看她，把她当做仙女看。妃子被领到王宫的时候，那疯狂的王子一见了她便大声嚷起来："我已经找着了！

她手里拿着龙珠跑出了宫门，一直浮上水面来

我已经找着了！"那停在他脑子里，使他癫痴的迷云一时消散了。他那双眼睛，以前是没有光辉的，现在便生动得像燃着两点理智的火。他的舌头，从前只能说"一会儿在这里，一会儿又走了！"现在已经解放了。总而言之，他自从见了妃子以后，一切都恢复到常人的状态。罗阇的喜悦自然是不可计量。全城的百姓也为王庆祝，并称赞八奇母的功劳。他们都希望王子和那位水仙早些结婚。妃子命老婆子对王说，如果要她和王子结婚，除非过一年才可以举行。因为她在水底已经有了一个丈夫，她试着要用一年的工夫将他忘却。她在这一年之内，无论如何，不能与任何人结婚。王子虽然很失望，他却深信俗语所说好事是越经折磨越甜美的。这一年的耽搁，便是妃子为他存贮将来快乐的时间。

妃子在被囚的时间，日夜悲啼，但也想不出逃脱的方法，她只怨恨她自己那没有用处的好奇心使她离开丈夫，自己浮上水面来。想着丈夫自己一人在水底，她就哭得更凄切。她所住的地方有重重的围墙，实在一步也不能跳出来。即使她能跳出城来，她也不能到水底去和她丈夫相会，因为那宝珠已不在她手里了。宫里的贵女们和八奇母用尽许多方法要使她快乐，可是都不成功。她现在看一切都是不可乐的，也很少与人谈话，每日每夜只哭得像泪人一般。一年的期限已经近了，她还是一样地悲伤，没有一点愉悦的神气。但无论如何，王子的大礼总是要举行的。罗阇集合许多星命家来占卜吉期和推定迎娶的时间。所有婚礼应办的事都陆续地预备好了。全城的糖果店为王子的婚事日夜忙着制造糖食；制乳厂忙着制造酥酪；爆竹店忙着制造焰火花盒。乐队在宫门口奏乐，一阵一阵悠扬的声音绕缭着全城。那日，全城真是充满了宴乐和畅快的气氛。

再讲到那位公子自离开他住在水底的朋友以后，一路平安回到本国。他于约定的时间领着象、马和侍从等来到池边，要接王子和妃子回去。他自别后到回来，中间已经过了好几个月。回来的时候，因为领着一大队象、马、人等，所以耽搁了些时日。他到池边，正是城里的王宫为纳妃子的盛典热闹的时候。那时距离王子迎娶的吉期不过两三日的工夫。好在池边连着一个檬果林，他便命侍从等把帐幕支在林下，把人和牲口安置在那里。公子独自在池边瞭望着。约定的日期已经到了，可是水底一点动静都没有。公子很忧闷地望那天上的太阳渐渐从山头沉落下去。他一连等候了两三天，水里还没有一点动静。他心里自问，我的朋友和他美丽的妻子，不晓得又遇见什么意外的事呢？他们是死了么？莫不是龙母回来把王子和妃子杀掉了？莫不是他们把宝珠丢了，所以不能浮上来？莫不是他们浮上水面来游玩被人捉了去？种种疑问都萦回于公子心中。他悲伤极了，不晓得要怎样办。他在池边发愁的时候，听见一阵一阵的乐音从远地送到耳边，他想着必是城里有了什么庆典，于是问了附近的乡人。乡人对他说，城里的王子近日要迎娶一个很美丽的水仙，就是从这个水池里浮上来，被王的侍从擒住的。她被捕的时候，正站在公子所站的石阶上。这事乡人也对他说了。他还告诉公子王子的吉期就在后天。公子听了乡人所说的话，就知道妃子已经被捕，把王子留在池底。他决定要进城去探听这事的究竟，还试着找一个方法去把妃子救出来。他吩咐侍从领着牲口回国，因为他不晓得要耽搁多少时日才能把妃子救出。他对于这事完全没有把握。人马走了以后，他独自一人进城去探听消息，后来他便在一个婆罗门人的家里留宿。

公子在婆罗门人的家里吃过晚饭以后，便故意问他的主人城中一阵一阵的音乐到底是什么意思。婆罗的门人问他："你是从哪一国来的呢？你不曾听见过我们的国王后天要为他的王子举行婚礼么？你不知道那位新妃子是从城外大池里浮上来，极其美丽的水仙么？"

公子回答说："不，我一点也不知道。我是从一个很远的国土来的，这样的奇事还没传到那里。请你把这事详细地告诉我吧。"

婆罗门人说："去年差不多在这个时候，罗阇的儿子出城去打猎。他在城外那个大池旁边支起帐幕做歇息的地方。有一天，他正走近池旁，可巧看见一个少女，或是神女，长得非常美丽，从池水中央浮现出来。那神女在水面停了不久又沉下去了。王子看见她那么俊美，心里非常眷慕。她忽然沉下去，使他的热爱立时变成疯狂。回宫以后什么话他都不能说，只说：'一会儿在这里，一会儿又走了！'王召集了国内的名医来治他，可是都不能把他治好。于是王命人在四城擂鼓，召那能医治王子的人，应许如果把他治好，就要把公主许给他为妻，并且分给他国土的一半。有一个老婆子名叫八奇母，走去摩触那鼓，说她有医治王子的本领。她命王为她搭了一座草舍在池边，在离池不远的地方又伏着些侍从听候她的差遣。听说那神女再浮上水面来，八奇母便把她留住，命侍从用肩舆把她抬进王宫去。王子因为见着那所爱的神女，他的病立时好了。当时王就要与他们成亲，但那神女不愿意，因为她还有一位丈夫在水底，如必要她与王子结婚时，就得容她用一年的时间来把前夫忘却，所以延迟到现在。现在你所听的乐音就是从宫门口送出来的。这就是这段奇事的大概情形。"

公子问："这真是一段奇遇！不晓得八奇母受了什么赏赐没有？"

婆罗门人说："还没有。王本应许要将公主许给治好王子的人，可是八奇母是个女人，她请求王把所应许的赐给他的儿子八奇珍。可是八奇珍是个心志不定几类疯癫的人。他出外已经一年多了。现在也没有人知道他在哪里。他常常是这样，出外很久，忽然就回家来看他的母亲，忽然就去了。现在我想他有娶公主和领受国土的福分，他的母亲一定希望他回来。"

公子问："他的模样是怎样的？他回家的时候都做些什么事体？"

婆罗门人说："不错，他就像你这样的身体，不过年纪轻一点。他不常穿衣服，只围一条布在腰上，用灰涂身，拿着一根树枝在手里。他到他母亲的家，必在门外舞一阵，口里还唱着，'嗒！嗒！嗒！'的声调。他说话也很不清楚。当他的母亲对他说：'八奇儿，同我住几天吧，'他必回答说：'不，不，我不住，我不住。'他若是对于他母亲的要求要应许的时候，必定说，'哼，'意思就是'好吧。'"

公子自从听了婆罗门人所说的话，把事情的原委探究出来。他断定妃子是自己一个因着宝珠的能力浮上水面来，被老婆子捉住的。他的朋友王子必定还在水底，而那颗宝珠必定是在老婆子手里。他想他的朋友丢了那颗宝珠一定没法逃出来，一种失望的悲伤不觉涌上他的心头。他整夜里深深地出神，试要想出一个方法来救他的朋友。他想除非得再从老婆子手里夺回那颗宝珠。想来想去，妙计就出来了！他想着八奇母这时一定很盼望她的儿子回来，何不假装八奇珍到她家里，相机行事。用这个方法，他想，或者可以把水底的王子救出来，也可以使困在宫里的妃子得以解脱。第二天，他辞了婆罗门人，跑到城外一个偏僻的地方，扮成八奇珍的模样。他照着昨晚上那位婆罗门人所说的话打扮起来。把衣服脱掉，只围着一幅布在腰上，下垂不过膝头，用灰涂抹他的身体，拿着一根树枝在手里，疯疯癫癫地一直到八奇母的门口。他在那里做很强烈的舞蹈，嘴里唱着"嗒！嗒！嗒！"的声调。老婆子在屋里觉得儿子又回来在门外舞着，赶紧跑出来说："我的八奇珍儿，你回来啦！我的宝贝，进来吧，诸天最终赐给我们许多福分呢。"那位假的八奇珍在门外舞得更剧烈，手里不住地摇着树枝，嘴里发出不明了的回答："哼。"

"在这个时候，你应当不要再走了，你应当回来和我住在一起。"

公子说："不，不，我不住，我不住。"

"同我住在一块儿吧。我要你和公主结婚。我的儿八奇珍呀，你娶她不娶呢？"

"哼，哼。"公子回答完，舞得像狂人一般。

"你同我到王宫去好不好？我领你去看那从水底上来的那位美

丽的妃子。"

"哼，哼。"这回答从公子的嘴里哼出来，随着唱那"嗒！嗒！嗒！"的歌调，双脚舞得更起劲。

"我的儿子，你见过值得七王所有宝藏的摩尼宝珠吗？我有一颗，你看不看。"老婆子觉得儿子什么都应许他，高兴起来，就要拿那颗宝珠出来眩惑他。

"哼，哼。"公子发出这样的回答。

老婆子把宝珠拿起来，放在儿子的手中。公子取过来看过之后，把它紧紧地卷藏在腰间的布里头。八奇母喜欢到了不得，因为她的儿子来得正是时候。她跑到宫里去报告，说她儿子八奇珍已经回来了，她要领他去见见从水底上来的妃子。八奇母自从有了捉住水仙的功劳，凡她所请求，王没有不答应的。她和假儿子来到宫里，随即领他去见水仙。妃子自然很不喜欢见着一个狂人在她面前，一半裸着体，全身涂着灰，乱舞乱叫地闹，可是她也没法拒绝。黄昏到了，八奇母催着她的儿子回家。但公子又装出疯狂的样子对她说："不，我不回去，我不回去。"八奇母知道他平素的性情，不敢强迫他。她问他不回去要在哪里歇。他说要留在妃子的屋里，好看着她。八奇母于是吩咐宫中的侍者和阍者好好地照顾着她的儿子，凡事听从他，因为不久他便是驸马。她吩咐完，自己便回家去了。

　　夜阑人静的时候，假的八奇珍悄悄地走到妃子面前，用原来的声音叫一声："妃子！你还认得我么？我就是信义公子，你丈夫的朋友。"妃子惊喜非常，对着他，嘴里带着愉快、希望和安慰说："你！你是公子吗？我丈夫的挚友，快把我救出这可厌的宫廷吧，我在这里比死还苦。我恨我的命运，因为从前完全是我做错了，才会到今日这步田地。好朋友，救一救我吧，救一救我吧。"她哭起来了。公子安慰她说："不要太伤心。我当尽我的力量去做，希望今晚上能够把你救出去；不过，你必要听我的话，我叫你做什么，你就做什么。"妃子说："好，我必听从你。你叫我怎样做，我就怎样做。"假的八奇珍说了这话，立刻离开妃子的住处。他在宫里的院子走来走去。人把宫门关了，他又命人开了，说他要出去一会儿就回来。他们都道八奇珍是个疯子，又不敢违忤他，便开门由他出去。在不久的时间，他果然回来。过一会儿，他又要出去。阍者问他，他又说："哼！哼！我出去一会儿就回来。"阍者又开门让他出去。停了一会儿，他又回来了。他一连出入了好些次，把阍者都闹乏了。他们彼此商议说："这个疯子八奇珍，今晚上要不歇地走出去和走进来的，不如由他自己开门出去，由他自己回来吧。我们没有那么精神来招呼他。谁能整夜不睡，尽管给他开门和关门呢？"公子还是一会儿出去，一会儿进来，阉者也不理会他，由着他自己爱出便出，爱进便进。他觉得救妃子的机会到了。在天快亮的时候，阉者都昏昏地睡着了，他忙跑进妃子的房里，对妃子说："妃子，现在可以逃走了。阉者都睡熟啦。你伏在我的背上，把你的头发围在我的脖上，双手紧搭着我。"妃子照样地办。在黑夜里只看见他背着一团东西，并看不出是一个人。他把妃子驮出院子，没人来盘问他。到了宫门，阉者都已睡熟了，即使有半醒的，微睁眼睛一看，见是八奇珍，也就由他自己开门出去了。一路上没人盘问，守城的都知道八奇珍就是那样疯疯癫癫的，所以也没有盘问他，就放他过去。他走到池边，才把妃子放下来。妃子站着，两条腿因着逃脱的愉快就抖擞起来。公子从腰间把宝珠取出来，带着妃子沉入水底的宫里。王子在水底时时都在失望的境地里，现在忽然看见他们回来，自然是喜欢到不可言状。他因为失了妃子，一年的工夫，几乎使他葬在悲伤和绝望的深渊里，现在他的精神才复活过来。三个人相见时，几乎因喜而狂。他们住在水底三天的工夫，将一切的遭遇细细地说给王子听。王子和妃子都说公子是一个有勇、有信、有义的好朋友。一切的事情都是得着他的帮助。他们求他时常跟他们住在一起，凡事要顾问他，要听他的指导。

他们起首计划回国的计策，因为公子带来的人马都被遣回去了，他们不得不步行。公子和王子本是长处安乐不惯步行的。尤其以妃子为更吃亏。她几曾走过远道，几曾用她细腻的脚去接触那粗硬不平的道路？她的脚走得肿破了。王子有时负着她在肩上，使她双腿分垂在他的胸前，好像骑马一样。那种办法在长途上走，于妃子固然是很安适，于王子却是一种甜爱而累赘的负载。所以妃子还是自己走的时候多。

有一天晚上，他们在一棵树下露宿，四围不见人烟。公子对王子和妃子说："你们睡吧，容我看守着你们，如有什么意外的危险，我可以保护你们。"他们两人紧紧地互搂着，便在树上睡着了。公子不敢睡，只是守望着。那棵树上可巧有一个鸟巢，巢里住着一对仙鸟，雄的名叫毘韩笈摩，雌的名叫毘韩笈弥。它们不但能够说人所说的话，并且知道个人将来的命运。公子正在守望着上下四围，忽然听见像两人谈话的声音从树上传下来，抬头一看，原来是那对仙鸟在巢里夜谈。他于是静听着它们所说的话。

毘韩笈摩："那位公子为保护他的朋友王子的性命，甚至情愿失掉他自己，可是他最终难以救护王子。"

毘韩笈弥："为什么？"

"王子的命运该遇见许多危险。这一次回国，王听见了，必定遣派象、马来迎接他们，仆从和象、马必定很多，保护得也必很周到，可是王子必要从象亭上摔下而死。"

"如果有人不叫王子乘象，叫他骑马，他不就可以得到平安吗？"

"那么，他就不至于摔死。然而别的危险又来了。当王子走近王宫时，必要穿过宫外的狮子门。正在他通过的时候，狮子门便倒下来，把他压死。"

"如果有人在王子未到以前，把狮子门拆毁下来，王子不就没有危险了么？"

"那么，他就不至于被压而死。可是别的危险又等着他去经历。王子到宫里时，王必为他们设筵，其中有一盘烧鱼头是特为王子预备的。王子吃那个鱼头的时候，就要被鱼骨哽死。"

"如果那时候有人在旁边快把鱼头夺去，不要使鱼头沾着王子的嘴，那不就没有危险了么？"

"若是有人把鱼头夺去，王子自然可以远离哽死的惨事。可是他还要渡过一件最危险的事情。到散席的时候，王子和妃子要回到他们的寝宫，正当他们睡着的时候，一条毒蛇要来到床上把他咬死。"

"如果有人先在宫里等候，一见那毒蛇就把它砍死，他不就平安了么？"

"若是有人把那条毒蛇砍死，王子自然没有性命的危险。但是那为救王子而斩毒蛇的人把我们现在所说的话对王子说，他必要变为石像。"

　　"若是他变为石像，就没有方法使他复活么？"

　　"有方法，如果王子肯把妃子将要生出来的儿子舍掉，将婴儿的血涂在那石像上头，他就可以复活。"

　　雌雄仙鸟谈完不久，晨鸦就啼起来了。东方的红光渐渐发射出来，树下一对睡着的旅客也被太阳光明的手摇醒了。公子把那对仙鸟所说的话牢记在心头，一点声色也不显露出来。他们三人在一清早又上了旅途，可幸走了不远就遇见一大队的马、象和仆从。因为有人到王那里去报信，说公子和王子夫妇快要到了，所以王就派遣他们到郊外迎接。大队中有一只象，背上的亭子铺着非常华丽的毯毹，是特为王子设备的，王为妃子预备的是一乘彩舆，用银镶得很精细。为公子预备的只是一匹骏马，当王子要升上象亭时，公子急急地阻止他说："容我坐在象亭上，你骑我的马吧。"王子念着他的劳绩，听见他这样要求，也不介意就让给他坐上，自己骑着那匹马。但是他在马上，心里总觉得公子的要求过分了一点。他又回想着他们夫妇的性命是他救出来的，也许他要借此要求乘坐象亭进城的荣耀当作酬报。大队向王城进行，已经看见宫门了。公子看见狮子门上结了彩，是专为王子和妃子回国而装饰的。他不等王子经过，便命人赶快把门上一切容易掉下来的装饰品都拆卸下来。王子问他为什么这样做。他却不能将理由说出，只说拆了更好。王子很不满意他这样做，可是念着他的功劳，还是容忍他，不对他露出什么形色。不一会儿，狮子门和上头的彩饰都被拆下来，他们才顺着次序通行过去。

他们来到宫里了，王为他们设欢迎的筵席。王子、妃子和公子都依次坐着。他们谈起一路上的经过和妃子的境遇，王更是敬重公子的忠义和勇敢多智。宫里的贵女们看见妃子那么美丽，认为是从来所未曾见，都加以赞叹。她们眼中的妃子，就是擅于说话的人来说，也说不出来，只见她的面庞是由乳酪和胭脂混合而成；她的脖项像天鹅的一样，又白又圆又细腻；她的眼睛好像小羚羊的，那么清秀流动；她的唇好像苹果那么红润而弯曲；她的双颊好像莲花那么娇红；她的鼻又高又直；她的头发垂到脚跟，她的脚步稳重得像小象一样。她全身的美丽，在一班宫人当中没有一个能够同她比较。她们围着她，问她的家世；问她为什么住在水底的宫里；问她毒龙怎么把她的亲人害死；种种问题都争着从她们的口中发出来。宴会的时候到了，所有的肴馔都是用金盘捧出来的。在桌上，罗列了许多珍奇的食点，最令人注意的就是特为王子预备的那盘烧鱼

他赶快从藏身处跑出来，用宝剑杀死了那条蛇

头。他们吃着，公子忽然把放在王子面前那个金盘上的烧鱼头夺来，不由分说便自己吃着。他对王子说："王子，容我吃这个鱼头吧。"王子看他这样行为，心里非常不高兴，可是他并不说什么。公子也看出王子心里的委屈，可是他也不能把理由告诉他。因为一说出来，他立时要变成石像，不但不能救他朋友的命，连自己的命也要丢了。

筵席散了，公子请求王子容他回家去。在平常的日子，王子一定是不答应的，不过今天看见他那么跋扈，心里早已不痛快，巴不得他立刻就走，所以不迟疑地应许他，其实公子并不是要先回家，他只为救他的朋友的缘故，先行跑进王子的卧室藏在一个隐蔽的地方。他身上本来有一把剑，在卧室只有床后可以做藏身的地方，因为床上的帐是用金丝织成的，一个人藏在里面，必不能被人发现。不久，王子和妃子都从设筵的宫廷回到寝室来。他们解衣睡去，公子还在帐后，一声也不响。到了夜半，公子看见一条很大的毒蛇从宫中水门进来，慢慢爬到床沿。他赶快从帐后跑出来，用剑向蛇狠狠地砍下去，把它切成许多段，放在床前一个金的槟榔盘上。当公子斩蛇的时候，不幸蛇血喷了一点在妃子的胸前，他想那血也是很毒的，若是救了王子而害了妃子，岂不是把从前为他们谋的幸福都废弃掉？他想定了，除非用舌头轻轻地把它舐干净，不能找出一个更好的方法。可是在黑夜里用口挨近一个年轻而半裸着的女人已是不合适，何况又是躺在床上的？他于是定看了有血的部分，再用布把眼睛包了七重，轻轻地把血舐净。当他舐着的时候，妃子惊醒了，就大叫起来。在她旁边的王子也醒了。王子看见公子，心里已动了气，因为他说要回家，现在却伏在妃子身上做那怪样子。他要起来杀公子。公子把他止住，对他说："朋友，我这样做，是要救你们的性命。"

"我不明白你的意思。"王子这样回答。他继续说，"自我们从水底回来，你就一天骄傲似一天。最初你把象亭抢去坐，那原是为我预备的，你也不觉得僭分，就自己乘起来了。我因念着你的功劳未曾发作，你又命人把狮子门拆去。在席上，你很无礼，把为我预备的鱼头夺去自己受用。席散之后，你说要回家，我因为你那么可恶，所以许你回去，不料你整夜未出宫门，跑到我的卧室来调戏我的妻子。你这样做，还说是救我的性命，难道破坏我妻子的贞洁便是救我的性命么？"

"唉，请你不要那样想。诸天知道我的心是纯洁的。他们知道我这样做是为救你的性命。你看我平日的行为还不知道我的为人么？如果我能自由地把我所做的都明白地说出来，我必要说出来，可惜我不能呀。"

"你为什么不能？谁把你的嘴堵住呢？"王子这样问。

"命运使我的口不能自由地说话。若是我说了，我必会立刻变成石人。"公子这样回答。

"你立刻变成石人！你以为我是个呆子，能受你的骗术么？这种废话，少说吧。"

"我的朋友，你愿意我说出来么？你若是要我说的话，就得记住你的朋友会变成石像呀。"

王子说："说吧，不然你就该死。"

公子为要辩白他的纯洁行为，想把一切的事由说给王子听。但他在没说以前，再三央求王子不要叫他说，而王子必不肯信，非迫着他说来不可。他正说到毘韩笈摩和毘韩笈弥对说的情形，他的双脚已变成石了。他说："看哪，朋友，我的脚已变成石头了。"王子不管他，只说："说下去吧。"公子顺着次序说，身体从底下渐渐坚硬，直到说吃鱼头事的时候，他的肩脖已变成石头了。他说："朋友，现在你看我全身都变成石，只剩下我的脖项和头部，如果你再要我说，我的全身便要化成石了。你愿意我说下去么？"王子回答说："说吧，说吧。"公子说："好吧好吧。我必把全部的事由说尽。但在我变了石像以后，你如果念着我们的旧谊，要我复活的时候，你必要把头生的婴儿杀掉，用他的血来涂我这变石的身体。妃子不久将要生子，你要我复活，必要牺牲了你的婴儿。这是我再三叮咛的话。"他把斩蛇的事由说了，全身便化了石，只剩下两片唇和一条舌头还很柔软。到他说完不作声时，连唇舌也坚硬起来。公子不见了，只见一个大理石像立在床前。王子和妃子下了床，摸摸那石像，冷得怪可怕的。他们揭开槟榔盘一看，果然有一段一段的蛇体放在盘中间。王子和妃子现在才理会公子的忠义和贞正，但已是迟而又迟了。他们对着那石像恸哭，却不能使它走动。他们于是把石像存放在屋里，等着要杀所生的婴儿来使它再变为人。

时间过得很快。妃子果然生出一个很美丽的婴儿，容貌和她一样。王子和妃子虽然舍不得害了自己美丽的儿子，可是舍此以外，并没有别的方法可以救他们的朋友。王子狠心地把婴儿杀死，将他的血涂在石像上头，公子果然复活过来。他把置在地上的儿尸抱起来，用布把尸上的血迹拭净，他要想个方法使婴儿复活。

公子为婴儿的缘故，遍访国中的名医，但他们都说他是个呆子。世间上，病人或者可以医治，哪有医治死人的？公子不得已，把婴儿的尸首抱回家交给他的妻子，看她有什么方法。他的妻子是崇拜黑母的。那时妻子已住在外家，所以他就抱着婴尸走到城外岳父家里。岳父的房子旁边有一所花园，他把婴尸用布裹好，挂在树上。他妻子看见丈夫回来，喜极到欢地，但觉得他很忧郁，不晓得是为什么缘故。她问他，他又不说。那一晚上，当他们在一起睡的时候，公子已睡着了，忽开门的声音把他惊醒。他静静地看他妻子从房门走出去。他本来心里挂念着那婴儿的尸体，心里很不自在，加以在那危险的深夜，妻子偷着走出去，叫他不能不起来，远远跟着她，看她到哪里去。他的妻子不晓得丈夫跟随着，自己来到黑母的庙里。那庙离她父亲的房子不远。她用香花和梅檀供奉黑母，祈求她说："迦梨①母呀！可怜我吧，救我脱离现在的困难吧。"女神说："什么？你还有困难么？你求我使你丈夫回来，现在他不是回来了么？"妻子说："是，他已经回来了。可是他心里很不舒坦，问他，他又不肯说。我的神母，他不理我，只睡在一边，叫我怎么办才好？"黑母说："你回去问你丈夫到底为什么那么不舒坦，然后再来告诉我吧。"公子在后面听了妻子和迦梨母所说的话，可是不露脸，赶紧回到自己的卧房来。第二天早晨，妻子问他有什么委屈，他便把王子将婴孩杀掉来使他复活的事情说给她听，还表示他愿意使婴儿复活的意思。那晚上，妻子又跑到黑母庙里去，说明丈夫忧郁的理由。女神说："你把婴孩的尸体抱来吧，我使他复活就是了。"第二天晚上，她就抱婴孩的尸体到庙里，女神果然使他复

① 原文为"诃利"（Kali），现通译为"迦梨"，是印度教三大主神之一湿婆神妃帕尔瓦蒂产生的化身，亦称"时母"，印度神话中既造福生灵，也能毁灭生灵的女神。——编者注

活过来。

现在他们都平安了。公子把活泼的婴孩抱到王宫。王子和妃子看见他们的儿子复活过来，自然喜欢到不可名状。他们做了一辈子的好朋友，直到各人老死的时候。


我的故事说到这里算完了，

那提耶也枯萎了。

那提耶呵，你为什么枯萎呢？

你的牛为什么要我用草来喂它？

牛呵，你为什么要人喂？

你的牧者，为什么不看护我？

牧者呵，你为什么不去看牛？

你的儿媳妇为什么不把米给我？

儿媳妇呵，你为什么不给米呢？

我的孩子为什么哭呢？

孩子呵，你为什么哭呢？

蚂蚁为什么要咬我呢？

蚂蚁呵，你为什么要咬人呢？

喀！喀！喀！

三　三宝罐

从前有一个婆罗门人，他有一个妻子和四个孩子。他的家境很穷，自己没有什么财产，只靠着富人的施舍度日。凡遇婚丧的典礼，他便到办事的家求布施。可是他所住的城不能天天都有丧事，所以他想如果一日没有人死或没有人嫁娶，他便要守着五口子挨饿。他的妻子叱责他，说他没能耐，不能供给一家的活计，使他的孩子们没有东西吃，也没有衣服穿。婆罗门人虽然很穷，却是一个非常良善的人。他对于敬天的礼拜每日必依时举行。在他的一生里头，他没有一日不祈祷。他的保护神是湿婆①的配偶，女神杜尔迦②。他每天必用红朱把杜尔迦的圣名写一百零八遍然后饮食。他没有一天不祈祷说："杜尔迦呀！杜尔迦呀！杜尔迦呀！可怜可怜我吧。"他一想起他对于取得生活资料的无能，致使他一家的人受冻饿之苦，他就叫，"杜尔迦！杜尔迦！杜尔迦！"

　　有一天，他悲哀到极致，就跑到离他所住的村里好几十里的树林里去，在那里痛哭。他望空祈祷说："杜尔迦呀，大母薄伽婆帝呀，你为何不把我的悲苦除掉呢？如果只是我自己一个，我就不至于穷到这步田地，可是你已赐给我一个妻子和四个孩子，叫我实在没法供养他们。大母呀，赐给我一种养活他们的方法吧。"那天

---

　　①② 原文为"大自在天"（Siva），现通译为"湿婆"，印度教三大主神之一，为毁灭之神。原文为"都尔格"（Durga），现通译为"杜尔迦"，湿婆妻子帕尔瓦蒂的化身之一，主司女性的力量。——编者注

正值湿婆和他的配偶杜尔迦来到林中作早晨的散步。女神远远地便看见那忠诚的婆罗门人在那里向她祷告。她对她的丈夫说："开拉的主宰呀，你看见那婆罗门人没有？他时常叫我的名字来祈祷，求我拯救他，使他脱离贫乏的苦恼。我的夫主，我们能不能为他的穷乏想一个方法来救济他呢？他的家累实在太大。我想我们应当赐给他一切所需的。因为他和他的家人时常没有吃的，我想就给他一个会出甜炒米饼的土罐吧。"湿婆以他的配偶所说的为然，随即做出一个土罐，里面充满了甜炒米饼。杜尔迦于是把婆罗门人叫来对他说："婆罗门人呀，我对于你的请求时时想到。你反复地祈祷引动了我的慈悲。我现在赐给你这个土罐。如果你要用它的时候，只将它翻转过来摇摇，就会摇出不尽的甜炒米饼来，你如觉得够了，只将土罐翻正就可以。你，你的妻子和孩子们都可以尽量地吃从罐里摇出来的饼，剩下的还可以拿到市上去卖。"婆罗门人得到那宝贝，便向女神礼拜，把土罐捧在手里，一直向着家门飞跑。但他跑了不远，心里想试一试那土罐到底能出甜炒米饼不能，于是住了脚，把罐子摇起来。甜炒米饼从罐子里泻出许多来。他心里自然非常欢喜，把地下的饼捡起来藏在身边，又往前走。天色已经晚了，天上只露出一弯月牙，他也饿了，但他从来要在祈祷及沐浴以后才吃东西的。他看见一所客舍离池子不远，就想着先把土罐寄存在那里，自己去沐浴祈祷，再回来吃甜炒米饼。他于是走到客店，歇了一会儿，抽过烟，抹过芥子油，然后把土罐交给主人。他嘱咐主人要好好地看着那土罐，然后走到池边去洗澡。

婆罗门人走了以后，客店主人对于他的叮咛反觉得非常奇怪。他想着一个不值什么的土罐，怎么会宝贵成这样？因为好奇的缘故，他把土罐打开来看，也没看出有什么东西在里头，他更觉得奇怪了。他将土罐翻来覆去地观察，正当他翻转过来察看罐的时候，不尽的甜炒米饼就从罐里泻出来！店主人于是叫他的妻子和孩子来看。他们都以为这是天赐给他们的，就立意要把宝贵的土罐藏起来，把一个平常的、大小和原来一样的土罐，放在方才婆罗门人寄放的地方。不久，婆罗门人沐浴和祈祷完了。他回到客舍里，嘴里还背诵着《吠陀》圣典，衣服还是很湿。他把干净的衣服换上，把杜尔迦的名字写了一百零八遍，然后吃方才在道上摇出来的甜炒米饼。吃过之后，他就要启程回家了，他叫店主人把土罐拿来给回他。店主人就把那假的拿来，还对他说："这就是你的土罐，你自己放在那里以后就没有人去摩触过。"婆罗门人也不理会是真的或是假的，拿着土罐就往回家的道上走，自己还很得意，以为可以对得起妻子了。他在道上自言自语地说："我的妻子一定很惊讶。我的孩子们必定要喜欢从此罐里倒出来的食品！我还可以将剩下的卖钱！那么，我不久便要成为富翁了。"走了许久，归程已经尽了。他一进门就大声叫着妻子和孩子们，说："你们都来，看我今天得着一件宝贝！我们要成富翁了。这个土罐里头藏着不尽的甜炒米饼。当我把它翻过来时，你们都要预备把甜炒米饼捡起来吃。"他的妻子听见这套离奇的话，想着她的丈夫必是疯了。她看见他把罐翻过来，却倒不出什么甜炒米饼，更是怀疑她丈夫害了什么病。婆罗门人还在那里尽管使劲摇，却摇不出什么来。他到那时才觉得土罐一定是被店主人偷换去了。第二天他跑到客店去和店主人理论。店主人反生气起来，说他是有意诬赖，把他撵了出去。

婆罗门人被撵出来之后，心里自然非常忧郁，他想着不如再到树林里去向杜尔迦禀告他所经过的情形。他到树林的时候，可巧湿婆又和杜尔迦又在那里散步。女神对他说："你真的把土罐丢了！这里还有一个，你就拿去，好好地用吧。"他又得着一个土罐，心里极其愉快，又向着家门飞跑。他跑了不远，又要试试这个罐的甜炒米饼和那一个有什么不同。唉，可怕极了！他一摇就摇出许多凶恶的鬼怪来，什么形状都有。它们起首围在婆罗门人身边，用它们的残酷手段来戏弄他。他心里想着这是什么一回事，快把土罐反正，鬼怪也就一个一个地灭迹了。想了又想，他醒悟了这是女神命他拿去责罚店主人的。他于是将土罐捧在手里，安详地又来到店主

他一摇就摇出许多凶恶的鬼怪出来，什么形状都有

人这里。他再请求店主人把土罐放好，等他到池里沐浴和祈祷以后才回来取。店主人自然是很乐意，因为他想这个呆子又送宝贝来了。这一个定是比前一个更好的。他把妻子和孩子们叫来说："那个送甜炒米饼土罐的婆罗门人又另送我们一个来了。这个，我希望不是出甜炒米饼，乃是出酥酪的。你们快去预备盘子来盛吧，等你们预备好，我就把它翻转过来摇。"他们都去拿盘子和篮子了，预备要盛酥酪。可是店主人一摇，只摇出满天鬼怪！店主人和家人都受它们的蹂躏，全店的人没有一个得着安宁。婆罗门人这时慢慢地走回来，店主人哀求他把鬼怪撵走，情愿把那出炒米饼的土罐奉还。婆罗门人把鬼罐翻正，鬼怪一时都绝迹了。他拿着两罐子从容地回到家中。

他到家以后，把饼罐翻过来摇，果然泻出无量的炒米饼。那饼的气味，是一切饼师所不能调制的。他们自己吃了，剩下的就拿到市场去卖。他们赚了许多钱，渐渐自己预备盘子，就在家门口开了一个铺子。就在他们开张的那一天，已经赚了不少的钱财，因为远近的人都争着要来买那奇异的米饼。他们都没曾尝过那么好的饼，又白，又甜，又香，又大块。世间实在没有一个饼师能够做出那么好的饼而又卖得那么便宜。那婆罗门人的饼驰名远近，不久，他就变成富翁了。他新盖了一所房子，直和本地的绅士所住的一样。

有一天，因为婆罗门人不在家，他的孩子们把那鬼罐拿来玩。孩子们把罐翻过来，摇出许多怪物，几乎把全间房子都捣碎了。幸亏婆罗门人回来得早一点，不然，他的财产就要荡尽。他自那时，就把鬼罐藏在一个常锁着的屋里。

　　婆罗门人的家境一天好似一天，所有的财主都不能和他比。有一天，婆罗们人又出去了，孩子都争着要摇那饼罐。个个都喜欢看米饼从自己的手里摇出来。因为彼此争夺的缘故，把罐子摔在了地下。饼罐破了！婆罗门人回家以后，知道这桩事体，自然是很不高兴。可是罐子已经破了，他把孩子打骂也是没用处。过了几天，他又跑到树林里去祈祷，向杜尔迦致敬礼，用许多供品去供献给她。他又禀告那罐子被孩子们摔破的事。杜尔迦于是又给他一个罐子，说："婆罗门人，仔细用这个罐子吧。你若再不小心，把它丢失，或打破了，我就不再给你了。"婆罗门人喜欢到不得了，谢了她，一直跑回家中。

　　他到家的时候，妻子和孩子看见他又拿着一个土罐回来，各人非常欢喜，把盘子取过来，预备承受泻出来的米饼。这回可不是米饼，乃是极甘美的酥酪！各人又惊又喜。因为他们一向不曾见过那么好的酥酪。那实在不是人间的食品，乃是诸天的食品。他起首贩卖酥酪了。他的饼店一天发达似一天，到处都有他的货物。逢着婚事或节日，他的生意特别好。因为他的酥酪比别家格外好，所以远近的人都争着来买，他一天总要出许多罐的货。

婆罗门人的富厚，引起了本村村长的注意。他听人家说婆罗门人所卖的酥酪并不是人做的，乃是从一个土罐里摇出来的。那时正值他的儿子娶妻，村长为他预备筵席，自然要用许多酥酪。村长命婆罗门人把土罐带来，因为他要亲自看见酥酪从那神奇的器具泻出来。婆罗门人起先不愿意，怎奈村长必要他这样办，他只得遵命。其实村长并不存好心，他眼看婆罗门人把许多酥酪摇出来之后，就硬把土罐留住，并且将物主撵出去。婆罗门人也不声张，自己跑回家里把那鬼罐取出来，又一直地到村长那里去。他放出许多许多的妖魔，把村长的家宅嬲乱一场。所有的男女客人都被鬼怪打的打，扯的扯！尤其是女客们，直被他们拨弄得衣服也撕破，头发也散乱了。村长被鬼从这屋追到那屋，直如狂风卷败絮一般，滚来滚去，不由自主。村长眼看他的客人个个都被嬲得要死，自己更是受不了，于是向婆罗门人跪着求饶。婆罗门人把酥酪罐夺过来，然后把鬼怪收回去。自此以后，没有人敢存着霸占他那神奇土罐的心了。他的日子一天过得好似一天，成为一个极富有的人。

我的故事说到这里算完了，

那提耶也枯萎了。

那提耶呵，你为什么枯萎呢？

你的牛为什么要我用草来喂它？

牛呵，你为什么要人喂？

你的牧者为什么不看护我？

牧者呵，你为什么不去看牛？

你的儿媳妇为什么不把米给我？

儿媳妇呵，你为什么不给米呢？

我的孩子为什么哭呢？

孩子呵，你为什么哭呢？

蚂蚁为什么要咬我呢？

蚂蚁呵，你为什么要咬人呢？

咯！咯！咯！

四　罗刹国

从前有一个穷乏而少智的婆罗门人和他的妻子住在一起。他们没有子女。他越来越穷，甚至连妻子也养不起。最坏的就是他那样的懒惰。他不喜欢走远道去收纳富人们的施舍。如果他肯，他的妻子也不至于挨饿，并且可以同过很安适的生活。那时邻国的王母去世，国王为她举行很热闹的丧礼。婆罗门人与乞士们都从各国集聚在那都城，等候王的布施。少智而懒惰的婆罗门人被他的妻子所怂恿，命他也到邻国的都城去，希望可以得着些礼物，但他还是不愿意去。妇人用尽许多方法来刺激他，使他不能不应许。他最终应许要去。妇人于是把一棵芭蕉树砍下来，烧成灰，为的是要给她的丈夫洗衣服。因为她的丈夫要去王宫里求施舍，自然要穿得整齐白净。又因为他是个婆罗门人，衣服也应当比别人洁白，所以她不惜把那棵树砍下来应用。婆罗门人在那天一早就离开家，向着邻国的都城前行。他生来就很愚憨，在道上走，也不问问人应当往哪里去。他只照着他眼睛所看着的道路走。这样走，自然会走错了。他经过的地方，起先还有些居民，后来越走越远，人民越稀少起来，乃至走了半天，全然没曾遇见什么人。他也不觉得奇怪，只顾往前走。

　　他走到一条道上，看见道旁满是货贝，正要去捡，又看见前面堆满了铜币。到了堆满铜币的地方，他看见前面道旁都是银币堆成的小山。到了银币堆成的小山，他又看见前面堆着无数的金子。那些金币明亮得直像初出熔炉的颜色。靠近金币堆成小山前头有一座很华丽的宫殿，好像是国王的行宫。婆罗门人走到宫门口，看见一个女人正站在那里，容貌长得非常美丽。女人看见他走近时，便大声叫说："来吧，我亲爱的丈夫，我自幼年与你结婚之后，你从不曾来过我这里。我日夜在此地盼着你来咧。今天真是幸福，使我能够见着我的丈夫。我的心肝，进来吧，我替你把脚上的尘土洗净，你在长途中行走怪疲乏的，歇歇去吧。歇过之后，我给你端吃的和喝的，完了，我还与你一同快乐去。"

婆罗门人觉得非常奇怪。他总想不起他除了与现时在家里的那个女人结婚以外，还有这一件事。因为他是个枯林婆罗门人，他想也许是他父亲在他幼年已经为他娶了这个媳妇，所以他不知道。但无论他记得或是忘记，那妇人一口咬定了他是她的丈夫。婆罗门人心里想着有这样的妻子也不错，她的美貌直如因陀罗天中的女神，她的富裕自然也是和她的美丽相称。他定神看着那妇人发痴。妇人再对他说："你心里怀疑我不是你的妻么。我们行婚礼那时候是多么热闹，那时你都忘记了么？我所爱的，进来吧，这是你的家，凡属于我的，都为你所有，都是你的。"婆罗门人受了那妇人的劝请，随着她进到屋里。那房子并非平常，乃是一座王宫，房室厅堂

一个女人正站在宫门口，长得非常美丽

都陈设得非常华丽。只有一件事叫婆罗门人诧异的，便是那么大一座宫殿，除了那妇人以外，一个人也没有。他住在那里，早晚到花园散步，总不见有什么人。这个缘故，他不能解释。其实那妇人并不是人，乃是一个罗刹女。她霸占了这个宫殿，把从前住着的王、王后及他们的眷属都吃掉了。后来她又把全国的人民一个一个吞噬了。所以婆罗门人在道上走了半天，总看不见有什么居民。

婆罗门人和罗刹女住了差不多有七八天的工夫，罗刹女就对他说："我很愿意见见我的姊姊，你的那一位妻子。你务必把她带来，我们可以一同在这里过快活的日子。这美丽而宽敞的房舍都是我们自己的。你明天一早就去吧，为我带些珠宝和锦绣送给她。"第二天早晨，婆罗门人果然穿起极美的衣服，带上宝贵的装饰品起程回家。

再说婆罗门人的妻子见别的婆罗门人和教师们都从那举行丧礼的王都回来了，她的丈夫一去七八天总不见影儿，心里实在难过。她看见许多赴那丧礼的人都带着许多的礼物回来，一向他们打听，都说没有看见他在那里，也不晓得他的下落。妻子心里断定他一定是在道上被强盗害死了。她正在难过的时候，忽然听见人家说她丈夫穿戴得很华丽在村外走着。正在疑信参半的时候，她丈夫已经带着罗刹女所赠的珠宝服饰来到她面前。婆罗门人一见他妻子，便说："我最爱的妻子，同我来吧，我已经找着我的第一位妻子了。她住在一座很华丽的宫廷里，那里有金山和银山，我们可以受用不尽。你为什么要自己一个人在此地受苦呢？同我到我第一位妻子那里去吧，我们一同过快活日子去。"妇人起先听见他说的金山，银山和第一位妻子，以为她丈夫是疯了，可是她看见他身上的确穿得很整齐，手里又拿着许多礼物，丝绸珠宝，都是后妃所用的东西，心里就想着她丈夫恐怕是遇见罗刹女了。她不敢说，也不愿意去。她丈夫急了，说如果她不去，她可以在老家挨苦，他可要去跟着他第一位富有的妻子住，永远不回来。妇人无可奈何，只得跟着他去，心里也想看看这事的来历到底是怎样。第二天早晨他们就离开老家，向罗刹女那里的道上走。他们经过贝山，铜山，金山，可是妻子一点也不惊奇。不久他们到了宫门口，罗刹女已经在那里候着。妇人被她扑过来，搂着她说："我所爱的姊姊，我欢迎你来！这是我一生最快乐的日子！因为我能与我最爱的姊姊相见！"她一手挽着妇人，一手挽着男子，三个人一同进屋里去。

婆罗门人在那宫里过的日子实在是很舒服。他的日用饮食都像从咒术得来的。他两个妻子，一个是人，一个是罗刹，都很敬爱他，所以他现在是一个福分极大的人。他在这愉快的洋海中过日子，一瞬间已经过了十五六年。罗刹女生了一个儿子，模样儿直像一个天神，婆罗门人给他起个名字叫娑诃斯罗多罗，意思就是"千枝"。原来的妻子也生了一个儿子，比千枝小一岁，名叫赡波多罗，意思是"赡波迦花枝"。两个孩子彼此都很相爱，他们一同到很远的村塾念书，每日骑着轻快的小马去。

十几年来，赡波多罗的母亲常怀疑娑诃斯罗多罗的母亲不是一个人，乃是一个罗刹女。她从许多许多事实得着这样的结论，可是不能证实。罗刹女也很能够自己检点，凡一切人做的事，她都做到，一切非人所做的，她未尝做出来。可是破绽终归要露出来的。婆罗门人觉得太过闲适，很想出去打猎消遣。他第一天出去打猎，便猎得一只羚羊回来。他把死的野兽放在院子，自己进屋里去更换衣服。罗刹女看见羚羊，嘴边就不歇地流出涎沫来。因为凡是罗刹都是喜欢吃生肉的。她性急起来，不等人把羚羊煮熟了，自己便将它取到屋里去，张着大嘴，把生肉一下一下地撕下来吃。婆罗门妇人本来就窥伺着她的行动，今天忽然看见她把羚羊拉到房里，自然要躲在一个幽秘的地方看她怎样行为。她看见罗刹女把羚羊的腿撕下来，一直就往嘴里塞。她的嘴真大得可怕，模样也是怪凶的。后来她看见只剩下一点羚羊肉，就不敢再吃了。她把那块肉拿到厨房去。第二天和第三天婆罗门人都猎得羚羊，她一样地自己先拿到房里生吃了一大部分，然后拿到厨房去。一连三天她这样做，都被婆罗门妇人看见。她忍不住了，在第三天，就对她的罗刹同伴现出惊讶的神气说："怎么许多肉都不见了，每次只剩下这一点。"罗刹女听见她的话刺到心头，便含怒地回答说："难道我吃生肉吗？"婆罗门妇人说："也许你是吃生肉的，我决然知道你能吃。"罗刹女知道她所做的事被发现了，更是生气，存心要复仇。婆罗门妇人到底很聪明，她断定了她自己、她的丈夫和儿子，必定要遇见凶恶的命运。那晚上，她不敢睡，因为她想着第二天早晨她将要被吃，她的丈夫与儿子也要遇见同样的厄运。在第二天早晨，她当赡波多罗要去上学的时候，就从她乳房上挤出一些乳汁注在一个金瓶里，交给儿子说："儿呀，若是你看见瓶里的乳汁变成淡红色，就知道你父亲已被害。若是你看见它变得更红一些，就知道你母亲也被婆诃斯罗多罗的母亲害死了。你如看见这样的光景，就得赶快骑上你的小马逃命去，不然，你也要被她吞噬了。"

罗刹女从床上下地，对婆罗门人说她要同他到离宫不远一个水池去洗澡。她一整夜不许婆罗门人和他原来的妻子说话，对于她的要求，他也没法不依。他在道上走着，好像一只小绵羊跟着凶恶的屠夫一般。婆罗门妇人立刻看出她丈夫的厄运到了，可是她没有方法和能力可以阻止罗刹女不去做那残酷的事情。罗刹女走到河边，便露出原形，将她丑恶的脸翻过来，两只带着利爪的手提着婆罗门人，把他撕开，在那里慢慢地吃。吃完之后，她立刻跑回宫里，又把婆罗门妇人连衣服及身上的一切都吞进肚子里去。

赡波多罗在书房里，眼看着金瓶里的乳汁变了颜色，因为母亲曾告诉过他，所以他知道父亲已经被害。不到一会儿的工夫，乳汁变成绯红色，他就大哭起来，赶紧跑出书房，骑上小马，试要逃避这场灾难。他的兄弟娑诃斯罗多罗看见他走得匆促，就赶出来问他说："赡波，你要到哪里去？你哭什么？你要走，我跟着你走吧。"

"唉，求你不要来我这里！你的母亲把我的爹和妈都吃了。请你不要再把我吃掉。"

"不要害怕，我不会吃你。我要救你。"娑诃斯罗本就知道他母亲不是人类，现在看见她远远地露出原形在那里叫赡波多罗。他说，"容我到你那里，赡波不能去。"说着，他带着一把小剑，一直走到他母亲面前，出其不意，把她的头砍下来。

赡波多罗一听见罗刹女叫他的时候，便勒起马来，飞跑到很远的地方。娑诃斯罗回来，不见了弟弟，也赶紧拉过马来，骑上去，在后面追赶他。不久，他被娑诃斯罗追上了。他哥哥告诉他他怎样把自己的母亲杀死，他才明白他们彼此的友爱是真实的。他们所骑的马本是鸟王马种，所以在很短的时间已跑了数千里路途。在日落之前，他到了一个村落，向一家尊贵的主人求宿。那主人很喜悦地接待他们，为他们安排卧具，预备饮食。兄弟们在谈话间，发现了主人和他的眷属都带着很忧愁的神采。他们断定主人家中必定出了什么不幸的事情。因为他们看见家人交头接耳，好像商量要事似的，并且有人在一边哭泣。他们听见老主妇说："容我去吧。我是主妇，应当去。我年纪也老了，活够了，要活也不过是多两三年罢了。容我去吧。"家里一个幼女又争着说："容我去吧，我年纪又小，又不能助理家务。如果我死掉，家里也不见得有什么损失。"但主人说："我是一家之主，是代表一家事务，担当家中一切危难的，所以我应当去为你们丧命。"主人的弟弟对他说："你是一家的梁柱，绝对不能容你去，如果你一去，这一家就要毁坏了。容我去吧，你无论如何，是不能去的，容我去吧。我去了，家里也不至于有多少损失。"两个寄宿的兄弟听见主人与他的眷属说的这些话，心里非常诧异。他们不晓得到底是为什么。娑诃斯罗忍不住，最终问了主人他们彼此方才所商量的是什么事。主人不得已就对他们说："尊贵的客人，你们须知在这个国土里住着一个罗刹，她把国人吃了许多。这村的人不幸也要依次被她残害，于是我们的王求她的怜悯，应许每夜由王供献一个人民给她吃。罗刹女对王说，如果每夜王能够献给她一个人，不论男女老幼，将那牺牲者带到一个她常去的庙里等她来吃，她就不再吞噬别人。如不然，她必在一夜间把全国的人都害死。我们的王没有别的方策，只好照着她所要求的去办。人哪里能够与罗刹争强呢？从那天起，王命国中的人民，各家轮流每夜要送一个人到庙里去供养她。所有附近的邻舍都轮到了，今晚上该轮到我们这家，所以方才我们在商量谁应当去咧。我们的不幸，想现在你们能够体会。"

　　他们两弟兄彼此商量了一会儿，娑诃斯罗便对主人说："最尊敬的主人，请你不要为这事发愁。你曾善待我们，我们愿意替你到庙里去做那罗刹的食品。我们代表你去得啦。"主人和他的眷属都不赞同这个提议。他们说客人的尊贵是和天神一样的，岂可容他们来担当家里的困难？天下也没有叫客人为主人受苦之理，做主人的本有使客人安适的责任。但是无论他们怎样反对，娑诃斯罗和赡波一定要去，主人无奈，只得应许他们。

　　在掌灯时分，娑诃斯罗和赡波一同骑上马来到庙里，把大门关上。哥哥命弟弟先去睡，他自己一个人坐在殿上守着，等那凶恶的罗刹来到。赡波不久便睡着了，但娑诃斯罗还睁着眼睛，留神四围的动静。起先并不见有何等动静，可是一到王宫的锣敲了中夜的信息时，娑诃斯罗便听见一阵怪风随着一阵怪响从远地传到殿里来。他理会罗刹快要到了。他静候着，听见门外拍门的声音响得很厉害，还说着：

"后，亩，口！我闻见一个人的气味，在里面守着的是谁？"

娑诃斯罗在里面回答：

"娑诃斯罗多罗守着；赡波多罗守着；两匹飞马守着。"

罗刹一听见娑诃斯罗的声音，便知道他是罗刹种，她发了一声怪叫便走了。过了一会儿，罗刹又来，捶着门说：

"后，亩，口！我闻见一个人的气味，在里面守着的是谁？"

娑诃斯罗又回答说：

"娑诃斯罗多罗守着；赡波多罗守着；两匹飞马守着。"

罗刹听了，又发出怪响就走了。以后每一个时辰，她必来一次，作同样的问。娑诃斯罗也必用同样的话回答她。她最终不敢进到庙里来。娑诃斯罗疲乏得很，不能再振作精神了，他于是把赡波摇醒，教他罗刹来时怎样对付。他吩咐弟弟在回答中必要把娑诃斯罗的名字先说出来。到了天快亮的时候，罗刹又来了。她捶着大门，口里大声说：

"后，亩，口！我闻见一个人的气味，在里面守着的是谁？"

赡波听见那可怕的声音，身上直抖起来。他忘记了他哥哥告诉他的话，就回答说：

"赡波多罗守着；娑诃斯罗多罗守着；两匹飞马守着。"

罗刹听见他的回答，就大声嚷起来，把门破坏，跳了进来，大笑不止。她的笑声的可怕，只有鬼物才可以发出，人类从来不会那样笑。娑诃斯罗在睡眠中被她的笑声惊醒，赶紧起来，提着那杀过母亲的剑，飞跑过来，趁着她不提防，把那罗刹的头砍下来。她的身体从半空中掉下来，声音震动了全地。尸体横卧着，也占了好几亩地。娑诃斯罗把罗刹的头束在腰间，自己就安睡去。第二天早晨，有几个樵夫从庙旁经过，他们看见那罗刹的遗骸横卧在道边，就记起王曾出过命令说如果有人能把罗刹杀死，就要赐给他国土的一半，并且要将王女嫁给他。每个樵夫因为没看见谁是杀死罗刹的人，各人心里都想拿那尸体去报功求奖。于是每人把那尸体的肢节分解下来，你拿一块，他拿一块，争着跑到王朝里去。各人都说他是杀死罗刹的英雄。王因为要知道到底是谁的功劳，就问宰相，昨晚应当是哪一家轮到送人到庙里去的。宰相一查，立刻命人把昨晚轮到送人的主人带到王的面前。主人对王说是他二位从远道来的客人替他家人到庙里去的。王于是命人到庙里，看大门已经毁破，娑诃斯罗和赡波还在那里。因为罗刹的头是在娑诃斯罗的手里，所以王断定他是真正的英雄，于是把女儿许给他，并且赐给他国土的一半。赡波和他哥哥同住在宫里，享受一切的愉快。

　　可惜他们兄弟二人同住在宫里不久就发生了一点猜忌。因为有一个后母的侍女很得她女主人的宠爱。宫中一切的事情，王后的母亲非要她办不可。她的聪明和手艺，宫里的人没有一个能与她比较。如果她一日不在，宫中的秩序便要紊乱起来。因此王后的母亲常优待她，使她的地位高过一切宫人。可是这个女人不是人类，乃是一个罗刹所现少女的形状到宫里来的。在夜阑人静的时候，她必露出原形，到处找寻她的食品，因为日间一个女人的食量，不能使她饱满。赡波因为没有妻子，所以睡在宫外近大门的地方。只有他知道那侍女在晚间出去吃羊、马和大象。侍女不久也觉得赡波注意她的行动，心里想把他除掉。有一天，她在服侍王后母亲的时候，忽然对她说："母后呀！我不能再在宫里服侍你了。"后母诧异地问："为什么呢，女侍？我怎能容你走呢？你把你要走的理由说给我听吧。你有什么委屈？"侍女说："唉，事情闹到现在，使我不能再在此地久留了。你女婿的朋友赡波时常调戏我，用不好听的话对我说。所以我想我应当避开，不然我就会把我的贞洁丢了。如果赡波在这宫里住，我是一定要走的。"后母听见侍女一番说话，决定要把赡波撵走。她想着侍女比他有用处。于是命人把娑诃斯罗叫来，说他的兄弟不是好人，品行极坏，不应当再容他住在宫里。娑诃斯罗劝说了一番，终于无效。他自己不忍亲自对兄弟说后母的意思，只写了一封信给他，命他立刻离开王宫。信到的时候，赡波正在洗澡，等他从浴室出来看了信便带着愁容上了马出了宫门。

　　赡波的马跑得非常快，不一会儿已走了几千里路。他走到一座很华丽的宫廷，下了马，慢慢走进去。他在宫院走着，始终未曾遇见一个人。他进入宫里，从这间房穿到那间房，也不见有人，只见陈设得非常华丽。最后，他走到一间房里，看见一个绝世的美人躺在一张非常富丽的床上。她正睡着，像死人一样。赡波注视着那少女，身体觉得有点振动，因为他从来未曾见过这么好看的女人。在床边，少女的头上，放着两根杖，一根是银的，一根是金的。赡波不敢亲自用手去摇醒她，就拿起银杖来推她一下，可是没有效果。她还是睡着。他又把金杖取下来，把它放在少女身上。她忽然醒过来，很惊讶地注视着赡波，问他从哪里来，他是什么人。赡波把事由略述一遍。少女说："不幸的人，你来此地做什么？这里是罗刹国，在这宫中住着七百个罗刹。他们每日早晨到海洋边去找寻食物，到晚间才跑回来。我父亲原本是这国的王，所属有十万百姓，前几年忽然到了一群罗刹，把人民一个一个吃掉，渐次把我父母兄弟都杀害了。他们不但吃人，这国里的牲口也都被吃得干干净净。现在这国里除了我一个人还存在，其余的早已化为尘土了。我也几乎被吃，可幸一个老罗刹女非常爱我，把我留住。她不许别的罗刹走近我身边。每早她要出去的时候，必要把那银杖来触我，使我倒

她忽然醒过来，坐在她的床上很惊讶地注视着眼前的陌生人，问他是谁

下，到晚间回来，才用金杖把我叫醒。我不晓得要用什么方法救你脱离这场危难，如果他们回来，一看见你，你就是一个死人了。"

他们彼此对谈，情感渐次发生。他们躺在一起，试要想个方法避免要来的灾难。眼看七百罗刹回来的时间快到了，王女想起宫中有个湿婆神庙里头一棵三叶树下可以容身，因为罗刹们不敢到那里去。赡波问了王女叫什么名字。她说是客萨婆帝，意思是"长发"，因为她的头发特别长。赡波在离开长发公主之前，便用银杖触她。她立刻躺下，像死人一般。

黄昏到了，赡波在神庙里的三叶圣树下隐隐听见狂风大作。后来，渐次听见宫里发出许多怪音，他便知道罗刹们回来了。罗刹出外所求的食物不外是山羊、绵羊、牛、马、大象之类。各个吃得饱饱的，一回来都躺下睡觉。那个老罗刹跑到长发公主房里，用金杖触动她说：

"赫，弥，客！我闻见一个人的气味。"

长发公主回答她说："只有我一个人在此地，如果你喜欢，就把我吃掉吧。"那老罗刹说："我要吃你的仇敌，我为什么要吃你？"她躺在地上不久就睡着了。她的身体高大得像宾陀山一样。长发公主也装着睡去的模样，唯有赡波在神庙里抖搂了一夜，不敢出来，也不敢睡。第二早晨，罗刹们都出去了。老罗刹照常把银杖将长发公主触倒，也跟着群怪出去。赡波看见他们都去了，才慢慢从神庙出来，走到长发公主的房间，用金杖把她触醒。他们一同到园里散步，享受早晨的清风；一同到浴池去洗澡；同吃，同喝；整整过了一天的愉快生活。他们没有忘掉想出脱离这班鬼物的方法。赡波教长发公主用计问老罗刹，看他们的生命寄托在什么地方，或者可以从那方面处置他们。到日快西沉的时候，赡波仍然用银杖触她，使她倒下，自己再跑到神庙里去藏着。夜到了，罗刹们依时回来。老罗刹走进长发公主的房里说：

"赫，弥，客！我闻见一个人的气味。"

长发公主照常回答她说："除了我以外，哪里还有别的人在这里？如果你喜欢，可以把我吃掉。""我为什么要吃你，我的宝贝？容我吃你的仇敌。"她说完，又躺下睡着了。她的身体高大得像喜马拉雅山一般。长发公主拿了一瓶温暖的芥子油走到老罗刹的脚下说："母亲，你的脚板都走破了皮，等我用油来替你涂涂吧。"她说着，把油在罗刹脚上涂抹了一回。正在涂抹的时候，她的眼泪滴在那怪物的腿上。那怪物用舌头去舐，觉得是咸味，就说："我的宝贝，你为什么哭？什么事情使你不喜欢？"公主回答她说："母亲哪，我哭，因为你老了，如果你一死掉，我一定要被他们吃掉。""我死么！呆女儿，你要知道罗刹是永远不死的。我们虽然不是永远活着的，可是我们的生命是寄存在一种东西里，为人类所不知道的。我索性说给你知道吧。你知道那里有一个水池，池的中间有一根水晶柱子，柱头有两只马蜂，如果有人能够没入水底，把那两只马蜂捕上水面来，打死它们，我们就没命了。但入水和出水只要一气，不能做第二次的呼吸，把马蜂捉住，一出水就立刻把它们打死，也不能使半滴血滴落在地上。若不然，那滴血必要再化成千万个罗刹。你想人类之中，谁能做到这事呢？所以我的宝贝，你不用发愁，我是死不掉的。"长发公主把这个秘密记住，自己就上床睡觉去了。

第二天早晨，罗刹们照常出外去求食，赡波从神庙出来，把长发公主摇醒，彼此谈了一会儿。公主告诉他罗刹们的生命所寄托的地方。赡波立即预备要去做那伤害罗刹们的事。他带了一把刀和许多灰到所说的池边，把衣服脱下来，用两滴芥子油滴在耳里，因为怕水渗进耳朵里去，随即没入水的。果然池中深处有一根水晶柱子，在柱头歇着两只马蜂，他把它们拿住，一气泅上水面来。他用小刀在灰上把两只马蜂截为两段，蜂血滴在灰上，没有沾污了地面。当赡波拿住两只马蜂的时候，在很远的地方传来一阵可怕的声音。这声音是从罗刹们那里发出的。他们赶快跑回来，要保护那对马蜂。可是在他们到池边之前，那对马蜂已经被杀死了。马蜂一死，所有的罗刹都在各个所站的地方丧了命。瞻波和公主回来的时候，看见满路都堆满了罗刹的遗骸，连宫门也被堵住。有些已经走到宫门口了。

自从瞻波把七百个罗刹治死以后，他便和公主结婚。因为那里只有他们两人，所以只行交换华鬘的典礼。公主一向不曾离开宫廷，自然很愿意出外走走，看看外面的世界。他们两夫妇每日都出宫到处去游玩，朝出暮归，习以为常。有一天，他们走到一条大河岸边，公主想要下去洗一个澡。当她第一次在河边洗澡的时候，她掉了一根头发。凡女人所掉的头发要扔掉的时候，必得把它和别的东西放在一起。所以公主把她那根掉下来的头发缠在水边一个贝壳上，放在水面，由它流去。他们洗完澡就一同回家。

那缠着头发的贝壳顺下流过河边一个浴场。那浴场是娑诃斯罗所常到的。正当娑诃斯罗和他的朋友在那里洗澡的时候，他看见远地漂流着一样东西。他的好奇心使他对朋友们说："谁能够去把那东西取来，我必定有重重的报酬给他。我也与你们比赛。"他们听了，各人争着向贝壳漂流的水面泅去。娑诃斯罗最擅于泅水，贝壳最终还是被他取到。他拿到岸边一看，只见贝壳上缠着一根很长的头发，"呀，一根头发！"他们都很惊奇，因为他们一向不曾见过那么长的头发。它的长度足有七肘长。娑诃斯罗断定说，"有这根头发的，一定是个尊贵而有来历的女人，我一定要见着她。"娑诃斯罗从河边回到宫中，心心想念要见那有长头发的女人。他连早饭也不吃，只坐在宫廷外头的廊上出神。母后看见她女婿像有忧愁存在心里，就走来问他。他把那根长发给她看，并且说他非见着那人才安心。母后对他说："这个容易，我命人把她领到宫里便是了。我应许你把她带来，你别着急。"她说得很有把握，因为深信她那罗刹变形的侍女可以办得到。她把头发拿着，叫侍女来，问她能否把那人找出来给她的女婿。侍女不迟疑地答应说她可以办得到。她命人用诃耶木做船，用孟婆班木做桨。做好了，她便到河边，上了船，带着许多很奇怪的柳篮和一些掺杂了毒药的糖果。她用指头作了三下响声，便念咒说：

"诃耶木做的船，孟婆班木做的桨，送我到长发，洗澡的浴场。"

她一念了咒，那船便像电一样，在水面飞驶。船经过许多城邑，最后停在河边一个浴场。罗刹侍女知道已经到了长发洗澡的地方，便携着糖果上岸去。她一直访寻到宫门口，大声嚷说："长发呵，长发呀！我是你的姨母，我是你母亲的姊妹。我现在来看你哪。我的宝贝，我们离别已经好些年了。长发，你在里头么？"公主正在房里，一听见有人在外头嚷着，就立刻跑出来，搂着那罗刹侍女便与她接吻。罗刹侍女假装哭出来，长发公主也同情地流了一些愉快的眼泪。她一点也不怀疑那罗刹侍女是个假姨母。赡波本不大知道他妻子有多少亲戚，所以也没怀疑。他们同在一起吃中饭，各人都尽欢地受用。赡波的习惯，每在中饭后必要歇午的，所以一散席，他就自己到房里去了。到午后，那位假姨母对公主说："我们到河边去洗澡吧。"公主说："我丈夫现在睡着咧，我们怎能去呢？"假姨母说："不要紧，由他睡去吧。我把我带来的糖果放在他床边，他醒时就可以吃，所以不必再伺候他。"她们于是同到河边，那只船还系在那里。长发公主看见船里放着许多异样的柳篮，便对假姨母说："姨母，你看那些篮子多么美啊，我很愿意自己也有一个。""我的儿，去吧，你要多少，就可以拿多少。"公主原先不愿意到那船上去，可是姨母一味地鼓励着她，她们就一同上了船。她们一上船，罗刹侍女又用指头做了三下响声，念着咒说：

"诃耶木做的船，孟婆班木做的桨，送我到娑诃斯罗，洗澡的浴场。"

她一念完这咒，船便像箭一般，在水面飞驶。长发公主这时害怕起来，在船上大哭。可是那船不停地直驶过了许多城邑，最终停在娑诃斯罗常到的浴场旁边。罗刹侍女把长发带到宫中，娑诃斯罗惊叹她的美丽和特别长的头发。他命宫里的人用各种方法使她愉快，但她只是大哭，一心要回到她丈夫那里。她哭也没用，因为她觉得她现在是一个被捕而不能自由的人，姑且对宫里的侍从们说，容她自己住着六个月，以后再定夺她将来的生活路向。她于是被囚在一间小屋里；那屋正有一个小窗当着大道。她日夜困在那里，睡和吃都减少了，只有悲叹和掉泪是她常行的事。

再说赡波一醒过来，不见了妻子，心里非常忧闷。他想来想去，最终断定那所谓姨母一定是个骗子，把他的妻子骗走了。他看见床边放着些糖果，知道不是他们平常所有的，怀疑有毒，也不敢吃。他把那些糖果扔出院外，看见乌鸦飞下来啄食，一会儿都飞不动，掉在地上死了。他更深信他对于那假姨母的结论是不错的。他因为丢了妻子，精神非常错乱，行动如疯人一样。他把家中的一切都搁下，出了宫门，照眼睛所指导的路线，不问通不通，一直往前走。他一面走着，一面叫："长发呀，长发呀！"他日夜地走，不晓得过了多少城市，也不知道他要往哪里去。他走了六个月的工夫，正巧走到娑诃斯罗的王都。走近宫门时，看见大道旁边一个小窗露出他妻子的面庞。彼此相视了一会儿，他的精神已恢复过了一半，但当时不能直接地谈话，他们只能用眼神传递意思。赡波在城中到处打听，把所有的事实都了解了。他知道他妻子将于明日要遵守她的应许，因为六个月的期间已满了。凡这类事，常要用一个婆罗门人把她的应许宣布给大众知道，赡波心里想着他有资格去做宣布者。第二天早晨，国中击鼓求通学的婆罗门人来宣示长发的生平和她的应许。赡波向前去触动那鼓，表示他愿意承领这样的差遣。一般的百姓和贵人都聚集在宫里的院子。那院子搭着丝幔，很是华丽。娑诃斯罗那时已经为王，聚集了国中一切有学的婆罗门人，长发藏在幕后，因为她不能使粗鲁的民众看见。赡波以宣布人的资格坐在首席的平台上。他慢慢地把长发的生平诉说出来。说到他与她结婚的事，他把他家庭的历史说出来。他说："原先有一个穷乏而少智的婆罗门人……"他说时，便向幔后问长发说得对不对。里面必回答说："对的，好婆罗门人，往下说吧。"当他述说的时候，那罗刹侍女的颜色渐渐改变，她知道她将要被发现她不是人类。娑诃斯罗对于宣布者的说话也很奇怪，他不明白他怎样会知道他过去的历史。等他一说完，娑诃斯罗跳到首座上，搂着他说："你不是别人，一定是我的弟弟赡波。"于是他命人把罗刹侍女带到面前，叫人在地上挖了一个大坑把她活埋掉。在埋她之前，令她戴一顶棘冠，使她多受一点苦。此后娑诃斯罗和他的王后，赡波和他的长发公主一同住着，享受他们的天伦之乐。

　　我的故事说到这里算完了，

那提耶也枯萎了。

那提耶呵，你为什么枯萎呢？

你的牛为什么要我用草来喂它？

牛呵，你为什么要人喂？

你的牧者，为什么不看护我？

牧者呵，你为什么不去看牛？

你的儿媳妇为什么不把米给我？

儿媳妇呵，你为什么不给米呢？

我的孩子为什么哭呢？

孩子呵，你为什么哭呢？

蚂蚁为什么要咬我呢？

蚂蚁呵，你为什么要咬人呢？

喀！喀！喀！

五
鲛
人
泪

从前有一个富商独生一子，爱他像无价之宝一般。他的儿子要什么，他便给他什么，永远没有吝惜的意思。他儿子要在一个大园里盖一所美丽的房子，他就命人赶工把它盖起来。房子盖好的时候，商人子就搬到那里去住。那大园的风景非常幽静，所以他住在里头很是舒服。有一天，他在园子里散步，偶然看见一棵小树上有一个同同尼小鸟的巢，里头有一个小卵。他把它拿起来，因为觉得很好玩，就带到屋里，放在墙上一个壁橱里头。他把柜门关好，也就不再想起那小卵。

　　小卵在壁橱里渐渐孵化。但出来的不是小鸟乃是一个很美丽的女婴。她在橱里渐次长大起来，经过好几年的工夫，就长成一个童女。商人子自从放了小卵在壁橱里早就忘记了这件事。那橱门是没有锁的。女孩子看见没有人在的时候，便私自走出来。商人子本是自己住在园里，每日的饭食都是家里的母亲命人为他端来的。女孩子有一次出来，看见地上排着些食物，于是试拿一点放在嘴里。这件事情，让她发现了食物的甘美，她每日必要出来偷一点去吃。商人子一点也不知道那壁橱里住着一个美丽的少女。也不理会他的食物减少了。他的母亲觉得他近来食量增加，也就为他多预备一些。女孩子一天大似一天，食量也增加了。她有时连留给商人子的那一份儿也吃了些。商人子还以为是他母亲预备得不够，便命人回家告

086

壁橱少女

诉要多预备。女孩子每出来偷吃的时候，必看着没人在跟前，她才把各盘的菜和饭拣了些出来，把它们再安排好了，自己才回到壁橱里去。商人子见每顿饭都安排得很整齐，自然不会怀疑有人偷吃的事。可是他的母亲每次都为他多预备，他还说不够，总觉得他的食量异乎常时。她自己很知道她儿子能吃多少，并且每顿都是她亲手把饭菜安排在银盆上头的。因为她儿子屡次说不够，她就立意要把这事的真相发现出来。她吩咐儿子留神。看在饭前有什么人来偷吃。商人子在饭前每次要洗澡的，他遵从母亲的吩咐，这一次就不到浴池去，藏在一边守着放在地上的那盘食物。不久，他看见壁橱的门开了，走出一个少女来。她的年纪在十六岁左右，容貌非常美丽。一出来，她便坐在地上照常偷吃。他立刻跑出来，女孩子不及躲避，就被他拿住了。

"你是谁？你长得这么俊美，恐怕不是人生的吧。你是天神的女儿么？"商人子这样问她。

"我不晓得我是谁。我只知道我从小就长在那壁橱里，一直到如今。"

商人子这时候忽然记起十六年前他做小孩子的时候曾捡了一个同同尼鸟卵放在壁橱里。他理会这女孩子一定是从那卵化生出来的。他被她的美貌所诱，心里很想娶她为妻。自此以后，她就不再住在壁橱里了。商人子安置她在一间美丽的房里。

他命人告诉他母亲，说他在日内就要娶妻。母亲这才觉得儿子年纪大了，自己怎样没想到要与他物色一个配偶。她立刻命人送信给她儿子，说明天她必要教他父亲去找媒人到各城市去为他寻求相当的配偶。商人子对来人说他已有了意中人，如果父母不反对，他就要领她去拜见。他父母本很疼他，自然不加反对。他于是把壁橱少女带到父母面前。两位老人家一见女孩子那么俊美，温柔，可爱，没有问明她的来历，就为他们举行婚礼。

过了好些年，老商人和他的妻子相继去世。商人子也到了中年时代，与壁橱少女生了两个儿子，长子名斯卫德，次子名巴散达。他们两兄弟长得都很俊秀。斯卫德结婚不久，壁橱少女也去世了，斯卫德的父亲是不耐鳏居的，他很快又娶了一个后妻，长得也非常美丽。因为斯卫德的妻子比他的后母年纪大，所以家中一切的事情都由她掌管。那个后母，和一切的后母一样，憎恶他们两兄弟到极致，对于当家的媳妇，自然时常发生冲突。

有一天，一个渔夫打得一条非常美丽的鱼，就送到斯卫德的父亲那里去。那鱼是世人所未曾见过的。渔夫说它是一件宝贝，如果有人吃了它，他笑的时候，必会从口里掉出摩尼宝珠，他哭的时候，他的眼泪都是珠子。斯卫德的父亲听见他说得这么玄，立刻用一千卢比买了它。他把鱼交给儿媳妇，命她煮熟了就端来给他吃。他吩咐完了，就出外去。当家的媳妇，斯卫德的妻子，在渔夫述说那鱼的功效的时候，早已听得很详细。她想着不如私自煮给她丈夫和小叔吃了，另外为她公公预备一盘田鸡，哄他说那就是鱼肉。正当她把鱼和田鸡煮好的时候，她听见她小叔和她后婆吵闹起来。巴散达年纪还是很小，他喜欢养鸽子。这一次鸽子飞到他后娘的屋里，她便把鸽子藏在衣服里。巴散达跑到她屋里去要鸽子，她只装作不知道。斯卫德看见他后娘的行为，就跑过来从她怀里取出鸽子交还他弟弟。后娘老羞成怒，便咒骂他们说："你们等着吧，等家长回来，在我倒水给他喝之前，我必教他把你们杀掉。"斯卫德的妻子对她丈夫说："我最爱的夫主，那妇人是极坏不过的，她一定会在公公面前说我们的坏话，叫他处置我们。她一定能够让他伤害我们，所以我们的性命非常危险。我们不如先吃一点，三个人一同逃走吧。"斯卫德把弟弟叫来，对他说妻子的计划。他们约定了在黄昏前逃走。妇人把那鱼放在丈夫和叔叔面前叫他们快些吃完。她进到自己屋里把所有的珠宝都检点好了，放在一个小箱里。家里可巧只有一匹马，却很健壮，他们三个人就一同骑上去，哥哥在前头，嫂嫂在当中，弟弟在背后。

那马一直飞跑，不晓得经过多少城邑。到了中夜，他们走到靠近河边一个树林里。他们不能再走了，因为斯卫德妻子的产期到了。他们下了马，把妇人扶下来，不久，她就生了一个男孩。在密林中，他们兄弟二人对于这事实在不晓得要怎样办才好。头一件事一定是要生火，使产母和婴儿不至于受冻。可是到哪里去取火呢？在树林的附近一点人烟也没有。那时正当冬季，生火是必要的，不然，母子们必会丧亡。斯卫德叫他弟弟看顾着嫂嫂，他出林外找火去。

斯卫德在林中走了好几里路，在黑暗里瞎走。他总找不着有人居住的地方，直到启明星出现了，他借着星光辨认出一条路来。他向着那条路走，看见远地有一座大城。他非常欢喜，想着他妻子的救星到了。他正想着解救他妻子和新生儿子的困难，忽然看见前面站着一头大象。那象背上安置一座很华丽的亭子，亭里铺着金织的毾𣰯，好像是王家所御的。它拦住斯卫德的去路，用鼻子把他卷起来，放他在亭子里坐着。斯卫德也不知道为什么，只由着它。它飞跑到城中，到王宫里停住了。那时，他才理会座上放着一顶王冕，有人请他戴上。

原来那一国每天早晨必要选一个王。因为做王的常要在登极的晚上，进入王后宫里以后，第二天早晨必定要死在床上。国王的死因是没有人知道的。就是王后也不知道。每日换一次王，每个王都以同一王后为后，所以她也觉得很苦恼。选王的方法就是每晚由象

突然一头装饰华美的大象拦住了斯卫德的去路

王出去选相当的人物，把他驮回宫里，这次可巧驮着斯卫德。象王每早驮回来的新王，有时是从很远的地方请来的。但无论它驮的是谁，百姓没有不承认他为王的。斯卫德到了宫里，大臣们便拥他升了宝座，宣布他为王。百姓中有些庆祝他的，但有些为他悲哀，因为他们都知道他的寿命不能延到明天。他在那一天仔细地打听前头那些王致死的原因，可是没有人能告诉他。他到晚间，只好谨慎一点。夜到了，他必要到王后宫里去，他不明白这危险的真相，故得处处留神。他想着两件事是一定要做的，就是带着武器进去，和一夜不睡，观察动静。王后很年轻，并且很美丽，很温柔。从她的举止与言语看来，绝不是那杀害丈夫一流的女人。在她的屋里，斯卫德度了半夜，也不见有什么。王后陪他说话，到很累的时候就自己睡去了。新王自己在屋里四围观望，总看不出有什么动静。停了许久，他忽然看见王后的鼻孔伸出一条东西好像线一般。那线很细，几乎看不见。它渐渐伸出好几尺，最终全部落在床上。线渐渐粗大起来，不到几分钟已经变成一条很凶猛的大蛇。斯卫德知道一定是那东西作怪，赶快用刀挥过去，好容易把它杀死了。他还是坐着，看看还有别的危险没有，可是不见有什么。天已经亮了。王后睡的时间比平日长，因为据她身体为巢穴的毒蛇不再搔扰她，使她安然地睡。大臣都在宫门口要听候别的新王来，同时听昨日登基的王的死信。这一次，使宫里与朝中的人们大大地诧异，因为斯卫德安然地从王后的宫里走出来。他把夜间所遇见的事宣布给众人知道，全国的人都赞美他的智慧和勇敢。国人为他庆祝，因为从此以后，他们就有了一个永久的王。

斯卫德自入宫为王以后，很奇怪的事，就是他把从前的妻子和婴儿一概忘了。他忘掉他过去一切的事迹，连前晚为什么出了树林和命弟弟守着产母的事也记不清楚。巴散达在林中守着嫂嫂，指望他哥哥取火回来。已经天亮了，还不见他的影儿。早晨的阳光射入林中，他走到河边去望着河水，自己在那里悲伤。他不晓得他哥哥晚间遇见什么危险。想到种种事由，使他不由得不哭。正巧那时有一只商船泊在岸边。船里有一个从远国回来的商人。他看见巴散达在那里哭，就走上前要来安慰他。他一到巴散达跟前，看见满地都是圆亮的珠子。那都是巴散达的眼泪所变的。他起了贪心，想着如果把这个鲛人带回本国，就可以不必再出海去求宝了。想定了，他便吩咐船工把船撑过来，试要把巴散达拖到船上去。巴散达越哭得沉痛，地上的珠子越多。商人更是喜欢，巴不得他永远地哭。他最终上了船，因为抵抗不过许多人的推拉。商人把他击在船面的桅边。他在被囚的时候，更要想到哥嫂和他自己的境遇，所以哭得更厉害。商人想着他越哭越发能叫他发财，也由着他哭去。其实他连从岸边捡得的珠子与巴散达在船上继续着掉下来的，已经得了不少。商人回到本国，就把巴散达囚在一间小屋里。他用方法使巴散达每日哭着。商人因着珠子致富。也对他的仆人说："他哭的时候，眼泪会变珠子，看他笑的时候，会出什么。"那仆人受了主人的吩咐，便到屋里撩触他，使他咯吱地笑。巴散达一笑的时候，从口里掉下许多摩尼宝珠来。自从他们发现巴散达的一笑一哭于他们都有利益，于是无昼无夜，用方法使他一时哭，一时笑。商人贩卖摩尼，富厚到没人能和他比较。

现在我们再说斯卫德的妻子吧。她独自一人在林中，不见了丈夫和小叔子，身边卧着那头胎新产下来的婴孩，自然非常凄苦。她哭得眼泪成河，也不能使他们回来。因为过于疲乏和悲伤的缘故，使她昏睡过去。她抱着那新生的婴孩睡着了。她睡着的时候，赶巧巡查官从林中经过。那巡查官本来希望子息，因为他妻子每生产孩子必夭殇，养不起来。他这时又抱着死婴儿要到河边去埋葬。他走着，正好看见林中一个妇人抱着婴儿在那里睡。那婴孩长得非常秀美。他心里想，不如把死婴孩放在她身边，将她的活婴孩换过来。他把活的婴孩抱过来，把死的婴孩放在妇人臂上，一直走回家，告诉他妻子说婴孩在道上复活了。斯卫德的妻子醒过来之后，不知道别人偷换了她的婴孩，以为她那块肉是不幸死了。她的悲伤使她望着前途都是黑暗。她想来想去，总想不出解救的方法，只好想到自杀。她知道林外就是大河，就立意要去投水。她抱着她的珠宝箱到河边去。那里正好有一个老婆罗门人在河边行早晨的礼拜。他以为那妇人一清早到河边也是要行圣浴的，就没有拦阻她走入水里。后来他看见她越走越到没顶的深处，才觉她的行为有点不对。他停止了他的礼拜，大声嚷着叫那妇人回到岸边来。斯卫德的妻子回头看见是一个老婆罗门人，就停了步。她慢慢走上岸，到婆罗门人那里去。婆罗门人问她的事由，她把一切都告诉他，并且献上她的珠宝给他当作礼物。婆罗门人于是带她回家，命他的老妻以女儿的名分待她。

　　一年一年过去了，巡查官的儿子长大成为一个很勇敢的孩子。婆罗门人的家离巡查官所住的房子不远，所以孩子时常经过他真正母亲的家门。他自然不知道从前的事，总觉得老婆罗门的女儿很可爱。她虽然比他年纪大得多，可是他已爱上了她，愿意娶她为妻。他把这个意思说给巡查官知道，于是那老人便命人来到婆罗门人的家里要求这事。婆罗门人听见这种要求就非常生气。他说巡查官的儿子是什么东西，他敢想娶婆罗门人的女儿为妻！那真是一个矮人伸手想往空中捉月了！但无论如何，那巡查官的儿子必要娶她。他想着用强硬的手段去娶她。他怀着这个恶意，有一天晚上，他便私下爬上婆罗门人屋里，藏在牛圈的屋脊上头，意思要等到人静的时候，好下去把女人抢走。他正在候着的时候，就听见圈里两只小牛在那里谈话。

"人们常以我们为无知和没有道德，我想他们比我们还要坏五十倍。"

"我的兄弟，你为什么这样想？你今天看见什么人类的邪恶行为么？"

"你看，哪一个罪恶比现在藏在这间房子脊梁上那个孩子的更大呢？"

"什么？我只知道他是巡查官的儿子，我没有听过他有什么不好的行为。"

"你没曾听见么？我说给你听吧，那个邪恶的孩子现在正想娶他母亲为妻咧！"

第一只小牛便把斯卫德和巴散达兄弟的生平事迹说给它的同伴知道。孩子在房顶上听得最清楚的就是他母亲怎样逃避后婆，怎样在林中生产，他父亲怎样去做了王，他叔叔怎样被商人掳了去，他怎样被人抱走了，他母亲怎样到了婆罗门人的家。他听完之后，心里非常难过。他立刻回家，对他的义父说，他要去见王。巡查官虽然不允许，但他自己径自去了。他把从牛圈上听来的故事一一述说给王听，王才记得当初实在有这回事。王立刻命人到婆罗门家把他的旧妻迎接回来，封她为后，又封孩子为王子。他又派人去把弟弟巴散达找来，连那可恶的富商也被捕到王跟前。王命人将那富商活埋了，葬地的四围还围着荆棘。此后他们一家人一同在王宫里过着很快乐的日子。

我的故事说到这里算完了，

那提耶也枯萎了。

那提耶呵，你为什么枯萎呢？

你的牛为什么要我用草来喂它？

牛呵，你为什么要人喂？

你的牧者，为什么不看护我？

牧者呵，你为什么不去看牛？

你的儿媳妇为什么不把米给我？

儿媳妇呵，你为什么不给米呢？

我的孩子为什么哭呢？

孩子呵，你为什么哭呢？

蚂蚁为什么要咬我呢？

蚂蚁呵，你为什么要咬人呢？

喀！喀！喀！

六　吉祥子

从前凶运的神土星与吉运的神吉祥天在天上争吵。他们彼此争权位，土星说他比吉祥天高，吉祥天说她比他高。因为诸天在天上都是绝对平等的，他们中间没有一个敢出来评判。于是这两位神便约定到人间来求那负有智慧和公正的美名的人来断定谁高谁低。那时地上正住着一个富裕的人名叫吉祥子，为人极其公正且有智慧。两位天神于是选定他来做判断人。他们遣人去告诉吉祥子，说土星和吉祥天要来见他，命他解决他们的纷争。吉祥子知道这事是很为难的。如果他说土星的权位比吉祥天的高大，吉祥天必要因生气而不保佑他。如果他说吉祥天的权位比土星的高大，土星必要用他的恶眼看着他，使他遇见凶运。他想来想去，决定不直接说谁高谁低，只用他的行为使两位天神自己去理会。他做了两张凳子，一张是金的，一张是银的，把它们放在自己身边。当土星和吉祥天来到的时候，他请土星坐在银凳上，请吉祥天坐在金凳上。土星理会吉祥子的判断，就生气得像发狂一样，对着他说："好，你以为我比吉祥天低，我要用三年的时间将恶眼看着你。我要看你的结果如何。"他说完，气愤地便走了。吉祥天临走的时候，安慰吉祥子说："我的儿，你不要害怕。我必定保佑你。"她说完也走了。

　　吉祥子对他妻子真陀摩尼说："我最爱的，土星的恶眼一定要看着我，不如我走开，省得连累你。我知道如果我留在家里，一家也会不安宁，如果我自己一个人离开这里，那恶眼一定要跟着我离开。"真陀摩尼说："我可不能让你离开我。你到哪里，我定要跟你到哪里。你的命运就是我的命运。"丈夫用尽方法留妻子在家，无奈妻子执意要跟着他去。他们于是收拾卧具，把所有的财宝藏在里面。那一晚上，他们要离开故家的时候，吉祥子便祷告说："吉祥天母呀，土星的恶眼现时就要射到我身上。我们必要离开此地求你庇佑我们，照顾我们的家产。"吉祥天回答说："不要害怕。我必定庇佑你，一切的事情最终要顺利的。"他们听见这话就出门去了。吉祥子把卧具顶在头上，和妻子慢慢地走着。他们去了很远，来到一条河边。因为水深，他们不能涉水过去。可巧岸边有一只独木舟，里头坐着一个人，他们就向他求渡。舟中的人回答说他的小舟只能容一个搭客。他说："每次我只能渡一个人，现在你们两位连那卧具一共得分三次渡过去。"吉祥子求他第一次容他的妻子带着卧具过去，但是舟中人不答应。他说："容我把你的行李先载过去吧，我的小舟实在载不了这么重。"吉祥子不得已，只得遵从他。他把卧具搁上小舟，刚泛到河中，大风便刮起来，波腾浪涌，霎时把小舟、舟人和行李都漂没了。很奇怪的，就是不到一会儿的工夫那条河也不见了。他们方才所见的大河，现在已经变成坚实的土地。吉祥子于是理会这是土星的恶眼所致。

他们收拾行李准备出门远行

吉祥子夫妇二人身边一个钱也没有了。他们到了一个住着许多樵夫的村里。樵夫们在日出的时候都到林中砍柴去。他们每日将所得的柴送到附近的城市去卖。吉祥子对樵夫们说他也愿意跟着他们去砍柴。他们都应许了他。他入林中跟着大众砍柴，但他所砍的与别的樵夫不同。樵夫们砍的都是平常的柴火，他砍的都是檀香木。他每日不用气力，把些少檀香木带到市上去卖，很发了些财。别的樵夫每日使劲地挑柴火，卖不到多少钱，因此便妒嫉他，大家商量好了，要撵他离开那村。他和他的妻子最终被撵了。

　　他们又走到一个小村，村人都是以纺线为职业的。真陀摩尼想着她也可以纺线谋生。她的手艺比别人好，纺出来的线又细，又匀，又干净，所以她的棉线格外容易卖出去，赚钱也格外多。本村的女人又不高兴了。吉祥子为了使村中的人们喜欢他和他的妻子，就把所有的人都请来赴他的宴会。那筵席都是真陀摩尼预备的。真陀摩尼是一个擅于烹调的女人，做出来的菜，味道都很合适，没有一个人不喜欢吃。客人在散席以后，回家去，个个都说他的妻子不会做饭，叫他的妻子做不中用的女人。村里的女人为这事更是恨她。有一天，她同村里的女人们到河边洗澡去。岸边有一只船搁浅在那里，已有好几天。妇女们合力去推它，都推不动。可是真陀摩尼到那里只一触，船便退到水中去了。船主看见这桩奇事，就起了不良的心意。他想不如把她抢到船上，第二次搁浅的时候可以用得着她。船主于是命船上的伙伴把她捉住。妇女们巴不得她不在，也不喊救，由他们把她掳去。吉祥子听见他妻子被人抢走，心里自然非常难过。他离开村子，走到河边，沿着岸走，试要找到掳他妻子的船。他在岸边一直地走，已经走到天黑的时候，那里也没有房舍，他只找到一棵树，爬上去住一宿。第二天早晨，他从树上爬下来，看见树下有迦毗罗牛的脚迹。迦毗罗牛是一种永不产犊的母牛，它每时能够不歇地出乳。吉祥子于是把它找着，挤它的乳汁出来喝。他发现那母牛的粪是金黄色的，留神一验，果然是纯粹的金子。牛粪初出来的时候还很软和，他试把自己的名字画在上面。粪干了，果然是一块一块的金砖，每砖都刻上吉祥子的名字。那棵树此后便成为吉祥子的住处，母牛因为到河边喝水后常在树荫下歇息，所以他每日都可以喝它的奶，捡它的金粪。吉祥子决意就在那里等候那只把他妻子载走的船。一天等过一天，金砖越积越多。每块金砖都有他的名字，因为他每天早晚都忙着在牛粪上画字。金砖在河边堆起来，远看真像一座金山。

再说到真陀摩尼在船上，自己思想多半是因为她的俊美才会惹出这场灾祸。她便祈求吉祥天说："吉祥天母呀，怜悯我吧。你让我长得这么美丽，现在我因此就要丢了我的贞洁和庄重了。我求你，我的慈爱天母，让我变成丑陋吧，让我的身体遍处发生毛病吧，因为这个可以使船里的人们不敢亲近我。"吉祥天准了她的祈求，当船里的人搂着她的时候，一瞬间，她的美容立时变为恶臭，像尸体一般。他们于是把她放下舱底。因为她全身都长满了恶疮，并且发出难闻的气味，所以船里的人都不敢进到舱里。他们每日只从货舱的小窗递一些饭和水给她。她在舱底过着很痛苦的生活，但她宁愿如此，也不愿丢了她的贞洁。

　　船主到处把货卖完，又沿着大河回来。他远远看见岸上的树下有一堆金子，于是把船驶近岸边。吉祥子认得那只船，想着他妻子或者还在里头。船主上岸要搬那些金砖，吉祥子对他说那都是他的财产。船主看见只有他一人在那里，就命人把他搂入舱底，把金砖都搬到船上去。吉祥子被拘的地方正和他妻子的舱相离不远。他们彼此都认得。真陀摩尼虽然变了形状，丈夫还可以辨认。他们不敢直接说话，只用手势交流。船主和水手们都很喜欢掷骰子，他们觉得吉祥子是个斯文人，时常叫他来凑数。他很擅于掷骰子，每掷必赢。水手不高兴，就把他扔下水去。真陀摩尼在舱底的窗门看她丈夫被扔下水，赶紧把枕在她脑后的枕头扔出去给他。吉祥子借着枕头的浮力，顺流直下，晚间已流到岸边一个花园旁边。他爬上园里的一棵树，全身湿得使他不歇地哆嗦，可也无可奈何地过了一夜。那花园是属于一个老寡妇的。先几年她是王宫里的鲜花供奉。不晓得为什么，她园里的花果忽然都不开花结子，所以好几年的工夫，她不能去当鲜花供奉的职务。吉祥子那晚在她园里的树上睡，第二天早晨，树树都开花。老婆子看见满园的花，以为她是在梦境之中。她出来把每棵花木都检验过，才信是真的。她不知道这是什么缘故，随意向后边走来，忽然看见吉祥子卧在一棵树上，冷得发抖，几乎要死。她把他扶下来，引他到她的茅舍里，为他生火，并且告诉他她的来历，和她的花木怎样忽然开花。她理会开花的原因是吉祥子卧在树上的功德，所以极意奉承他。她自己走到王宫去报告，说她又可以当鲜花供奉，王立时赐她恢复原来的职分。吉祥子住在老婆子家里好几天，便请求她在王的大臣面前举荐他，为他安置一个职位。于是他被引领到王面前。王发现他是一个很有智慧的人。大臣见王喜欢他，便问他愿意当什么差使。他说他愿意当河上的税吏。他上了任以后，不到几天工夫，就看见掳他和他妻子的那只船来了。他把船扣留住，将船主拿到宫里，告他抢劫他的财宝。王亲自到河边来勘验，果然发现每块金砖都有"吉祥子"的字样。同时，吉祥子又告他掳他的妻子。王命人进舱底去检查，果然搜出一个很美丽的女人来。王听了吉祥子述说他的生平，就赐他好几天的筵宴。后来他又赐他们夫妇一群象和一群马，命人护送他们回本国去。

土星的恶眼现在已经满期了。他不再加害于吉祥子，所以他们夫妇二人在本乡重又过着很愉快的生活。他的名字是"吉祥天的儿子"，到这时才证实了。

我的故事说到这里算完了，

那提耶也枯萎了。

那提耶呵，你为什么枯萎呢？

你的牛为什么要我用草来喂它？

牛呵，你为什么要人喂？

你的牧者，为什么不看护我？

牧者呵，你为什么不去看牛？

你的儿媳妇为什么不把米给我？

儿媳妇呵，你为什么不给米呢？

我的孩子为什么哭呢？

孩子呵，你为什么哭呢？

蚂蚁为什么要咬我呢？

蚂蚁呵，你为什么要咬人呢？

喀！喀！喀！

七 七母子

从前有一个王娶了七个王后。他很忧愁，因为他七个王后都没有儿女。有一天，来了一个乞士，他告诉王说在某一个树林中有一棵檬果树，树上有一枝连结着七个檬果。如果他能够去把那七个檬果摘下来，分给七个王后吃，她们各人必定要怀胎。王听他的话，便到那树林里找，果然找出七个果子同生在一枝的檬果树。他摘回来，把檬果分给七位王后吃。此后不久，王便得着宫里报出来的喜信，说七位王后都怀了孕。

有一天，王出外去打猎，在道上看见一个少女从他面前经过。他一见便钟爱她，命人把她带回宫里，立时封她为第八位王后。那第八王后本不是人类，乃是一个罗刹。王自然不知道她的来历，他越与她亲近，越觉得她可爱。他爱这位新封的王后过于爱一切，凡她所求，无不应许。

第八王后有一天对王说："你说你爱我胜过一切的，我总有一点怀疑，我要试试看你是否真爱我。你若是爱我的话，就请把那七位王后的眼睛挖出，然后把她们杀掉。"

王听见她的要求，心里就非常纳闷，因为他也很爱七位王后，这时她们各人又都在孕期，怎舍得把她们杀掉。可是第八王后一定要他这样做，他不得已便命人把七位王后的眼睛挖出来，然后把她们交给宰相，命他杀死她们。

宰相是一个慈善的人，不忍见她们无辜受罪，就把她们送到一个山洞里藏着。日子过得快，第一位王后在洞里已生了一个婴孩。但她们都饿得很厉害，因为没人给她们送吃的，她们又瞎，不能出外讨东西吃。第一位王后对其余的说："我对于这个孩子要怎么办呢。我们都瞎了，又没东西吃，不如把他杀掉，我们大家分开来吃吧。"她把婴儿杀掉，把肉分给几个王后吃。第二王后又生了一个孩子，她也照样杀了，把肉分给大众吃。她们这样办，一直轮到第六位王后的婴儿也被杀来做食品。第七位王后总不敢吃人肉，她虽很饿，也把前头几位王后所给她的肉藏起来，一块也没吃。临到她生产的时候，前六位王后就要求她也把婴儿杀来分给大家吃。她舍不得杀自己的孩子，就将前六次她存起来六个婴儿肉分给她们。她们吃的时候，觉得肉很干就问她什么缘故。她把因由说给她们听，说她舍不得杀害她的婴孩。六位王后也很喜欢，个个答应要共同乳哺那婴儿。她们受尽千辛万苦，好容易把孩子养大起来，那孩子是七个母亲乳哺的，所以非常强壮。在世间里没有一个孩子能和他相比较。

　　罗刹王后把七位王后摆弄出宫，就将宫中一切的生灵渐渐吞噬起来。平常的饭菜是不够她吃的。她每夜必在宫中找王的侍从、象、马等来吃。她把一切都吃完了，所剩的只有她自己和王。她于是每夜出宫去，在王城内外噬杀民人。王自己在宫里，觉得没人服侍他，没人为他预备饭，也没人在他身边听候差遣。

那第七王后所生的王子这时已经很大了。他听见父王的事，就来到宫里请求做他的侍者。他为王做一切的事，用尽方法去阻止罗刹王后做害王的事。他每夜必在王宫守护着王，所以罗刹不能把他吃掉。罗刹王后于是非常憎恶大力王子，想方法要撵走他。因为他是一个侍者，可以听她的差遣的，所以她对他说她得了一种病，非得找一种瓜来治才能好。那一种瓜是十二肘长，可有十三肘的核，别的地方不能得，唯有住在隔洋，她母亲那里才有。她命王子为她去取来。其实她的意思是要撵走他，并且要让她国里的罗刹把他吃掉。她把一封信交在王子手里，告诉他怎样去。

王子心里明知她的诡计，为了要看她怎么办，所以将计就计，为她送信去取那十二肘长、有十三肘核的奇瓜。他走到海边，望着对海罗刹国大声嚷："祖母！祖母！来救你的女儿吧。她现在病得很沉重哪。"那边的老罗刹听见了，走过来见了孩子，问明因由，就把他带过洋去。王子到了罗刹国，果然看见那里有十三肘核的十二肘瓜。老罗刹把瓜摘下来给他，叫他赶快回去。但他说他很疲乏，要歇一天再走。老罗刹只得留他住一宿。他看见罗刹屋里挂着一根大棒和一条绳子，就问那些东西是干什么用的。罗刹对他说：

112

"孩子，那棒和绳是我用来渡海的。无论是谁，若把它们拿在手里，念着咒说：

'大棒呀！粗绳呀！立刻送我到那边的岸上去吧。'

棒和绳便会送他渡过大海，到那边的岸上。"他又看见房角悬着一个鸟笼，里头有一只怪鸟，便问那是什么鸟。老罗刹因为以为王子是自己的孙子，便对他说："孩子，那是不能告诉人类知道的。可是我怎能不对我的孙子说明呢？我的孩子，那只鸟就是你母亲的生命。如果人把那鸟杀死，你的母亲也要死的。"王子知道了这个秘密，就睡去了。

第二天，罗刹们都出外去求食，王子便把鸟笼取下来，拿着那棒和绳子，念咒说：

"大棒呀！粗绳呀！立刻送我到那边的岸上去吧。"

一瞬间，他已回到这边的岸上。他赶回宫中，把瓜交给罗刹王后，把鸟和棒绳秘密地藏起来。

在不久的时间，城里的居民每夜都见一只大怪鸟从宫中飞出来吃人。他们跑到王面前禀告说："每夜我们看见从王宫飞出一只大怪鸟来，在道上吞噬行人，如果永远是这样，这国就要没人民了。"王实在不晓得那怪鸟是什么样子，藏在哪里。王的侍者，大力王子说他知道，并且求王把王后请来，他要在大众跟前把那鸟杀

每夜从王宫飞出一只大怪鸟来

掉。王于是命人把王后请来，坐在他身边。王子把鸟拿来时，王后一见便晕倒过去。王子当作没看见，回头对王说："大王，你将要知道是谁每夜出宫去吞噬你的人民了。我把鸟的肢体撕开，那吃人的肢体也要同时分裂。"他说完，便撕那鸟，王后在王身边，手足都自然地掉下来。王子捏它的咽喉的时候，王后就断了气。王子把罗刹杀死以后，便将他的来历说给王听。王于是命人速把从前七位王后迎接回宫。她们的眼睛忽然再生回来，个个都如从前的俊美。王又封了王子为承继王位的储君。他们此后在宫中同过愉快的生活。

我的故事说到这里算完了，
那提耶也枯萎了。
那提耶呵，你为什么枯萎呢？
你的牛为什么要我用草来喂它？
牛呵，你为什么要人喂？
你的牧者，为什么不看护我？
牧者呵，你为什么不去看牛？
你的儿媳妇为什么不把米给我？
儿媳妇呵，你为什么不给米呢？

我的孩子为什么哭呢？

孩子呵，你为什么哭呢？

蚂蚁为什么要咬我呢？

蚂蚁呵，你为什么要咬人呢？

喀！喀！喀！

八　宝扇缘

从前有一个商人，生了七个女儿。有一天，商人问他七个女儿说："你们都是靠谁的命运活着的呢？"大女儿说："爸爸，我是依赖你的福分活着的。"二女儿，三女儿，一直到第六个女儿，都是这样回答。轮到第七个女儿，她却说："我依赖我自己的命运活着。"商人听了他第七个女儿的话，立时对她发怒，说："好，你既然这样不知恩义，说你是靠着你自己的命运活着的，我倒要看看你要怎样靠。今天你必须从我的家门出去，一点东西，一个钱也不许你带走，看你怎样。"他说了这话，立时叫舆夫预备一顶小轿，把他第七个女儿抬到大树林里舍弃掉。第七个女儿哀求她父亲许她带着她自己的针黹盒子，里面只有些针线。她父亲容她带那个盒子走，她于是上了轿，被抬走了。轿夫们抬着她，一面走着，一面喘气，发出"哼！哼！哼！哼！"的声调。他们走不远，就被一个老婆子拦住。老婆子原来是七姑娘的乳母，听见道上轿夫抬轿的声音，本要出来看是哪位贵人经过，想不到被抬的就是她的乳儿。她问轿夫们说："你们要把我的女儿抬到哪里去呢？"轿夫们说："商主叫我们把她抬到大树林里舍弃掉咧。"她问为什么缘故，七姑娘就对她说明方才得罪了她父亲的事由。她对轿夫们说："我一定要与我女儿一同去。"轿夫不答应，说："老太太，你别跟着吧，我们跑得快，你跟不上。"老婆子说："无论如何，我一定要跟我女儿去。"他们没法，只得容她们两人同坐一顶小轿里，慢慢地走。过了午刻，他们已经到了密林的深处，他们走了又走，一直走到积叶满地乱藤交错的地方，把两个女人放在一棵大树底下。他们走的时候已经快到黄昏了。

七姑娘虽然有她乳母做伴，可是两个弱女子在密林中是很危险的。她今年不过十四岁，在家又是被娇养惯的，现在坐在密林中一棵大树底下，身上一个钱也没有，一点吃的也没有，一点防身的东西也没有！她只有一个老态龙钟、手颤脚战的老婆子在身边伴着！在古时候，树也会说话的。她们背后那棵大树看见她们这样可怜，不由得伤心起来，因为它的根被她们的眼泪渗湿了，于是对七姑娘说："不幸的女子呀，我很可怜你！待会儿林中的野兽就要出来了。它们要嚎叫着来找食物。我知道它们见了你。一定要把你和你的同伴吃掉。容我救你吧。我把我的干部分开，容你们进来暂时避着吧。你一看见我的干部开了，就立刻进来，我就再把我的皮合上，你们在里头就不至于受野兽们的残害。"树干果然裂开了。七姑娘和乳母走进去，树皮又合起来，像原来一样。夜到了，所有的野兽都出来找食。那里有凶猛的老虎，这里有残暴的野熊；那里又来了勇健的犀牛，这里又来了醉狂的大象。那些吃肉的野兽都来嗅着这棵大树，因为它们觉得里头有人血的气味。七姑娘和乳母听见外面野兽咆哮的声音，都不敢动弹。那些野兽，有用角来触树干的，有把树皮咬破的，有把树枝咬断的。它们最终不能把树里的人取出来吃掉。天渐渐明亮，野兽都各自走了。大树对干部里的两个女人说："不幸的女人，那些野兽在搅扰我一夜以后，现在都走了。太阳已出来，你们也出来吧。"说完，树干好像大门一样分两边开着，让她们出来。她们出来以后坐在树根上，看见地上和树干上留下许多野兽搅扰的痕迹。树枝树叶有许多掉在地上，树干上有几部分掉了皮。七姑娘对大树说："大树母亲哪，谢谢你昨夜给我们一个安身的地方，避过种种危险。你在一夜中必定被扰不堪，很是痛苦。"她说着，便走到离树不远一个小池边去取一些泥土来为树的毁伤部分敷上。她做完这事，大树谢谢她说："多谢你，好姑娘，你这样做，叫我减少了许多痛苦。我实在为你们着急，你们昨晚没吃东西，现在一定很饿了，我能给你们什么呢？我自己是不结果子的。你把些钱给那老婆子，叫她去买一点东西回来给你吃吧。这里离城市不算很远。"她们都说她们身边一个铜钱也没有。七姑娘拿起她的针黹盒，翻来翻去，可巧翻出五个贝壳。五个小贝壳本可以当钱用，但所值非同小可。大树便叫老婆子到城里去买一点炒米回来。

老婆子拿着五个小贝壳到城里去，到了一家饼店要买炒米，她对饼商说："请给我值五个小贝壳的炒米。"饼商笑着鄙夷她说："走吧，丑老婆子，你想五个小贝壳能换多少炒米么？"她挨店问了好几家，都没人肯卖给她。最后到一家，主人见她那么老，可怜她，便收下那五个小贝壳，给她很多的炒米。

老婆子捧一掬炒米回到密林来。大树便对七姑娘说："姑娘，你们都吃一点，留一大半撒在树干的周围。"她们照着大树告诉她们的话去做，可不明白到底为什么缘故。一天的工夫就在忧愁饥饿之中过去了。她们晚间仍然被大树拥入干部里头。野兽在夜间依然出来，到大树的周围咆哮着。第二天早晨，树干渐渐开了，两个女人在没走出来的时候，就看见几百只孔雀围着树的四面，争着啄食地上的炒米。它们啄食的时候，有许多美丽的羽毛掉下来。大树告诉两个女人说："你们去把那些羽毛捡起来吧。那就是你们的财产。"七姑娘把捡得的孔雀翎选择过一遍，把那些精美的用针线缝起来，做成一把很好看的扇子。老婆子拿扇子进城去卖，走过王宫，王子看见那扇子非常悦目，就重价买去了。自此以后，七姑娘每天做孔雀扇叫老婆子拿进城去卖。她们每天早晨都可以捡得许多孔雀翎，因为孔雀们来啄炒米已经成了习惯。在不久的时候，她们两个女人已经成为富户。大树又叫她们在树下盖一所房子安住。她们于是找砖匠来烧砖，找木匠来伐木，找灰匠来炼

她们看见几百只美丽的孔雀聚集在大树底下争着啄食地上的炒米。

灰，找泥水匠来盖房子。不到几个月工夫，密林里竟然成了她们两个女人的小花园，野兽也被撵走了。她们的房子和王宫差不多，陈设得非常华丽。

那时七姑娘的父亲因为不受吉祥天的庇佑，把家财都散尽了。他的六个女儿也跟着他夫妇二人过穷苦的生活。他穷得连房子也变卖了，带着一家人漂泊到林外一个小村子住下。他听见林里的富户要招工进去凿一个水池，想着到那里去做小工。原来七姑娘因为林中没有清水，不能敷她们日常用度，她们就决定要在园后开一个水池，所以到四围的村庄去招工人。商人也去报名做一个日工，自早到晚在后园凿池子。他妻子想着自己也可以去干这样的活，于是随着丈夫也做工去。有一天，七姑娘正在窗边望外观赏园里的景色，蓦然看她父母赤着脖在太阳下做苦工。她不由得掉下许多眼泪，望着他们。他们实在穷得连衣服也没得穿，各自只围着一条破麻布。她叫仆人出去，把他们请进来，他们却非常害怕。因为水池快要完工了，古时的风俗，凡池子完工的那一天，必要用人去献祭，所以他们恐怕主人要了他们的命去做牺牲。仆人命他们把破麻布除下来，换上很美丽的衣服，他们更是害怕。女主人出来，他们都不敢抬头看她，后来她说明她就是他们的第七个女儿，彼此才抱头大哭了一场。七姑娘把在林中的经过都说给父母知道。到这时，商人才佩服他第七个女儿从前所说的话是对的。七姑娘给父亲许多钱财，叫他回到本城里重兴旧业。

商人不久又富裕起来了。那一天，他要到远国去做买卖，一切行色都预备好了，可是一上船，船却撑不动。船上的人都很奇怪，商人也很诧异，他最后想起一件事来，原来他在出发以前曾问过六位女儿要他带什么东西回来给她们，只有七姑娘不住在家里，他把她忽略了。他立刻叫人走到林中去问七姑娘要他带什么东西回来给她。仆人到的时候，七姑娘正在礼拜，听见父亲差人来，她只对他说："苏拔尔。"意思就是"等一等"。仆人以为七姑娘要的是"苏拔尔"，就一直跑到船上告诉了商人。船可以撑动了，商人在各港口都很获利，六位女儿所要的东西也都购置妥了。她们所要的东西无非是脂粉装饰物品，不难得到，唯有七姑娘的"苏拔尔"最不容易买。他从一个港口经过第二个港口，到处问有没有"苏拔尔"卖。所有的商人都对他说没有这样东西。他做完买卖快要回家，而"苏拔尔"还没办得，心里非常着急。他每经过一城，必在通衢大道上嚷着说："我要苏拔尔！我要苏拔尔！"最后来到一个王城，他依然在通衢上嚷。正巧王子从那里经过，他的名字就是苏拔尔。王子走近前，问他要苏拔尔干什么。他自然不知道那就是王子的名字，便对他说是他第七个女儿要的。王子于是从身边取出一

124

个小木盒来，对他说："这就是你女儿所要的'苏拔尔'，你带回去吧。"他把木盒子交给商人，没受他的报酬便去了。商人得着"苏拔尔"，就立刻扬帆回家。

商人到家后，把各位姑娘的礼物都分发了。七姑娘得着一个小木盒，以为是平常的东西，没打开看，就把它放在一边。有一天，她闲坐着没事，那盒正好搁在身边，她便把它拿过来，打开一看，原来是一把扇，扇上装着一面小镜子。那扇非常好看，她拿起来摇了一摇，忽然一个王子站在面前，他对七姑娘说："我就是王子苏拔尔，你要我，现在我在你面前了。你要什么东西呢？"七姑娘非常诧异，又看见他是一个美男子，心里反觉得愉快。她问他怎么会到这里来。他说那扇有能力使他从很远的国土来和她相会。如要见他时，只把扇子拿起来一摇就可以。七姑娘因为爱上他，留他在家住了两三天。以后他就时常被她用扇招来，彼此表示眷恋的情怀。王子应许要娶她为妃，他也和父王商量妥了。到要出嫁的时候，七姑娘就把父母和六位姊姊请来赴喜筵。他们看着她与王子苏拔尔结上合婚的结子。六位姊姊嫉妒她的幸运，心生毒计，要害死那贵人。她们把许多毒瓶子打碎，研成细末，暗地里拿去撒在新郎的床上。苏拔尔晚间躺在床上，不一会儿的工夫，全身都肿痛起来。因为药瓶细末的毒流遍了他的全身。王子感觉非常痛苦便嚷出来。他的侍从进来，立刻把他送回本国，找太医医治去。

苏拔尔回到宫中，父王母后召了许多太医来讨究他的病症，下的药都没功效。王子天天躺在床上呻吟，只剩下一丝残喘了。七姑娘自然非常悲伤，因为她还没过洞房的快乐，新郎便因病而被人送回国去医治。她虽不曾去过外国，却立定主意要到她丈夫那里去服侍他。她于是化装成一个男子，穿上修道士的衣服，手里拿着一把行者所用的铲子。她走了好些年，每日步行，累了便歇。

那一天，她已经走近苏拔尔所住的国土了。她在一棵树下歇息。在树顶上，有一个天鸟的巢，住着雄鸟毗韩笈摩和雌鸟毗韩笈弥。那时老鸟不在巢里，只剩下一对雏鸟。小鸟们忽然叫起来，因为它们看见一条蛇要上树去伤害它们。那位行者猛然起来用铲子将蛇截为两段，小鸟们就安静了。不久，毗韩笈摩夫妇飞回来。雌鸟在空中的道上对雄鸟说："我恐怕我们的儿女会被蛇、我们的仇敌吃掉吧。怎么我听不见它们的叫声？"雄鸟也很发愁。它们来到巢中，很欢喜见儿女们还活着。小鸟便把方才树下那位行者所做的事说给它们知道。它们果然看见地上有条蛇已截成两段。雄鸟看见树下的行者，早已知道她的来历。毗韩笈弥对它的同伴说："那位少年的行者救了我们的子女，我愿意为他做一点事来报答他。"

毗韩笈摩说："她是个女人，不是一个男行者。我们应当帮

126

助她，因为自从她嫁给苏拔尔王子以后，不到几刻，王子便得了恶疾。那是她的姊姊将毒瓶的粉末撒在新人床上所致，什么药都不能治得好的。他现在还躺在病床上哪。她是个有勇气的新妇，现在乔装要到她丈夫那里去服侍他。"

"那王子的病真的没有药可以治得好么？"

"有的，有药可以治好他，那就是我们的粪。"雄鸟这样回答。它接着说，"若是把我们放在地上的粪晒干了，研成粉末，洗澡以后敷在病人身上七次就可以了。但是用药后，必要再用七罐水与七罐乳去洗净他便可以把王子苏拔尔的病治好。"

"可是这位不幸的商人女怎能再走几天的路程呢？她到的时候，王子恐怕已经死掉咧。"

雄鸟说："我可以驮她到王子那里去。因为她是空身一个，很轻省，也不带什么礼物，所以我还可以送她回家去。"

那装作行者的七姑娘在树下把天鸟的话都听明白了，便求毘韩笈摩驮她到苏拔尔王子那里去。雄鸟立刻答应她。在骑上鸟背之前，她捡了许多鸟粪带在身边。鸟飞得非常快，一会儿便到了王宫。她下来，走到宫门口，对守卫的人说她有奇药可以治王子的病，请他入宫去禀报。王本急于为王子求医，现在听见外头有个行者说有奇药，在几刻中就可以使他儿子痊愈，立时召她进来。她到宫里把鸟粪如法制好，命人为王子洗澡，再用羽毛把药扫在他身上。过了一会儿，她又命人将七罐水和七罐乳依次淋在他身上。王子的身体到用过第七次的乳冲洗以后，便都复原了。王喜欢到极致问她要什么报酬，他都可以给她。可是她既然是个行者，所以拒绝一切礼物。她只求王子把手上的指环送给她作为纪念品。王子果然把指环给了她。他也不知道那行者就是他的妻子。

　　昆韩笈摩在海边等候七姑娘从宫里回来，就把她驮回林中。她安静地歇了一夜。第二天早晨，她拿起宝扇来一摇，王子苏拔尔立刻来到她跟前。他看见他妻子带着他昨天给那行者的指环，问起因由，才知道是他妻子把他的病治好的。他更是敬爱七姑娘，请她一同回到本国去。王子很大度，也不惩治他那几位大姨子。他们夫妇在宫中过着很美满的生活，一直到生子，生孙，还见得着了他们的曾孙。


　　我的故事说到这里算完了，

　　那提耶也枯萎了。

　　那提耶呵，你为什么枯萎呢？

　　你的牛为什么要我用草来喂它？

　　牛呵，你为什么要人喂？

你的牧者，为什么不看护我？

牧者呵，你为什么不去看牛？

你的儿媳妇为什么不把米给我？

儿媳妇呵，你为什么不给米呢？

我的孩子为什么哭呢？

孩子呵，你为什么哭呢？

蚂蚁为什么要咬我呢？

蚂蚁呵，你为什么要咬人呢？

喀！喀！喀！

九

阿芙蓉

从前在恒河岸边住着一个仙人，每日每夜不断地敬礼诸天，实行禅定，所以具有很大的神通能力。白天他只坐在河边礼拜。夜间他就在一间用棕榈叶搭成的小屋里住。那小屋是他亲手搭成的。屋的四围都是小丛林，相距好几里才有村落，所以他那里很是幽静。在小屋里有一只小家鼠，每晚出来吃仙人剩下的食物。仙人本来是不伤害生灵的，他不但不害它，并且时常同它玩。仙人对它，一半是因为善意对待动物，一半是因为他要个小伴侣来共谈。他用神通力使小家鼠会说人话。

　　有一天晚上，仙人从河边回来，小家鼠忽然立起来，合着前肢，像人礼拜一样。它向着仙人说："圣者，你曾施恩于我，使我能够说话。现在若是你喜欢的话，我还要请你再赐给我一样福气。"仙人说："你要什么？小家鼠，你要什么呢？你把你所要的说出来吧。"小家鼠回答说："当圣者你日间到河边去礼拜和静坐时，这里常有一只猫走来想要捉我。若不是敬畏圣者你的缘故，它早已把我吃掉了，我怕终有一天会被它吃掉。我求圣者赐我变成一只小猫，具有和我的仇敌一样的能力。"仙人可怜小鼠的被欺，就把圣水浇在它身上，口里念了些真言，立时把它化成小猫。

　　隔了许多晚上，仙人又问小猫说："小猫，你对于现在的生活喜欢不喜欢呢？"小猫摇着头回答他说："圣者，我不大喜欢。"

132

仙人问："为什么呢？你不是很强健，足以战胜世间一切的猫么？"小猫说："不错。圣者，你使我化成一只足以战胜同类的强健的猫，可是我又有了新的仇敌。每逢圣者你到河边去的时候，一只狗王常跑到屋里来狂吠，我怕它，怕得几乎丢了性命。如果圣者你不厌弃我，敢求再使我也变成一只狗。"仙人于是对它发出命令的语气说："变成一只狗吧。"那小猫立时变成一只大狗。

日子过得快，大狗也过腻了。在一个晚间，它又对仙人说："我想圣者你对待我还不算圆满。从前我不过是一只小家鼠，你使我说话，又使我变成猫，现在又使我变成狗。我做狗，有了许多困难，头一样每天你所吃剩下的老不够我吃饱。我只依赖你吃剩的度活，可是你使我变成一只具有野兽食量的狗，叫我怎能过日子呢？我在林中，看见树上那些小猕猴过着很快活的日子。它们从这棵树跳过那棵树，爱吃哪一个果子就吃哪一个。它们能够遍尝一切的果子，它们的生活真是令我羡慕啊！圣者，你如果不对我发怒，我要求你把我也变成一只猕猴。"仙人顺从它的意思，立时把它变成猕猴。

大狗现在又变成小猕猴了，它很喜欢它的新生活，从一棵树攀过另一棵树，随意吃它所喜欢吃的果子。可惜一切的满足和愉快都是不长久的，小猕猴对于它的生活又厌烦了。夏天来到，又热又旱，猕猴常觉得渴和热，它很不容易到池里去喝水。它看见野猪整日躺在湿泥里，不觉得热，也不觉得渴，心里就非常羡慕。它嚷着说："呀，那班野猪多么快活呢！它们整日泡在水里，老不觉得热。我愿意我也变成一只野猪。"那一晚上，它回到小屋里来，求仙人使它变成一只野猪。仙人的仁爱是无限量的，凡有所求，他没有不照办的，他又命小猕猴变成了一只野猪。

野猪在淤泥中滚了两天，觉得很舒服，它满足极了。第三天，它正在泥中游戏，蓦然看见远地来了一只大象。象的全身装饰得很庄严。它的背上坐着一位大王。国王是出来打猎路过那里的。野猪看见王的技艺很娴熟，射杀许多野兽。野猪在泥中险些被他看见。若是它被王和他的侍从发现，它的命一定也要丢掉。它自己想来，觉得野猪的生活也是非常危险的。它想王所坐的象一定很快活，回家以后便请求仙人把它也变成一只象王。

象王在林中遨游，一心等王来捕它。有一天，王果然又出来打猎，象王故意跑到王跟前。王在远处早已看见它，觉得它长得非常健壮和美丽，现在见它跑到跟前，就叫人把它拿住，带回宫里豢养去。过了好些日子，王后想到恒河去洗澡。王说他也愿意与她一同去。于是命人把那新驯的象王装饰起来，把象亭安在它背上。王和王后出来，侍从先把王后扶上去，然后王也上去。人都以为象王现在可满足它的心愿了。其实不然！它觉得被女人骑在自己背上总有点不合适，虽然她是个王后，也没有好处。它想着它的身份太低了，——叫一个女人骑在背上！它一发怒，就把王和王后从亭子上摔下来。王赶紧把王后扶起来，安慰她说象王是新捕来的，还没驯熟。他搂着她，问她受了伤没有，他为她拍掉身上的尘土。他命人去取衣服来给王后换，用他自己的手帕来拭掉她面上和手上的尘垢，他还搂着她吻唼了一百多次。

象王站在一边，仔细看见王对待王后那么温存体贴，它想着世间唯有王后是最快乐的了。它想定了，不顾一切危险，撇下王和他的侍从们，飞跑到林中。它一面跑一面对自己说："我今天才理会王后是一切生灵中最快乐的。她受人家多么满足的爱护呢！王把她扶起来，搂着她，慰问她，亲手为她拂拭尘土，且吻唼了她一百多次！做一个王后真是快乐呀！我一定要请仙人把我变成一个王后！"象王自己打定了主意，便从林中跑回仙人所住的小屋。太阳下去了，仙人从河边回来。象王俯伏在他面前，做请求的姿态。仙人问它："今天又有什么趣味的消息呢？你为什么又离开王的象坊，跑回来呢？"象王说："我还能说什么呢？你待我这么好，使我不敢再有所请求。不过，凡我所求的你都应许了我，现在我大胆敢再求一样，我自变成象王以后，身体虽加大了，福乐却一点也不见得增加。我觉得在一切生灵中，王后是最幸福的。我神圣的父亲，求你把我变成一个王后。"仙人回答它说："呆子，我怎能使你变成一个王后呢？我到哪里去找一个有国土、有权位的王来做你的丈夫呢？我最多可以使你变成一个非常美丽的女子。你的美丽温柔很够得上受一个王或王子的眷恋，若是诸天赐福与你，遣一个大王来与你相会，你的机会便到了。"象王听见仙人所说的话，也很情愿变成一个美女。仙人立时运用他的神通，把它变成一个非常俊美的女子。他给她取一个名字叫普斯陀摩尼，意思便是"罂粟女"。我们可以叫她阿芙蓉。

阿芙蓉住在仙人的小屋里，每日以种木栽花为自己的娱乐。有一天，仙人已到河边去了，她自己一个人坐在小屋外头。正在出神，忽然来了一位贵人，身上穿戴得非常华丽，举止也很大方。她站起来，问他需要什么。贵人说他是出来打猎，追逐一群麋鹿到此地来，追不上它们，由它们逃了。现在他又疲乏，又口渴，所以走来看看有人能够供给他一点水和一点食物没有。

阿芙蓉说："贵客，请暂时以这间破屋为你的家吧，我要为你做一切能够使你安适的事情。我很抱歉的是我们很穷，不能供给你平日所需要的东西。我想你必定是一位有权位的大王吧。"

贵人微笑一下，也没有回答她。阿芙蓉去把水壶端来，蹲在他面前，要为他洗脚。她以王的礼遇待他。可是王说："圣女，请不要触摸我的脚，我不过是一个萨帝利人而已。你是圣人的女儿，切不可如此。"

阿芙蓉说："贵人，我并非仙人的女儿，也不是婆罗门女，所以我为你洗脚，是没有伤害的。再者，你是我的客人，我有为你洗脚的义务。"

王问她："请你饶恕我的无礼。敢问你是属于哪一种姓的呢？"

阿芙蓉回答说："我曾听见仙人说我的父母属于萨帝利种姓的。"

王问："你可以容我问你，你的父亲是一位大王么？你非常美丽的容貌和你的庄重态度表明你不是一个常人，必定是生于王家的。"

阿芙蓉没回答他，走进屋里端出一盘香美的鲜果来放在王面前。王一定要她回答他的问题才吃她端来的水果。女孩子不得已，便扭怩地说："仙人说我父亲是一个国王。因为和邻国争战，打败了，与我母亲同逃到林中。我的父亲在林中不久就被老虎吃掉了。我母亲那时正拥抱着我，在林中草地上卧着，因为我还是一个新生的婴儿，一见父王死掉，她便吓坏了。我睁开眼的时候，正是她永

王对阿芙蓉说，她必能使那大有权势的大王的宫殿增加荣耀

远闭着眼睛的时候！很可幸的就是在我躺着的地方，有一个蜜蜂窝挂在枝上。过剩的蜂蜜滴下来，正落在我嘴里。我因此得以活着，直到仙人把我捡回来，当作义女养我到如今。这就是站在大王面前那个薄命的孤女生平的略历。"

王说："要说你是薄命的孤女，在我眼中，你是一个最可爱、最俊美的女子。你若肯，必能使那大有权势的大王的宫殿增加荣耀。"

王爱上了阿芙蓉，直等到仙人回来，对他说明他的意思。仙人于是为他们二人行合婚礼。自此以后，阿芙蓉便住在宫中。王也不理他原来的王后，一心只宠爱她。

所有的愉快都是不能长久的，阿芙蓉的幸福到这时快要享尽了。有一天她正走到井边，忽然脑晕起来，向前一扑，便掉进井底，她被水淹死了。王命人把仙人请来说明这事。仙人安慰王，请他不用悲伤。他说："大王，过去的事不要再想了，命运所定的事情，一定要经过的。方才淹死的王后并非萨帝利种，她不过是我屋里一只小家鼠而已。她在小鼠时代请求我把她变成猫、狗、猕猴、野猪、象王乃至成为一个美女。我都顺着她的意思，使她去享受她理想的生活。现在她享受够了，请你再立从前那位王后为第一王后吧。不过，她既然在名分上是我的义女，我不能不使她的名字永留于人间。请王不要把她的尸身捞上来，只命人挑土倒进井里，把它填满了。以后她的骨肉要化成很美丽的植物，就命名它做阿芙蓉花。从阿芙蓉花的果实中，可以取出一种药材。那药是在一切时地，治一切病，最有功效的。它可以用火烧着吸着吃，或做成丸子吞下去。吸食阿芙蓉的人要得着阿芙蓉一生所经历诸野兽和王后的性格。他一吸了，要像小家鼠那么会酿灾害；像猫那么喜欢喝奶；像狗那么爱争辩；像猕猴那么淫鄙；像野猪那么蛮横；像王后那么好使性子。"

这就是我们现在做药材的鸦片烟的来历。


我的故事说到这里算完了，

那提耶也枯萎了。

那提耶呵，你为什么枯萎呢？

你的牛为什么要我用草来喂它？

牛呵，你为什么要人喂？

你的牧者为什么不看护我？

牧者呵，你为什么不去看牛？

你的儿媳妇为什么不把米给我？

儿媳妇呵，你为什么不给米呢？

我的孩子为什么哭呢?

孩子呵, 你为什么哭呢?

蚂蚁为什么要咬我呢?

蚂蚁呵, 你为什么要咬人呢?

喀! 喀! 喀!

# FOLK–TALES OF BENGAL

Lal Behari Day

# PREFACE

In my *Peasant Life in Bengal* I make the peasant boy Govinda spend some hours every evening in listening to stories told by an old woman, who was called Sambhu's mother, and who was the best story-teller in the village. On reading that passage, Captain R. C. Temple, of the Bengal Staff Corps, son of the distinguished Indian administrator S. Richard Temple, wrote to me to say how interesting it would be to get a collection of those unwritten stories which old women in India recite to little children in the evenings, and to ask whether I could not make such a collection. As I was no stranger to the Mährchen of the Brothers Grimm, to the *Norse Tales* so admirably told by Dasent, to Arnason's *Icelandic Stories* translated by Powell, to the *Highland Stories* done into English by Campbell, and to the fairy stories collected by other writers, and as I believed that the collection suggested would be a contribution, however slight, to that daily increasing literature of folk lore and comparative mythology which, like comparative philosophy, proves that the swarthy and half-naked peasant on the banks of the Ganges is a cousin, albeit of the hundredth remove, to the fair-skinned and well-dressed Englishman on the banks of the Thames, I readily caught up the idea and cast about for materials. But where was an old story-telling woman to be got? I had myself, when a little boy, heard hundreds—it would be no exaggeration to say thousands—of fairy tales from that same old woman, Sambhu's mother—for she was no fictitious person; she actually lived in the flesh and bore that name; but I had nearly forgotten those stories, at any rate they had all got confused in my head, the tail of one story being joined to the head of another, and the head of a third to the tail of a fourth. How I wished that poor Sambhu's mother had been alive! But she had gone long, long ago, to that bourne from which no traveller returns, and her son Sambhu, too, had followed her thither. After a great deal of search I found my Gammer Grethel—though not half so old as the Frau Viehmännin of Hesse-Cassel—in the person of a Bengali Christian woman, who, when a little girl and living in her heathen home, had heard many stories from her old grandmother. She was a good story-teller, but her stock was not large; and after I had heard ten from her I had to look about for fresh sources. An old Brahman told me two stories; an old barber, three; an old servant of mine told me two; and the rest I heard from another old Brahman. None of my authorities knew English; they all told the stories in Bengali, and I translated them into English when I came home. I heard many more stories than those contained in the following pages; but I rejected a great many, as they appeared to me to contain spurious additions to the original stories which I had heard when a boy. I have reason to believe that the stories given in this book area genuine sample of the old stories told by old Bengali women from age to age through a hundred generations.

Sambhu's mother used always to end every one of her stories—and every orthodox Bengali story-teller does the same—with repeating the following formula—

Thus my story endeth,
The Natiya-thorn withereth.
"Why, O Natiya-thorn, dost wither?"
"Why does thy cow on me browse?"
"Why, O cow, dost thou browse?"
"Why does thy neatherd not tend me?"
"Why, O neatherd, dost not tend the cow?"
"Why does thy daughter-in-law not give me rice?"
"Why, O daughter-in-law, dost not give rice?"
"Why does my child cry?"
"Why, O child, dost thou cry?"
"Why does the ant bite me?"

"Why, O ant, dost thou bite?"

*Koot! Koot! Koot!*

What these lines mean, why they are repeated at the end of every story, and what the connection is of the several parts to one another, I do not know. Perhaps the whole is a string of nonsense purposely put together to amuse little children.

LAL BEHARI DAY.
HOOGHLY COLLEGE,
February 27, 1883.

# CHAPTER I
## LIFE'S SECRET

There was a king who had two queens, Duo and Suo.[①] Both of them were childless. One day, a Faquir (mendicant) came to the palace gate to ask for alms. The Suo queen went to the door with a handful of rice. The mendicant asked whether she had any children. On being answered in the negative, the holy mendicant refused to take alms, as the hands of a woman unblessed with child are regarded as ceremonially unclean. He offered her a drug for removing her barrenness, and she expressing her willingness to receive it, he gave it to her with the following directions:—"Take this nostrum, swallow it with the juice of the pomegranate flower; if you do this, you will have a son in due time. The son will be exceedingly handsome, and his complexion will be of the colour of the pomegranate flower; and you shall call him Dalim Kumar.[②] As enemies will try to take away the life of your son, I may as well tell

---

① Kings, in Bengali folk-tales, have invariably two queens—the elder is called Duo, that is, not loved; and the younger is called suo, that is, loved.

② *Dalim* or *dadimba* means a pomegranate, and kumara son.

you that the life of the boy will be bound up in the life of a big *boal* fish which is in your tank, in front of the palace. In the heart of the fish is a small box of wood, in the box is a necklace of gold, that necklace is the life of your son. Farewell."

In the course of a month or so it was whispered in the palace that the Suo queen had hopes of an heir. Great was the joy of the king. Visions of an heir to the throne, and of a never-ending succession of powerful monarchs perpetuating his dynasty to the latest generations, floated before his mind, and made him glad as he had never been in his life. The usual ceremonies, performed on such occasions were celebrated with great pomp; and the subjects made loud demonstrations of their joy at the anticipation of so auspicious an event as the birth of a prince. In the fulness of time, the Suo queen gave birth to a son of uncommon beauty. When the king the first time saw the face of the infant, his heart leaped with joy. The ceremony of the child's first rice was celebrated with extraordinary pomp, and the whole kingdom was filled with gladness.

In course of time Dalim Kumar grew up a fine boy. Of all sports he was most addicted to playing with pigeons. This brought him into frequent contact with his stepmother, the Duo queen, into whose apartments Dalim's pigeons had a trick of always flying. The first time the pigeons flew into her rooms, she readily gave them up to the owner; but the second time she gave them up with some reluctance. The fact is that the Duo queen, perceiving that Dalim's pigeons had this happy knack of flying into her apartments, wished to take advantage of it for the furtherance of her own selfish views. She naturally hated the child, as the king, since his birth, neglected her more than ever, and idolised the fortunate mother of Dalim. She had heard, it is not known how, that the holy mendicant that had given the famous pill to the Suo queen had also told her of a secret connected with the child's life. She had heard that the child's life was bound up with something—she did not know with what. She determined to extort that secret from the boy. Accordingly, the next time the pigeons flew into her rooms, she refused to give them up, addressing the child thus:—"I won't give the pigeons up unless you tell me one thing."

*Dalim.*—"What thing, mamma?"

*Duo.*—"Nothing particular, my darling; I only want to know in what your life is."

*Dalim.*—"What is that, mamma? Where can my life be except in me?"

*Duo.*—"No, child, that is not what I mean. A holy mendicant told your mother that your life is bound up with something. I wish to know what that thing is."

*Dalim.*—"I never heard of any such thing, mamma."

*Duo.*—"If you promise to inquire of your mother in what thing your life is, and if you tell me what your mother says, then I will let you have the pigeons, otherwise not."

*Dalim.*—"Very well, I'll inquire, and let you know. Now, please, give me my pigeons."

*Duo.*—"I'll give them on one condition more. Promise to me that you will not tell your mother that I want the information."

*Dalim.*—"I promise."

The Duo queen let go the pigeons, and Dalim, overjoyed to find again his beloved birds, forgot every syllable of the conversation he had had with his stepmother. The next day, however, the pigeons again flew into the Duo queen's rooms. Dalim went to his stepmother, who asked him for the required information. The boy promised to ask his mother that very day, and begged hard for the release of the pigeons. The pigeons were at last delivered. After play, Dalim went to his mother and said—"Mamma, please tell me in what my life is contained." "What do you mean, child?" asked the mother, astonished beyond measure at the child's extraordinary question. "Yes, Mamma," rejoined the child, "I have heard that a holy mendicant told you that my life is contained in something. Tell me what that thing is." "My pet, my darling, my treasure, my golden-moon, do not ask such an inauspicious

152

question. Let the mouth of my enemies be covered with ashes, and let my Dalim live forever," said the mother, earnestly. But the child insisted on being informed of the secret. He said he would not eat or drink anything unless the information was given him. The Suo queen, pressed by the importunity of her son, in an evil hour told the child the secret of his life. The next day the pigeons again, as fate would have it, flew into the Duo queen's rooms. Dalim went for them; the stepmother plied the boy with sugared words, and obtained the knowledge of the secret.

The Duo queen, on learning the secret of Dalim Kumar's life, lost no time in using it for the prosecution of her malicious design. She told her maid-servants to get for her some dried stalks of the hemp plant, which are very brittle, and which, when pressed upon, make a peculiar noise, not unlike the cracking of joints of bones in the human body. These hemp stalks she put under her bed, upon which she laid herself down and gave out that she was dangerously ill. The king, though he did not love her so well as his other queen, was in duty bound to visit her in her illness. The queen pretended that her bones were all cracking; and sure enough, when she tossed from one side of her bed to the other, the hemp stalks made the noise wanted. The king, believing that the Duo queen was seriously ill, ordered his best physician to attend her. With that physician the

Duo queen was in collusion. The physician said to the king that for the queen's complaint there was but one remedy, which consisted in the outward application of something to be found inside a large *boal* fish which was in the tank before the palace. The king's fisherman was accordingly called and ordered to catch the *boal* in question. On the first throw of the net the fish was caught. It so happened that Dalim Kumar, along with other boys, was playing not far from the tank. The moment the *boal* fish was caught in the net, that moment Dalim felt unwell; and when the fish was brought up to land, Dalim fell down on the ground, and made as if he was about to breathe his last. He was immediately taken into his mother's room, and the king was astonished on hearing of the sudden illness of his son and heir. The fish was by the order of the physician taken into the room of the Duo queen, and as it lay on the floor striking its fins on the ground, Dalim in his mother's room was given up for lost. When the fish was cut open, a casket was found in it; and in the casket laid a necklace of gold. The moment the necklace was worn by the queen, that very moment Dalim died in his mother's room.

When the news of the death of his son and heir reached the king he was plunged into an ocean of grief, which was not lessened in any degree by the intelligence of the recovery of the Duo queen. He wept over his dead Dalim so bitterly that his courtiers were apprehensive of a permanent derangement of his mental powers. The king would not allow the dead body of his son to be either buried or burnt. He could not realize the fact of his son's death; it was so entirely causeless and so terribly sudden. He ordered the dead body to be removed to one of his garden-houses in the suburbs of the city, and to be laid there in state. He ordered that all sorts of provisions should be stowed away in that house, as if the young prince needed them for his refection. Orders were issued that the house should be kept locked up day and night, and that no one should go into it except Dalim's most intimate friend, the son of the king's prime minister, who was intrusted with the key of the house, and who obtained the privilege of entering it once in twenty-four hours.

As, owing to her great loss, the Suo queen lived in retirement, the king gave up his nights entirely to the Duo queen. The latter, in order to allay suspicion, used to put aside the gold necklace at night; and, as fate had ordained that Dalim should be in the state of death only during the time that the necklace was round the neck of the queen, he passed into the state of life whenever the necklace was laid aside. Accordingly Dalim revived every night, as the Duo queen every night put away the necklace, and died again the next morning when the queen put it on. When Dalim became re-animated at night he ate whatever food he liked, for of such there was a plentiful stock in the garden-house, walked about on the premises, and meditated on the singularity of his lot. Dalim's friend, who visited him only during the day, found him always lying a lifeless corpse; but what struck him after some days was the singular fact that the body remained in the same state in which he saw it on the first day of his visit. There was no sign of putrefaction. Except that it was lifeless and pale, there were no symptoms of corruption—it was apparently quite fresh. Unable to account for so strange a phenomenon, he determined to watch the corpse more closely, and to visit it not only during the day but sometimes also at night. The first night that he paid his visit he was astounded to see his dead friend sauntering about in the garden. At first he thought the figure might be only the ghost of his friend, but on feeling him and otherwise examining him, he found the apparition to be veritable flesh and blood. Dalim related to his friend all the circumstances connected with his death; and they both concluded that he revived at nights only because the Duo queen put aside her necklace when the king visited her. As the life of the prince depended on the necklace, the two friends laid their heads together to devise if possible some plans by which they might get possession of it. Night after night they consulted together, but they could not think of any feasible scheme. At length the gods brought about the deliverance of Dalim Kumar in a wonderful manner.

Some years before the time of which we are speaking, the

sister of Bidhata-Purusha[①] was delivered of a daughter. The anxious mother asked her brother what he had written on her child's forehead; to which Bidhata-Purusha replied that she should get married to a dead bridegroom. Maddened as she became with grief at the prospect of such a dreary destiny for her daughter, she yet thought it useless to remonstrate with her brother, for she well knew that he never changed what he once wrote. As the child grew in years she became exceedingly beautiful, but the mother could not look upon her with pleasure in consequence of the portion allotted to her by her divine brother. When the girl came to marriageable age, the mother resolved to flee from the country with her, and thus avert her dreadful destiny. But the decrees of fate cannot thus be overruled. In the course of their wanderings, the mother and daughter arrived at the gate of that very garden-house in which Dalim Kumar lay. It was evening. The girl said she was thirsty and wanted to drink water. The mother told her daughter to sit at the gate, while she went to search for drinking water in some neighbouring hut. In the meantime the girl through curiosity pushed the door of the garden-house which opened of itself. She then went in and saw a beautiful palace, and was wishing to come out when the door shut itself of its own accord, so that she could

---

① Bidhata-Purusha is the deity that predetermines all the events of the life of man or woman, and writes on the forehead of the child, on the sixth day of its birth, a brief precis of them.

not get out. As night came on the prince revived, and, walking about, saw a human figure near the gate. He went up to it, and found it was a girl of surpassing beauty. On being asked who she was, she told Dalim Kumar all the details of her little history—how her uncle, the divine Bidhata-Purusha, wrote on her forehead at her birth that she should get married to a dead bridegroom, how her mother had no pleasure in her life at the prospect of so terrible a destiny, and how, therefore, on the approach of her womanhood, with a view to avert so dreadful a catastrophe, she had left her house with her and wandered in various places, how they came to the gate of the garden-house, and how her mother had now gone in search of drinking water for her. Dalim Kumar, hearing her simple and pathetic story, said, "I am the dead bridegroom, and you must get married to me, come with me to the house." "How can you be said to be a dead bridegroom when you are standing and speaking to me?" said the girl. "You will understand it afterwards," rejoined the prince, "come now and follow me." The girl followed the prince into the house. As she had been fasting the whole day, the prince hospitably entertained her. As for the mother of the girl, the sister of the divine Bidhata-Purusha, she returned to the gate of the garden-house after it was dark, cried out for her daughter, and getting no answer, went away in search of her in the huts in the neighbourhood. It is said that after this she was not seen anywhere.

While the niece of the divine Bidhata-Purusha was partaking of the hospitality of Dalim Kumar, his friend as usual made his appearance. He was surprised not a little at the sight of the fair stranger; and his surprise became greater when he heard the story of the young lady from her own lips. It was forthwith resolved that very night to unite the young couple in the bonds of matrimony. As priests were out of the question, the hymeneal rites were performed à *la Gandharva*.[1] The friend of the bridegroom took leave of the newly-married couple and went away to his house. As the happy pair had spent the greater part of the night in wakefulness, it was long after sunrise that they awoke from their sleep;—I should have said that the young wife woke from her sleep, for the prince had become a cold corpse, life having departed from him. The feelings of the young wife may be easily imagined. She shook her husband, imprinted warm kisses on his cold lips, but in vain. He was as lifeless as a marble statue. Stricken with horror, she smote her breast, struck her forehead with the palms of her hands, tore her hair and went about in the house and in the garden as if she had gone mad. Dalim's friend did not come into the house during

---

[1] There are eight forms of marriage spoken of in the Hindu Sastras, of which the Gandharva is one, consisting in the exchange of garlands.

the day, as he deemed it improper to pay a visit to her while her husband was lying dead. The day seemed to the poor girl as long as a year, but the longest day has its end, and when the shades of evening were descending upon the landscape, her dead husband was awakened into consciousness; he rose up from his bed, embraced his disconsolate wife, ate, drank, and became merry. His friend made his appearance as usual, and the whole night was spent in gaiety and festivity. Amid this alternation of life and death did the prince and his lady spend some seven or eight years, during which time the princess presented her husband with two lovely boys who were the exact image of their father.

It is superfluous to remark that the king, the two queens, and other members of the royal household, did not know that Dalim Kumar was living, at any rate, was living at night. They all thought that he was long ago dead and his corpse burnt. But the heart of Dalim's wife was yearning after her mother-in-law whom she had never seen. She conceived a plan by which she might be able not only to have a sight of her mother-in-law, but also to get hold of the Duo queen's necklace on which her husband's life was dependent. With the consent of her husband and of his friend she disguised herself as a female barber. Like every female barber she took a bundle containing the following articles:—an iron instrument for pairing nails, another iron instrument for scraping off the superfluous flesh of the soles of the feet, a piece of jhama or burnt brick for rubbing the soles of the feet with, and *alakta*[①] for painting the edges of the feet and toes with. Taking this bundle in her hand she stood at the gate of the king's palace with her two boys. She declared herself to be a barber, and expressed a desire to see the Suo queen, who readily gave her an interview. The queen was quite taken up with the two little boys, who, she declared, strongly reminded her of her darling Dalim Kumar. Tears fell profusely from her eyes at the recollection of her lost treasure; but she of course had not the remotest idea that the two little boys were the sons of her own dear Dalim. She told the supposed barber that she did not require her services, as, since the death of her son, she had given up all terrestrial vanities and among others the practice of dyeing her feet red; but she added that, nevertheless, she would be glad now and then to see her and her two fine boys. The female barber, for so we must now call her, then went to the quarters of the Duo queen and offered her services. The queen allowed her to pare her nails, to scrape off the superfluous flesh of her feet, and to paint them with *alakta*, and was so pleased with her skill, and the sweetness of her disposition, that she ordered her to wait upon her

---

① *Alakta* is leaves or flimsy paper saturated with lac.

periodically. The female barber noticed with no little concern the necklace round the queen's neck. The day of her second visit came on, and she instructed the elder of her two sons to set up a loud cry in the palace, and not to stop crying till he got into his hands the Duo queen's necklace. The female barber, accordingly, went again on the appointed day to the Duo queen's apartments. While she was engaged in painting the queen's feet, the elder boy set up a loud cry. On being asked the reason of the cry, the boy, as previously instructed, said that he wanted the queen's necklace. The queen said that it was impossible for her to part with that particular necklace, for it was the best and most valuable of all her jewels. To gratify the boy, however, she took it off her neck, and put it into the boy's hand. The boy stopped crying and held the necklace tight in his hand. As the female barber after she had done her work was about to go away, the queen wanted the necklace back. But the boy would not part with it. When his mother attempted to snatch it from him, he wept bitterly, and showed as if his heart would break. On which the female barber said—"Will your Majesty be gracious enough to let the boy take the necklace home with him? When he falls asleep after drinking his milk, which he is sure to do in the course of an hour, I will carefully bring it back to you." The queen, seeing that the boy would not allow it to be taken away from him, agreed to the proposal of the female barber, especially reflecting that Dalim, whose life depended on it, had long ago gone to the abodes of death.

Thus possessed of the treasure on which the life of her husband depended, the woman went with breathless haste to the garden-house and presented the necklace to Dalim, who had been restored to life. Their joy knew no bounds, and by the advice of their friend they determined the next day to go to the palace in state, and present themselves to the king and the Suo queen. Due preparations were made; an elephant, richly caparisoned, was brought for the prince Dalim Kumar, a pair of ponies for the two little boys, and a *ckaturdala*[①] furnished with curtains of gold lace for the princess. Word was sent to the king and the Suo queen that the prince Dalim Kumar was not only alive, but that he was coming to visit his royal parents with his wife and sons. The king and Suo queen could hardly believe in the report, but being assured of its truth they were entranced with joy; while the Duo queen, anticipating the disclosure of all her wiles, became overwhelmed with grief. The procession of Dalim Kumar, which was attended by a band of musicians, approached the palace-gate; and the king and Suo queen went out to receive their long-lost son. It is needless to

---

① A sort of open Palki, used generally for carrying the bridegroom and bride in marriage processions.

163

say that their joy was intense. They fell on each other's neck and wept. Dalim then related all the circumstances connected with his death. The king, inflamed with rage, ordered the Duo queen into his presence. A large hole, as deep as the height of a man, was dug in the ground. The Duo queen was put into it in a standing posture. Prickly thorn was heaped around her up to the crown of her head; and in this manner she was buried alive.

Thus my story endeth,
The Natiya-thorn withereth:
"Why, O Natiya-thorn, dost wither?"
"Why does thy cow on me browse?"
"Why, O cow, dost thou browse?"
"Why does thy neatherd not tend me?"
"Why, O neatherd, dost not tend the cow?"
"Why does thy daughter-in-law not give me rice?"
"Why, O daughter-in-law, dost not give rice?"
"Why does my child cry?"
"Why, O child, dost thou cry?"
"Why does the ant bite me?"
"Why, O ant, dost thou bite?"
*Koot! Koot! Koot!*

# CHAPTER II
## PHAKIR CHAND

There was a king's son, and there was a minister's son. They loved each other dearly; they sat together, they stood up together, they walked together, they ate together, they slept together, they got up together. In this way they spent many years in each other's company, till they both felt a desire to see foreign lands. So one day they set out on their journey. Though very rich, the one being the son of a king and the other the son of his chief minister, they did not take any servants with them; they went by themselves on horseback. The horses were beautiful to look at; they were *pakshirajes*, or kings of birds. The king's son and the minister's son rode together many days. They passed through extensive plains covered with paddy; through cities, towns, and villages; through waterless, treeless deserts; through dense forests which were the abode of the tiger and the bear. One evening they were overtaken by night in a region where human habitations were not seen; and as it was getting darker and darker, they dismounted beneath a lofty tree, tied their horses to its trunk, and, climbing up, sat on its branches covered with thick foliage. The tree grew near a large tank, the water of which was as clear as the eye of a crow. The king's son and the minister's son made themselves as comfortable as they could on the tree, being determined to spend on its branches the livelong night. They sometimes chatted together in whispers on account of the lonely terrors of the region; they sometimes sat demurely silent for some minutes; and anon they were falling into a doze, when their attention was arrested by a terrible sight.

A sound like the rush of many waters was heard from the middle of the tank. A huge serpent was seen leaping up from under the water with its hood of enormous size. It "lay floating many a rood", then it swam ashore, and went about hissing. But what most of all attracted the attention of the king's son and the minister's son was a brilliant *manikya* (jewel) on the crested hood of the serpent. It shone like a thousand diamonds. It lit up the tank, its embankments, and the objects round about. The serpent doffed the jewel from its crest and threw it on the ground, and then it went about hissing in search of food. The two friends sitting on the tree greatly admired the wonderful brilliant, shedding ineffable lustre on everything around. They had never before seen anything like it; they had only heard of it as equaling the treasures of seven kings. Their admiration, however, was soon changed into sorrow and fear; for the serpent came hissing to the foot of the tree on the branches of which they were seated, and swallowed up, one by one, the horses tied to the trunk. They feared that they themselves would be the next victims, when, to their infinite relief, the gigantic cobra turned away from the tree, and went about roaming to a great distance. The minister's son seeing this, bethought himself of taking possession of the lustrous stone. He had heard that the only way to hide the brilliant light of the jewel was to cover it with cow-dung or horse-dung, a quantity of which latter article he perceived lying at the foot of the tree. He came down from the tree softly, picked up the horse-dung, threw it upon the precious stone, and again climbed into the tree. The serpent, not perceiving the light of its head-jewel, rushed with great fury to the spot where it had been left. Its hissings, groans, and convulsions were terrible. It went round and round the jewel covered with horse-dung, and then breathed its last. Early next morning the king's son and the minister's son alighted from the tree, and went to the spot where the crest-jewel was. The mighty serpent lay there perfectly lifeless. The minister's son took up in his hand the jewel covered with horse-dung; and both of them went to the tank to wash it. When all the horse-dung had been washed off, the jewel shone as brilliantly as before. It lit up the entire bed of the tank, and exposed to their view the innumerable fishes swimming about in the waters. But what was their astonishment when they saw, by the light of the jewel, in the bottom of the tank, the lofty walls of what seemed a magnificent palace. The venturesome son of the minister proposed to the prince that they should dive into the waters and get at the palace below. They both dived into the waters—the jewel' being in the hand of the minister's son—and in a moment stood at the gate of the palace. The gate was open. They saw no being, human or superhuman. They went inside the gate, and saw a beautiful garden laid out on the ample grounds round about the house which was in the centre. The king's son and the minister's son had never seen such a profusion of flowers. The rose with its many varieties, the jessamine, the *bel*, the *mallika*, the *king of smells*, the lily of the valley, the *Champaka*, and a thousand other sorts of sweet-scented flowers were there. And of each of these flowers there seemed to be a large number. Here were a hundred rose-bushes, there many acres covered with the delicious jessamine, while yonder were extensive plantations of all sorts of flowers. As all the plants were begemmed with flowers, and as the flowers were in full bloom, the air was loaded with rich perfume. It was a wilderness of sweets.

Through this paradise of perfumery they proceeded towards the house, which was surrounded by banks of lofty trees. They stood at the door of the house. It was a fairy palace. The walls were of burnished gold, and here and there shone diamonds of dazzling hue which were stuck into the walls. They did not meet with any beings, human or other. They went inside, which was richly furnished. They went from room to room, but they did not see any one. It seemed to be a deserted house. At last, however, they found in one room a young lady lying down, apparently in sleep, on a bed of golden framework. She was of exquisite beauty; her complexion was a mixture of red and white; and her age was apparently about sixteen. The king's son and the minister's son gazed upon her with rapture; but they had not stood long when this young lady of superb beauty opened her eyes, which seemed like those of a gazelle. On seeing the strangers she said: "How have you come here, ye unfortunate men? Begone, begone! This is the abode of a mighty serpent, which has devoured my father, my mother, my brothers, and all my relatives; I am the only one of my family that he has spared. Flee for your lives, or else the serpent will put you both in its capacious maw." The minister's son told the princess how the serpent bad breathed its last; how he, and his friend had got possession of its head-jewel, and by its light had come to her palace. She thanked the strangers for delivering her from the infernal serpent, and begged of them to live in the house, and never to desert her. The king's son and the minister's son gladly accepted the invitation. The king's son, smitten with the charms of the peerless princess, married her after a short time; and as there was no priest there, the hymeneal knot was tied by a simple exchange of garlands of flowers.

The king's son became inexpressibly happy in the company of the princess, who was as amiable in her disposition as she was beautiful in her person; and though the wife of the minister's son was living in the upper world, he too participated in his friend's happiness. Time thus passed merrily, when the king's son bethought himself of returning to his native country; and as it was fit that he should go with his princess in due pomp, it was determined that the minister's son should first ascend from the subaqueous regions, go to the king, and bring with him attendants, horses, and elephants for the happy pair. The snake-jewel was therefore had in requisition. The prince, with the jewel in hand, accompanied the minister's son to the upper world, and bidding adieu to his friend returned to his lovely wife in the enchanted palace. Before leaving, the minister's son appointed the day and the hour when he would stand on the high embankments of the tank with horses, elephants, and attendants, and wait upon the prince and the princess, who were to join him in the upper world by means of the jewel.

Leaving the minister's son to wend his way to his country and to make preparations for the return of his king's son, let us see how the happy couple in the subterranean palace were passing their time. One day, while the prince was sleeping after his noonday meal, the princess, who had never seen the upper regions, felt the desire of visiting them, and the rather as the snake-jewel, which alone could give her safe conduct through the waters, was at that moment shedding its bright effulgence in the room. She took up the jewel in her hand, left the palace, and successfully reached the upper world. No mortal caught her sight. She sat on the flight of steps with which the tank was furnished for the convenience of bathers, scrubbed her body, washed her hair, disported in the waters, walked about on the water's edge, admired all the scenery around, and returned to her palace, where she found her husband still locked in the embrace of sleep. When the prince woke up, she did not tell him a word about her adventure. The following day at the same hour, when her husband was asleep, she paid a second visit to the upper world, and went back unnoticed by mortal man. As success made her bold, she repeated her adventure a third time. It so chanced that on that day the son of the Rajah, in whose territories the tank was situated, was out on a hunting excursion, and had pitched his tent not far from the place. While his attendants were engaged in cooking their noon-day meal, the Rajah's son sauntered about on the embankments of the tank, near which an old woman was gathering sticks and dried branches of trees for purposes of fuel. It was while the Rajah's son and the old woman were near the tank that the princess paid her third visit to the upper world. She rose up from the waters, gazed around, and seeing a man and a woman on the banks again went down. The Rajah's son caught a momentary glimpse of the princess, and so did the old woman gathering sticks. The Rajah's son stood gazing on the waters. He had never seen such a beauty. She seemed to him to be one of those *deva–kanyas*, heavenly goddesses, of whom he had read in old books, and who are said now and then to favour the lower world with their visits which, like angel visits, are "few and far between". The unearthly beauty of the princess, though he had seen her only for a moment, made a deep impression on his heart, and distracted his mind. He stood there like a statue, for hours, gazing on the waters, in the hope of seeing the lovely figure again. But in vain. The princess did not appear again. The Rajah's son became mad with love. He kept muttering—"Now here, now gone! Now here, now gone!" He would not leave the place till he was forcibly removed by the attendants who had now come to him. He was taken to his father's palace in a state of hopeless insanity. He spoke to nobody; he always sobbed heavily; and the only words which proceeded out of his mouth—and he was muttering them every minute—were, "Now here, now gone! Now here, now gone!" The Rajah's grief may well be conceived. He could not imagine what should have deranged his son's mind. The words, "Now here, now gone," which ever and anon issued from his son's lips, were a mystery to him; he could not unravel their meaning; neither could the attendants throw any light on the subject. The best physicians of the country were consulted, but to no effect. The sons of Aesculapius could not ascertain the cause of the madness, far less could they cure it. To the many inquiries of the physicians, the only reply made by the Rajah's son was the stereotyped words—"Now here, now gone! Now here, now gone!"

The Rajah, distracted with grief on account of the obscuration of his son's intellects, caused a proclamation to be made in the capital by beat of drum, to the effect that, if any person could explain the cause of his son's madness and cure it, such a person would be rewarded with the hand of the Rajah's daughter, and with the possession of half his kingdom. The drum was beaten round most parts of the city, but no one touched it, as no one knew the cause of the madness of the Rajah's son. At last, an old woman touched the drum, and declared that she would not only discover the cause of the madness, but cure it. This woman, who was the identical woman that was gathering sticks near the tank at the time the Rajah's son lost his reason, had a crackbrained son of the name of Phakir Chand, and was in consequence called Phakir's mother, or more familiarly Phakre's mother. When the woman was brought before the Rajah, the following conversation took place:—

*Rajah.*—"You are the woman that touched the drum—you know the cause of my son's madness?"

*Phakir's Mother.*—"Yes, oh, incarnation of justice, I know the cause, but I will not mention it, till I have cured your son."

*Rajah.*—"How can I believe that you are able to cure my son, when the best physicians of the land have failed?"

*Phakir's Mother.*—"You need not now believe, my lord, till I have performed the cure. Many an old woman knows secrets with which wise men are unacquainted."

*Rajah.*—"Very well, let me see what you can do. In what time will you perform the cure?"

*Phakir's Mother.*—"It is impossible to fix the time at present; but I will begin work immediately with your lordship's assistance."

*Rajah.*—"What help do you require from me?"

*Phakir's Mother.*—"Your lordship will please order a hut to be raised on the embankment of the tank where your son first caught the disease. I mean to live in that hut for a few days. And your lordship will also please order some of your servants to be in attendance at a distance of about a hundred yards from the hut, so that they might be within call."

*Rajah.*—"Very well; I will order that to be immediately done. Do you want anything else?"

*Phakir's Mother.*—"Nothing else, my lord, in the way of preparations. But it is as well to remind your lordship of the conditions on which I undertake the cure. Your lordship has promised to give to the performer of the cure the hand of your daughter and half your kingdom. As I am a woman and cannot marry your daughter, I beg that, in case I perform the cure, my son Phakir Chand may marry your daughter and take possession of half your kingdom."

*Rajah.*—"Agreed, agreed."

A temporary hut was in a few hours erected on the embankment of the tank, and Phakir's mother took up her abode in it. An outpost was also erected at some distance for servants in attendance who might be required to give help to the woman. Strict orders were given by Phakir's mother that no human being should go near the tank excepting herself. Let us leave Phakir's mother keeping watch at the tank, and hasten down into the subterranean palace to see what the prince and the princess are about. After the mishap which had occurred on her last visit to the upper world, the princess had given up the idea of a fourth visit. But women generally have greater curiosity than men; and the princess of the underground palace was no exception to the general rule. One day, while her husband was asleep as usual after his noonday meal, she rushed out of the palace with the snake-jewel in her hand, and came to the upper world. The moment the upheaval of the waters in the middle of the tank took place, Phakir's mother, who was on the alert, concealed herself in the hut and began looking through the chinks of the matted wall. The princess, seeing no mortal near, came to the bank, and sitting there began to scrub her body. Phakir's mother showed herself outside the hut, and addressing the princess, said in a winning tone—"Come, my child, thou queen of beauty, come to me, and I will help you to bathe." So saying, she approached the princess, who, seeing that it was only a woman, made no resistance. The old woman, while in the act of washing the hair of the princess, noticed the bright jewel in her hand, and said—"Put the jewel here till you are bathed." In a moment the jewel was in the possession of Phakir's mother, who wrapped it up in the cloth that was round her waist. Knowing the princess to be unable to escape, she gave the signal to the attendants in waiting who rushed to the tank and made the princess a captive.

Great were the rejoicings of the people when the tidings reached the city that Phakir's mother had captured a water-nymph from the nether regions. The whole city came to see the "daughter of the immortals", as they called the princess. When she was brought to the palace and confronted with the Rajah's son of obscured intellect, the latter said with a shout of exultation—"I have found! I have found!" The cloud which had settled on his brain was dissipated in a moment. The eyes, erewhile vacant and lustreless, now glowed with the fire of intelligence; his tongue, of which he had almost lost the use—the only words which he used to utter being, "Now here, now gone!"—was now relaxed; in a word, he was restored to his senses. The joy of the Rajah knew no bounds. There was great festivity in the city; and the people who showered benedictions on the head of Phakir Chand's mother, expected the speedy celebration of the marriage of the Rajah's son with the beauty of the nether world. The princess, however, told the Rajah, through Phakir's mother, that she had made a vow to the effect that she would not, for one whole year, look at the face of another man than that of her husband who was dwelling beneath the waters, and that therefore the marriage could not be performed during that period. Though the Rajah's son was somewhat disappointed, he readily agreed to the delay, believing, agreeably to the proverb, that delay would greatly enhance the sweetness of those pleasures which were in store for him.

It is scarcely necessary to say that the princess spent her days and her nights in sorrowing and sighing. She lamented that idle curiosity which had led her to come to the upper world, leaving her husband below. When she recollected that her husband was all alone below the waters she wept bitter tears. She wished she could run away. But that was impossible, as she was immured within walls, and there were walls within walls. Besides, if she could get out of the palace and of the city, of what avail would it be? She could not gain her husband, as the serpent jewel was not in her possession. The ladies of the palace and Phakir's mother tried to divert her mind, but in vain. She took pleasure in nothing; she would hardly speak to any one; she wept day and night. The year of her vow was drawing to a close, and yet she was disconsolate. The marriage, however, must be celebrated. The Rajah consulted the astrologers, and the day and the hour in which the nuptial knot was to be tied were fixed. Great preparations were made. The confectioners of the city busied themselves day and night in preparing sweetmeats; milkmen took contracts for supplying the palace with tanks of curds; gunpowder was being manufactured for a grand display of fireworks; bands of musicians were placed on sheds erected over the palace gate, who ever and anon sent forth many "a bout of linked sweetness"; and the whole city assumed an air of mirth and festivity.

It is time we should think of the minister's son, who, leaving his friend in the subterranean palace, had gone to his country to bring horses, elephants, and attendants for the return of the king's son and his lovely princess with due pomp. The preparations took him many months; and when everything was ready he started on his journey, accompanied by a long train of elephants, horses, and attendants. He reached the tank two or three days before the appointed day. Tents were pitched in the mango-topes adjoining the tank for the accommodation of men and cattle; and the minister's son always kept his eyes fixed on the tank. The sun of the appointed day sank below the horizon; but the prince and the princess dwelling beneath the waters made no sign. He waited two or three days longer; still the prince did not make his appearance. What could have happened to his friend and his beautiful wife? Were they dead? Had another serpent, possibly the mate of the one that had died, beaten the prince and the princess to death? Had they somehow lost the serpent-jewel? Or had they been captured when they were once on a visit to the upper world? Such were the reflections of the minister's son. He was overwhelmed with grief. Ever since he had come to the tank he had heard at regular intervals the sound of music coming from the city which was not distant. He inquired of passers-by what that music meant. He was told that the Rajah's son was about to be married to some wonderful young lady, who had come out of the waters of that very tank on the bank of which he was now seated, and that the marriage ceremony was to be performed on the day following the next. The minister's son immediately concluded that the wonderful young lady of the lake that was to be married was none other than the wife of his friend, the king's son. He resolved therefore to go into the city to learn the details of the affair, and try if possible to rescue the princess. He told the attendants to go home, taking with them the elephants and the horses; and he himself went to the city, and took up his abode in the house of a Brahman.

After he had rested and taken his dinner, the minister's son asked the Brahman what the meaning was of the music that was heard in the city at regular intervals. The Brahman asked, "From what part of the world have you come that you have not heard of the wonderful circumstance that a young lady of heavenly beauty rose out of the waters of a tank in the suburbs, and that she is going to be married the day after tomorrow to the son of our Rajah?"

*Minister's Son.*—"No, I have heard nothing. I have come from a distant country whither the story has not reached. Will you kindly tell me the particulars?"

*Brahman.*—"The Rajah's son went out for a hunting about this time last year. He pitched his tents close to a tank in the suburbs. One day while the Rajah's son was walking near the tank, he saw a young woman, or rather goddess, of uncommon beauty rise from the waters of the tank. She gazed about for a minute or two and disappeared. The Rajah's son, however, who had seen her, was so struck with her heavenly beauty that he became desperately enamoured of her. Indeed, so intense was his passion that his reason gave way; and he was carried home hopelessly mad. The only words he uttered day and night were—'Now here, now gone!' The Rajah sent for all the best physicians of the country for restoring his son to his reason; but the physicians were powerless. At last he caused a proclamation to be made by beat of drum to the effect that if anyone could cure the Rajah's son, he should be the Rajah's son-in-law and the owner of half his kingdom. An old woman, who went by the name of Phakir's mother, took hold of the drum, and declared her ability to cure the Rajah's son. On the tank where the princess had appeared was raised for Phakir's mother a hut in which she took up her abode; and not far from her hut another hut was erected for the accommodation of attendants who might be required to help her. It seems the goddess rose from the waters; Phakir's mother seized her with the help of the attendants, and carried her in a *palki* to the palace. At the sight of her the Rajah's son was restored to his senses; and the marriage would have been celebrated at that time but for a vow which the goddess had made that she would not look at the face of any male person till the lapse of a year. The year of the vow is now over; and the music which you have heard is from the gate of the Rajah's palace. This, in brief, is the story."

*Minister's Son.*—"A truly wonderful story! And has Phakir's mother, or rather Phakir Chand himself, been rewarded with the hand of the Rajah's daughter and with the possession of half the kingdom?"

*Brahman.*—"No, not yet. Phakir has not been got hold of. He is a half-witted lad, or rather quite mad. He has been away for more than a year from his home, and no one knows where he is. That is his manner; he stays away for a long time, suddenly comes home, and again disappears. I believe his mother expects him soon."

*Minister's Son.*—"What like is he? And what does he do when he returns home?"

*Brahman.*—"Why, he is about your height, though he is somewhat younger than you. He puts on a small piece of cloth round his waist, rubs his body with ashes, takes the branch of a tree in his hand, and, at the door of the hut in which his mother lives, dances to the tune of *dhoop, dhoop, dhoop!* His articulation is very indistinct; and when his mother says—'Phakir! Stay with me for some days,' he invariably answers in his usual unintelligible manner, 'No, I won't remain, I won't remain.' And when he wishes to give an affirmative answer, he says, 'hoom,' which means 'yes.'"

The above conversation with the Brahman poured a flood of light into the mind of the minister's son. He saw how matters stood. He perceived that the princess of the subterranean palace must have alone ventured out into the tank by means of the snake-jewel; that she must have been captured alone without the king's son; that the snake-jewel must be in the possession of Phakir's mother; and that his friend, the king's son, must be alone below the waters without any means of escape. The desolate and apparently hopeless state of his friend filled him with unutterable grief. He was in deep musings during most part of the night. Is it impossible, thought he, to rescue the king's son from the nether regions? What if, by some means or other, I contrive to get the jewel from the old woman? And can

I not do it by personating Phakir Chand himself who is expected by his mother shortly? And possibly by the same means I may be able to rescue the princess from the Rajah's palace. He resolved to act the rôle of Phakir Chand the following day. In the morning he left the Brahman's house, went to the outskirts of the city, divested himself of his usual clothing, put round his waist a short and narrow piece of cloth which scarcely reached his knee-joints, rubbed his body well with ashes, took in his hand a twig which he broke off a tree, and thus accoutred, presented himself before the door of the hut of Phakir's mother. He commenced operations by dancing, in a most violent manner, to the tune of *dhoop, dhoop, dhoop!* The dancing attracted the notice of the old woman who, supposing that her son had come, said—"My son Phakir, are you come? Come, my darling; the gods have at last become propitious to us." The supposed Phakir Chand uttered the monosyllable "hoom," and went on dancing in a still more violent manner than before, waving the twig in his hand. "This time you must not go away," said the old woman, "you must remain with me." "No, I won't remain, I won't remain," said the minister's son. "Remain with me, and I'll get you married to the Rajah's daughter. Will you marry, Phakir Chand?" The minister's son replied—"hoom, hoom," and danced on like a madman. "Will you come with me to the Rajah's house? I'll show you a princess of uncommon beauty who has risen from the waters." "Hoom, hoom," was the answer that issued from his lips, while his feet tripped it violently to the sound of *dhoop, dhoop!* "Do you wish to see a *manik*, Phakir, the crest jewel of the serpent, the treasure of seven kings?" "Hoom, hoom," was the reply. The old woman brought out of the hut the snake-jewel, and put it into the hand of her supposed son. The minister's son took it, and carefully wrapped it up in the piece of cloth round his waist. Phakir's mother delighted beyond measure at the opportune appearance of her son, went to the Rajah's house, partly to announce to the Rajah the news of Phakir's appearance, and partly to show Phakir the princess of the waters. The supposed Phakir and his mother found ready access to the Rajah's palace, for the old woman had, since the capture of the princess, become the most important person in the kingdom. She took him into the room where the princess was, and introduced him to her. It is superfluous to remark that the princess was by no means pleased with the company of a madcap, who was in a state of semi-nudity, whose body was rubbed with ashes, and who was ever and anon dancing in a wild manner. At sunset the old woman proposed to her son that they should leave the palace and go to their own house. But the supposed Phakir Chand refused to comply with the request; he said he would stay there that night. His mother tried to persuade him to return with her, but he persisted in his determination. He said he would remain with the princess. Phakir's mother therefore went away, after giving instructions to the guards and attendants to take care of her son.

When all in the palace had retired to rest, the supposed Phakir coming towards the princess said in his own usual voice— "Princess! Do you not recognize me? I am the minister's son, the friend of your princely husband." The princess, astonished at the announcement, said—"Who? The minister's son? Oh, my husband's best friend, do rescue me from this terrible captivity, from this worse than death. O fate! It is by my own fault that I am reduced to this wretched state. Oh, rescue me; rescue me, thou best of friends!" She then burst into tears. The minister's son said, "Do not be disconsolate. I will try my best to rescue you this very night; only you must do whatever I tell you." "I will do anything you tell me, minister's son; anything you tell me." After this the supposed Phakir left the room, and passed through the courtyard of the palace. Some of the guards challenged him, to whom he replied, "hoom, hoom. I will just go out for a minute and again come in presently." They understood that it was the madcap Phakir. True to his word he did come back shortly, and went to the princess. An hour afterwards he again went out and was again challenged, on which he made the same reply as at the first time. The guards who challenged him began to mutter between their teeth—"This madcap of a Phakir will, we suppose, go out and come in all night. Let the fellow alone; let him do what he likes. Who can be sitting up all night for him?" The minister's son was going out and coming in with the view of accustoming the guards to his constant egress and ingress, and also of watching for a favourable opportunity to escape with the princess. About three o'clock in the morning the minister's son again passed through the courtyard, but this time no one challenged him as all the guards had fallen asleep. Overjoyed at the auspicious circumstance, he went to the princess. "Now princess, is the time for escape. The guards are all asleep. Mount on my back, and tie the locks of your hair round my neck, and keep tight hold of me." The princess did as she was told. He passed unchallenged through the courtyard with the lovely burden on his back, passed out of the gate of the palace—no one challenging him, passed on to the outskirts of the city, and reached the tank from which the princess had risen. The princess stood on her legs, rejoicing at her escape, and at the same time trembling. The minister's son untied the snake-jewel from his waist-cloth, and descending into the waters, both he and she found their way to the subterranean palace. The reception which the prince in the subaqueous palace gave to his wife and his friend may be easily imagined. He had nearly died of grief, but now he suffered a resurrection. The three were now mad with joy. During the three days that they remained in the palace they again and again told the story of the egress of the princess into the upper world, of her seizure, of her captivity in the palace, of the preparations for marriage, of the old woman, of the minister's son personating Phakir Chand, and of the successful deliverance. It is unnecessary to add that the prince and the princess expressed their gratitude to the minister's son in the warmest terms, declared him to be their best and greatest friend, and vowed to abide always, till the day of their death, by his advice, and to follow his counsel.

Being resolved to return to their native country, the king's son, the minister's son and the princess left the subterranean palace, and, lighted in the passage by the snake-jewel, made their way good to the upper world. As they had neither elephants nor horses, they were under the necessity of travelling on foot; and though this mode of travelling was troublesome to both the king's son and the minister's son, as they were bred in the lap of luxury, it was infinitely more troublesome to the princess, as the stones of the rough road,

*"Wounded the invisible*
*Palms of her tender feet where'er they fell."*

When her feet became very sore, the king's son sometimes took her up on his broad shoulders on which she sat astride; but the load, however lovely, was too heavy to be carried any great distance. She, therefore, for the most part, travelled on foot.

One evening they bivouacked beneath a tree, as no human habitations were visible. The minister's son said to the prince and princess, "Both of you go to sleep, and I will keep watch in order to prevent any danger." The royal couple were soon locked in the arms of sleep. The faithful son of the minister did not sleep, but sat up watching. It so happened that on that tree swung the nest of the two immortal birds, Bihangama and Bihangami, who were not only endowed with the power of human speech, but who could see into the future. To the no little astonishment of the minister's son the two prophetical birds joined in the following conversation:—

*Bihangama.* "The minister's son has already risked his own life for the safety of his friend, the king's son but he will find it difficult to save the prince at last."

*Bihangami.*—"Why so?"

*Bihangama.*—"Many dangers await the king's son. The prince's father, when he hears of the approach of his son, will send for him an elephant, some horses, and attendants. When the king's son rides on the elephant, he will fall down and die."

*Bihangami.*—"But suppose someone prevents the king's son from riding on the elephant, and makes him ride on horseback, will he not in that case be saved?"

*Bihangama.*—"Yes, he will in that case escape that danger, but a fresh danger awaits him. When the king's son is in sight of his father's palace, and when he is in the act of passing through its lion-gate, the lion-gate will fall upon him and crush him to death."

*Bihangami.*—"But suppose someone destroys the lion-gate before the king's son goes up to it; will not the king's son in that case be saved?"

*Bihangama.*—"Yes, in that case he will escape that particular danger, but a fresh danger awaits him. When the king's son reaches the palace and sits at a feast prepared for him, and when he takes into his mouth the head of a fish cooked for him, the head of the fish will stick in his throat and choke him to death."

*Bihangami.*—"But suppose someone sitting at the feast snatches the head of the fish from the prince's plate, and thus prevents him from putting it into his mouth, will not the king's son in that case be saved?"

*Bihangama.*—"Yes, in that case he will escape that particular danger, but a fresh danger awaits him. When the prince and princess after dinner retire into their sleeping apartment, and they lie together in bed, a terrible cobra will come into the room and bite the king's son to death."

*Bihangami.*—"But suppose someone lying in wait in the room cut the snake into pieces, will not the king's son in that case be saved?"

*Bihangama.*—"Yes, in that case the life of the king's son will be saved; but if the man who kills the snake repeats to the king's son the conversation between you and me, that man will be turned into a marble statue."

*Bihangami.*—"But is there no means of restoring the marble statue to life?"

*Bihangama.*—"Yes, the marble statue may be restored to life if it is washed with the life-blood of the infant which the princess will give birth to, immediately after it is ushered into the world."

The conversation of the prophetical birds had extended thus far when the crows began to caw, the east put on a reddish hue, and the travellers beneath the tree bestirred themselves. The conversation stopped, but the minister's son had heard it all.

The prince, the princess, and the minister's son pursued their journey in the morning; but they had not walked many hours when they met a procession consisting of an elephant, a horse, a *palki*, and a large number of attendants. These animals and men had been sent by the king, who had heard that his son, together with his newly married wife and his friend the minister's son, were not far from the capital on their journey homewards. The elephant, which was richly caparisoned, was intended for the prince; the *palki*, the framework of which was silver and was gaudily adorned, was meant for the princess; and the horse for the minister's son. As the prince was about to mount on the elephant, the minister's son went up to him and said—"Allow me to ride on the elephant, and you please ride on horseback." The prince was not a little surprised at the coolness of the proposal. He thought his friend was presuming too much on the services he had rendered; he was therefore nettled, but remembering that his friend had saved both him and his wife, he said nothing, but quietly mounted the horse, though his mind became somewhat alienated from him. The procession started, and after some time came in sight of the palace, the lion-gate of which had been gaily adorned for the reception of the prince and the princess. The minister's son told the prince that the lion-gate should be broken down before the prince could enter the palace. The prince was astounded at the proposal, especially as the minister's son gave no reasons for so extraordinary a request. His mind became still more estranged from him; but in consideration of the services the minister's son had rendered, his request was complied with, and the beautiful lion gate, with its gay decorations, was broken down.

The party now went into the palace, where the king gave a warm reception to his son, to his daughter-in-law, and to the minister's son. When the story of their adventures was related, the king and his courtiers expressed great astonishment, and they all with one voice extolled the sagacity, prudence, and devotedness of the minister's son. The ladies of the palace were struck with the extraordinary beauty of the new comer; her complexion was milk and vermilion mixed together; her neck was like that of a swan; her eyes were like those of a gazelle; her lips were as red as the berry *bimba*; her cheeks were lovely; her nose was straight and high; her hair reached her ankles; her walk was as graceful as that of a young elephant—such were the terms in which the connoisseurs of beauty praised the princess whom destiny had brought into the midst of them. They sat around her and put her a thousand questions regarding her parents, regarding the subterranean palace in which she formerly lived, and the serpent which had killed all her relatives. It was now time that the new arrivals should have their dinner. The dinner was served up in dishes of gold. All sorts of delicacies were there, amongst which the most conspicuous was the large head of a *rohita* fish placed in a golden cup near the prince's plate. While they were eating, the minister's son suddenly snatched the head of the fish from the prince's plate, and said, "Let me, prince, eat this *rohita's* head." The king's son was quite indignant. He said nothing, however. The minister's son perceived that his friend was in a terrible rage; but he could not help it, as his conduct, however strange, was necessary to the safety of his friend's life; neither could he clear himself by stating the reason of his behaviour, as in that case he himself would be transformed into a marble statue. The dinner over, the minister's son expressed his desire to go to his own house. At other times the king's son would not allow his friend to go away in that fashion; but being shocked at his strange conduct, he readily agreed to the proposal. The minister s son, however, had not the slightest notion of going to his own house; he was resolved to avert the last peril that was to threaten the life of his friend. Accordingly, with a sword in his hand, he stealthily entered the room in which the prince and the princess were to sleep that night, and ensconced himself under the bedstead, which was furnished with mattresses of down and canopied with mosquito curtains of the richest silk and gold lace. Soon after dinner the prince and princess came into the bedroom, and undressing themselves went to bed. At midnight, while the royal couple were asleep, the minister's son perceived a snake of gigantic size enter the room through one of the water-passages, and climb up the tester-frame of the bed. He rushed out of his hiding-place, killed the serpent, cut it up in pieces, and put the pieces in the dish for holding betel-leaves and spices. It so happened, however, that as the minister's son was cutting the serpent into pieces, a drop of blood fell on the breast of the princess, and the rather as the mosquito curtains had not been let down. Thinking that the drop of blood might injure the fair princess, he resolved to lick it up. But as he regarded it as a great sin to look upon a young woman lying asleep half naked, he blindfolded himself with seven-fold cloth, and licked up the drop of blood. But while he was in the act of licking it, the princess awoke and screamed, and her scream roused her husband lying beside her. The prince seeing the minister's son, who he thought had gone away to his own house, bending over the body of his wife, fell into a great rage, and would have got up and killed him, had not the minister's son besought him to restrain his anger, adding—"Friend, I have done this only in order to save your life." "I do not understand what you mean," said the prince, "ever since we came out of the subterranean palace you have been behaving in a most extraordinary way. In the first place, you prevented me from getting upon the richly caparisoned elephant, though my father, the king, had purposely sent it for me. I thought, however, that a sense of the services you had rendered to me had made you exceedingly vain; I therefore let the matter pass, and mounted the horse. In the second place, you insisted on the destruction of the fine lion-gate, which my father had adorned with gay decorations; and I let that matter also pass. Then, again, at dinner you snatched away, in a most shameful manner, the *rohita's* head which was on my plate, and devoured it yourself, thinking, no doubt that you were entitled to higher honors than I. You then pretended that you were going home, for which I was not at all sorry, as you had made yourself very disagreeable to me. And now you are actually in my bedroom, bending over the naked bosom of my wife. You must have had some evil design; and you pretend that you have done this to save my life. I fancy it was not for saving my life, but for destroying my wife's chastity." "Oh, do not harbour such thoughts in your mind against me. The gods know that I have done all this for the preservation of your life. You would see the reasonableness of my conduct throughout if I had the liberty of stating my reasons." "And why are you not at liberty?" asked the prince, "who has shut up your mouth?" "It is destiny that has shut up my mouth," answered the minister's son, "if I were to tell it all, I should be transformed into a marble statue." "You would be transformed into a marble statue!" exclaimed the prince, "you must take me to be a simpleton to believe this nonsense." "Do you wish me then, friend," said the minister's son, "to tell you all? You must then make up your mind to see your friend turned into stone." "Come, out with it," said the prince, "or else you are a dead man." The minister's son, in order to clear himself of the foul accusation brought against him, deemed it his duty to reveal the secret at the risk of his life. He again and again warned the prince not to press him. But the prince remained inexorable. The minister's son then went on to say that, while bivouacking under a lofty tree one night, he had overheard a conversation between Bihangama and Bihangami, in which the former predicted all the dangers that were to threaten the life of the prince. When the minister's son had related the prediction concerning the mounting upon the elephant, his lower parts were turned into stone. He then, turning to the prince said, "See, friend, my lower parts have already turned into stone." "Go on, go on," said the prince, "with your story." The minister's son then related the prophecy regarding the destruction of the lion-gate, when half of his body was converted into stone. He then related the prediction regarding the eating of the head of the fish, when his body up to his neck was petrified. "Now, friend," said the minister's son, "the whole of my body, excepting my neck and head, is petrified; if I tell the rest, I shall assuredly become a man of stone. Do you wish me still to go on?" "Go on," answered the prince, "go on." "Very well, I will go on to the end," said the minister's son, "but in case you repent after I have become turned into stone, and wish me to be restored to life, I will tell you of the manner in which it may be effected. The princess after a few months will be delivered of a child; if immediately after the birth of the infant you kill it and besmear my marble body with its blood, I shall be restored to life." He then related the prediction regarding the serpent in the bedroom; and when the last word was on his lips the rest of his body was turned into stone, and he dropped on the floor a marble image. The princess jumped out of bed, opened the vessel for betel-leaves and spices, and saw there pieces of a serpent. Both the prince and the princess now became convinced of the good faith and benevolence of their departed friend. They went to the marble figure, but it was lifeless. They set up a loud lamentation; but it was to no purpose, for the marble moved not. They then resolved to keep the marble figure concealed in a safe place, and to besmear it with the blood of their first-born child when it should be ushered into existence.

In process of time the hour of the princess's travail came on, and she was delivered of a beautiful boy, the perfect image of his mother. Both father and mother were struck with the beauty of their child, and would fain have spared its life; but recollecting the vows they had made on behalf of their best friend, now lying in a corner of the room a lifeless stone, and the inestimable services he had rendered to both of them, they cut the child into two, and besmeared the marble figure of the minister's son with its blood. The marble became animated in a moment. The minister's son stood before the prince and princess, who became exceedingly glad to see their old friend again in life. But the minister's son, who saw the lovely new-born babe lying in a pool of blood, was overwhelmed with grief. He took up the dead infant, carefully wrapped it up in a towel, and resolved to get it restored to life.

The minister's son, intent on the re-animation of his friend's child, consulted all the physicians of the country; but they said that they would undertake to cure any person of any disease so long as life was in him, but when life was extinct, the case was beyond their jurisdiction. The minister's son at last bethought himself of his own wife who was living in a distant town, and who was a devoted worshipper of the goddess Kali, who, through his wife's intercession, might be prevailed upon to give life to the dead child. He, accordingly, set out on a journey to the town in which his wife was living in her father's house. Adjoining that house there was a garden where upon a tree he hung the dead child wrapped up in a towel. His wife was overjoyed to see her husband after so long a time; but to her surprise she found that he was very melancholy, that he spoke very little, and that he was brooding over something in his mind. She asked the reason of his melancholy, but he kept quiet. One night while they were lying together in bed, the wife got up and opening the door went out. The husband, who had little sleep any night in consequence of the weight of anxiety regarding the re-animation of his friend's child, perceiving his wife go out at that dead hour of night, determined to follow her without being noticed. She went to a temple of the goddess Kali which was at no great distance from her house. She worshipped the goddess with flowers and sandal-wood perfume, and said, "O mother Kali! Have mercy upon me, and deliver me out of all my troubles." The goddess replied, "Why, what further grievances have you? You long prayed for the return of your husband, and he has returned; what aileth thee now?" The woman answered, "True, O Mother, my husband has come to me, but he is very moody and melancholy, hardly speaks to me, takes no delight in me, and only sits moping in a corner." To which the goddess rejoined, "Ask your husband what the reason of his melancholy is, and let me know it." The minister's son overheard the conversation between the goddess and his wife, but he did not make his appearance, he quietly slunk away before his wife and went to bed. The following day the wife asked her husband of the cause of his melancholy, and he related all the particulars regarding the killing of the infant child of the prince. Next night, at the same dead hour, the wife proceeded to Kali's temple and mentioned to the goddess the reason of her husband's melancholy; on which the goddess said, "Bring the child here and I will restore it to life." On the succeeding night the child was produced before the goddess Kali, and she called it back to life. Entranced with joy, the minister's son took up the re-animated child, went as fast as his legs could carry him to the prince and princess, and presented to them their child alive and well. They all rejoiced with exceeding great joy, and lived together happily till the day of their death.

Thus my story endeth,
The Natiya-thorn withereth, &c.

# CHAPTER III
## THE INDIGENT BRAHMAN

There was a Brahman who had a wife and four children. He was very poor. With no resources in the world, he lived chiefly on the benefactions of the rich. His gains were considerable when marriages were celebrated, or funeral ceremonies were performed; but as his parishioners did not marry every day, neither did they die every day, he found it difficult to make the two ends meet. His wife often rebuked him for his inability to give her adequate support, and his children often went about naked and hungry. But though poor he was a good man. He was diligent in his devotions; and there was not a single day in his life in which he did not say his prayers at stated hours. His tutelary deity was the goddess Durga, the consort of Siva, the creative Energy of the Universe. On no day did he either drink water or taste food till he had written in red ink the name of Durga at least one hundred and eight times; while throughout the day he incessantly uttered the ejaculation, "O Durga! O Durga! Have mercy upon me." Whenever he felt anxious on account of his poverty and his inability to support his wife and children, he groaned out—"Durga! Durga! Durga!"

One day, being very sad, he went to a forest many miles distant from the village in which he lived, and indulging his grief wept bitter tears. He prayed in the following manner:—"O Durga! O Mother Bhagavati! Wilt thou not make an end of my misery? Were I alone in the world, I should not have been sad on account of poverty, but thou hast given me a wife and children. Give me, O Mother, the means to support them." It so happened that on that day and on that very spot, the god Siva and his wife Durga were taking their morning walk. The goddess Durga, on seeing the Brahman at a distance, said to her divine husband —"O Lord of Kailas! Do you see that Brahman? He is always taking my name on his lips and offering the prayer that I should deliver him out of his troubles. Can we not, my lord, do something for the poor Brahman, oppressed as he is with the cares of a growing family? We should give him enough to make him comfortable. As the poor man and his family have never enough to eat, I propose that you give him a *handi*[①] which should yield him an inexhaustible supply of *mudki*[②]." The lord of Kailas readily agreed to the proposal of his divine consort, and by his decree created on the spot a *handi*

---

① *Handi* is an earthen pot, generally used in cooking food.
② Mudki, fried paddy boiled dry in treacle or sugar.

203

possessing the required quality. Durga then, calling the Brahman to her, said,—"O Brahman! I have often thought of your pitiable case. Your repeated prayers have at last moved my compassion. Here is a *handi* for you. When you turn it upside down and shake it, it will pour down a never-ceasing shower of the finest *mudki*, which will not end till you restore the *handi* to its proper position. Yourself, your wife, and your children can eat as much *mudki* as you like, and you can also sell as much as you like." The Brahman, delighted beyond measure at obtaining so inestimable a treasure, made obeisance to the goddess, and, taking the *handi* in his hand, proceeded towards his house as fast as his legs could carry him. But he had not gone many yards when he thought of testing the efficacy of the wonderful vessel. Accordingly he turned the *handi* upside down and shook it, when, lo, and behold! A quantity of the finest *mudki* he had ever seen fell to the ground. He tied the sweetmeat in his sheet and walked on. It was now noon, and the Brahman was hungry; but he could not eat without his ablutions and his prayers. As he saw in the way an inn, and not far from it a tank, he purposed to halt there that he might bathe, say his prayers, and then eat the much-desired *mudki*. The Brahman sat at the innkeeper's shop, put the *handi* near him, smoked tobacco, besmeared his body with mustard oil, and before proceeding to bathe in the adjacent tank gave the *handi* in charge to the innkeeper, begging him again and again to take especial care of it.

When the Brahman went to his bath and his devotions, the innkeeper thought it strange that he should be as careful as to the safety of his earthen vessel. There must be something valuable in the *handi*, he thought, otherwise why should the Brahman take so much thought about it? His curiosity being excited he opened the *handi*, and to his surprise found that it contained nothing. What can be the meaning of this? Thought the innkeeper within himself. Why should the Brahman care so much for an empty *handi*? He took up the vessel, and began to examine it carefully; and when, in the course of examination, he turned the *handi* upside down, a quantity of the finest *mudki* fell from it, and went on falling without intermission. The innkeeper called his wife and children to witness this unexpected stroke of good fortune. The showers of the sugared fried paddy were so copious that they filled all the vessels and jars of the innkeeper. He resolved to appropriate to himself this precious *handi*, and accordingly put in its place another *handi* of the same size and make. The ablutions and devotions of the Brahman being now over, he came to the shop in wet clothes reciting holy texts of the Vedas. Putting on dry clothes, he wrote on a sheet of paper the name of Durga one hundred and eight times in red ink;

after which he broke his fast on the *mudki* his *handi* had already given him. Thus refreshed, and being about to resume his journey homewards, he called for his *handi* which the innkeeper delivered to him, adding—"There, sir, is your *handi*; it is just where you put it; no one has touched it." The Brahman, without suspecting anything, took up the *handi* and proceeded on his journey; and as he walked on, he congratulated himself on his singular good fortune. "How agreeably," he thought within himself, "will my poor wife be surprised! How greedily the children will devour the *mudki* of heaven's own manufacture! I shall soon become rich, and lift up my head with the best of them all." The pains of travelling were considerably alleviated by these joyful anticipations. He reached his house, and calling his wife and children, said—"Look now at what I have brought. This *handi* that you see is an unfailing source of wealth and contentment. You will see what a stream of the finest *mudki* will flow from it when I turn it upside down." The Brahman's good wife, hearing of *mudki* falling from the *handi* unceasingly, thought that her husband must have gone mad; and she was confirmed in her opinion when she found that nothing fell from the vessel though it was turned upside down again and again. Overwhelmed with grief, the Brahman concluded that the innkeeper must have played a trick with him; he must have stolen the *handi* Durga had given him, and put a common one in its stead. He went back the next day to the innkeeper, and charged him with having changed his *handi*. The innkeeper put on a fit of anger, expressed surprise at the Brahman s impudence in charging him with theft, and drove him away from his shop.

The Brahman then bethought himself of an interview with the goddess Durga who had given him the *handi*, and accordingly went to the forest where he had met her. Siva and Durga again favoured the Brahman with an interview. Durga said—"So, you have lost the *handi* I gave you. Here is another, take it and make good use of it." The Brahman, elated with joy, made obeisance to the divine couple, took up the vessel, and went on his way. He had not gone far when he turned it upside down, and shook it in order to see whether any *mudki* would fall from it. Horror of horrors! Instead of sweetmeats about a score of demons, of gigantic size and grim visage, jumped out of the *handi*, and began to belabour the astonished Brahman with blows, fisticuffs and kicks. He had the presence of mind to turn up the *handi* and to cover it, when the demons forthwith disappeared. He concluded that this new *handi* had been given him only for the punishment of the innkeeper. He accordingly went to the innkeeper, gave him the new *handi* in charge, begged of him carefully to keep it till he returned from his ablutions and prayers.

The innkeeper, delighted with this second godsend, called his wife and children, and said—"This is another *handi* brought here by the same Brahman who brought the *handi* of *mudki*. This time, I hope, it is not *mudki* but *sandesa*[①]. Come, be ready with baskets and vessels, and I'll turn the *handi* upside down and shake it." This was no sooner done than scores of fierce demons started up, who caught hold of the innkeeper and his family and belaboured them mercilessly. They also began upsetting the shop, and would have completely destroyed it, if the victims had not besought the Brahman, who had by this time returned from his ablutions, to show mercy to them and send away the terrible demons. The Brahman acceded to the innkeeper's request, he dismissed the demons by shutting up the vessel; he got the former *handi*, and with the two *handi*s went to his native village.

On reaching home the Brahman shut the door of his house, turned the *mudki-handi* upside down and shook it; the result was an unceasing stream of the finest *mudki* that any confectioner in the country could produce. The man, his wife, and their children, devoured the sweetmeat to their hearts' content; all the available earthen pots and pans of the house were filled with it; and the Brahman resolved the next day to turn confectioner, to open a

---

① A sort of sweetmeat made of curds and sugar.

shop in his house, and sell *mudki*. On the very day the shop was opened, the whole village came to the Brahman's house to buy the wonderful *mudki*. They had never seen such *mudki* in their life, it was so sweet, so white, so large, so luscious; no confectioner in the village or any town in the country had ever manufactured anything like it. The reputation of the Brahman's *mudki* extended, in a few days, beyond the bounds of the village, and people came from remote parts to purchase it. Cartloads of the sweetmeat were sold every day, and the Brahman in a short time became very rich. He built a large brick house, and lived like a nobleman of the land. Once, however, his property was about to go to wreck and ruin. His children one day by mistake shook the wrong *handi*, when a large number of demons dropped down and caught hold of the Brahman's wife and children and were striking them mercilessly, when happily the Brahman came into the house and turned up the *handi*. In order to prevent a similar catastrophe in future, the Brahman shut up the demon-*handi* in a private room to which his children had no access.

Pure and uninterrupted prosperity, however, is not the lot of mortals; and though the demon-*handi* was put aside, what security was there that an accident might not befall the *mudki-handi*? One day, during the absence of the Brahman and his wife from the house, the children decided upon shaking the *handi*; but as each of them wished to enjoy the pleasure of shaking it there was a general struggle to get it, and in the mêlée the *handi* fell to the ground and broke. It is needless to say that the Brahman, when on reaching home he heard of the disaster, became inexpressibly sad. The children were of course well cudgelled, but no flogging of children could replace the magical *handi*. After some days he again went to the forest, and offered many a prayer for Durga's favour. At last Siva and Durga again appeared to him, and heard how the *handi* had been broken. Durga gave him another *handi*, accompanied with the following caution— "Brahman, take care of this *handi*; if you again break it or lose it, I'll not give you another." The Brahman made obeisance, and went away to his house at one stretch without halting anywhere. On reaching home he shut the door of his house, called his wife to him, turned the *handi* upside down, and began to shake it. They were only expecting *mudki* to drop from it, but instead of *mudki* a perennial stream of beautiful *sandesa* issued from it. And such *sandesa*! No confectioner of Burra Bazar ever made its like. It was more the food of gods than of men. The Brahman forthwith set up a shop for selling *sandesa*, the fame of which soon drew crowds of customers from all parts of the country. At all festivals, at all marriage feasts, at all funeral celebrations, at all *Pujas*, no one bought any other *sandesa* than the Brahman's. Every day, and every hour, many jars of gigantic size, filled with the delicious sweetmeat, were sent to all parts of the country.

The wealth of the Brahman excited the envy of the Zemindar of the village who, having heard that the *sandesa* was not manufactured but dropped from a *handi*, devised a plan for getting possession of the miraculous vessel. At the celebration of his son's marriage he held a great feast, to which were invited hundreds of people. As many mountain-loads of *sandesa* would be required for the purpose, the Zemindar proposed that the Brahman should bring the magical *handi* to the house in which the feast was held. The Brahman at first refused to take it there; but as the Zemindar insisted on its being carried to his own house, he reluctantly consented to take it there. After many Himalayas of *sandesa* had been shaken out, the *handi* was taken possession of by the Zemindar, and the Brahman was insulted and driven out of the house. The Brahman, without giving vent to anger in the least, quietly went to his house, and taking the demon-*handi* in his hand, came back to the door of the Zemindar's house. He turned the *handi* upside down and shook it, on which a hundred demons started up as from the vasty deep and enacted a scene which it is impossible to describe. The hundreds of guests that had been bidden to the feast were caught hold of by the unearthly visitants and beaten; the women were dragged by their hair from the Zenana and dashed about amongst the men; while the big and burly Zemindar was driven about from room to room like a bale of cotton. If the demons had been allowed to do their will only for a few minutes longer, all the men would have been killed, and the very house razed to the ground. The Zemindar fell prostrate at the feet of the Brahman and begged for mercy. Mercy was shown him and the demons were removed. After that the Brahman was no more disturbed by the Zemindar or by anyone else, and he lived many years in great happiness and enjoyment.

Thus my story endeth,
The Natiya-thorn withereth, &c.

# CHAPTER IV
## THE STORY OF THE RAKSHASAS

There was a poor half-witted Brahman who had a wife but no children. It was only with difficulty he could supply the wants of himself and his wife. And the worst of it was that he was rather lazily inclined. He was averse to taking long journeys, otherwise he might always have had enough, in the shape of presents from rich men, to enable him and his wife to live comfortably. There was at that time a king in a neighbouring country who was celebrating the funeral obsequies of his mother with great pomp. Brahmans and beggars were going from different parts with the expectation of receiving rich presents. Our Brahman was requested by his wife to seize this opportunity and get a little money, but his constitutional indolence stood in the way. The woman however gave her husband no rest till she extorted from him the promise that he would go. The good woman, accordingly, cut down a plantain tree and burnt it to ashes with which ashes she cleaned the clothes of her husband, and made them as white as any fuller could make them. She did this because her husband was going to the palace of a great king, who could not be approached by men clothed in dirty rags; besides, as a Brahman, he was bound to appear neat and clean. The Brahman at last one morning left his house for the palace of the great king. As he was somewhat imbecile, he did not inquire of any one which road he should take; but he went on and on, and proceeded whithersoever his two eyes directed him. He was of course not on the right road, indeed he had reached a region where he did not meet with a single human being for many miles, and where he saw sights which he had never seen in his life. He saw hillocks of *cowris* (shells used as money) on the roadside: he had not proceeded far from them when he saw hillocks of pice, then successively hillocks of four-anna pieces, hillocks of eight-anna pieces, and hillocks of rupees. To the infinite surprise of the poor Brahman, these hillocks of shining silver coins were succeeded by a large hill of burnished gold-mohurs, which were all as bright as if they had been just issued from the mint. Close to this hill of gold-mohurs was a large house which seemed to be the palace of a powerful and rich king, at the door of which stood a lady of exquisite beauty. The lady seeing the Brahman, said, "Come, my beloved husband; you married me when I was young, and you never came once after our marriage, though I have been daily expecting you. Blessed be this day which has made me see the face of my husband. Come, my sweet, come in, wash your feet and rest after the fatigues of your journey; eat and drink, and after that we shall make ourselves merry." The Brahman was astonished beyond measure. He had no recollection of having been married in early youth to any other woman than the woman who was now keeping house with him. But being a Kulin Brahman, he thought it was quite possible that his father had got him married when he was a little child, though the fact had made no impression on his mind. But whether he remembered it or not, the fact was certain, for the woman declared that she was his wedded wife,—and such a wife! As beautiful as the goddesses of Indra's heaven, and no doubt as wealthy as she was beautiful. While these thoughts were passing through the Brahman's mind, the lady said again, "Are you doubting in your mind whether I am your wife? Is it possible that all recollection of that happy event has been effaced from your mind—all the pomp and circumstance of our nuptials? Come in, beloved; this is your own house, for whatever is mine is thine." The Brahman succumbed to the loving entreaties of the fair lady, and went into the house. The house was not an ordinary one—it was a magnificent palace, all the apartments being large and lofty and richly furnished. But one thing surprised the Brahman very much, and that was that there was no other person in the house besides the lady herself. He could not account for so singular a phenomenon; neither could he explain how it was that he did not meet with any human being in his morning and evening walks. The fact was that the lady was not a human being. She was a *Rakshasi* [①]. She had eaten up the king, the queen, and all the members of the royal family, and gradually all his subjects. This was the reason why human beings were not seen in those parts.

The Rakshasi and the Brahman lived together for about a week, when the former said to the latter, "I am very anxious to see my sister, your other wife. You must go and fetch her, and we shall all live together happily in this large and beautiful house. You must go early tomorrow, and I will give you clothes and jewels for her." Next morning the Brahman, furnished with fine clothes and costly ornaments, set out for his home. The poor woman was in great distress; all the Brahmans and Pandits that had been to the funeral ceremony of the king's mother had returned home loaded with largesses; but her husband had not returned,—and no one could give any news of him for no one had seen him there. The woman therefore concluded that he must have been murdered on the road by highwaymen. She was in this terrible suspense, when one day she heard a rumour in the village that her husband was seen coming home with fine clothes and costly jewels for his wife. And sure

---

① *Rakshasas* and *Rakshasis* (male and female) are in Hindu mythology huge giants and giantesses, or rather demons. The word means literally *raw-eaters*; they were probably the chiefs of the aborigines whom the Aryans overthrew on their first settlement in the country.

enough the Brahman soon appeared with his valuable load. On seeing his wife the Brahman thus accosted her:—"Come with me, my dearest wife; I have found my first wife. She lives in a stately palace, near which are hillocks of rupees and a large hill of gold-mohurs. Why should you pine away in wretchedness and misery in this horrible place? Come with me to the house of my first wife, and we shall all live together happily." When the woman heard her husband speak of his first wife, of hillocks of rupees and of a hill of gold-mohurs, she thought in her mind that her half-witted good man had become quite mad; but when she saw the exquisitely beautiful silks and satins and the ornaments set with diamonds and precious stones, which only queens and princesses were in the habit of putting on, she concluded in her mind that her poor husband had fallen into the meshes of a Rakshasi. The Brahman, however, insisted on his wife's going with him, and declared that if she did not come she was at liberty to pine away in poverty, but that for himself he meant to return forthwith to his first and rich wife. The good woman, after a great deal of altercation with her husband, resolved to go with him and judge for herself how matters stood. They set out accordingly the next morning, and went by the same road on which the Brahman had travelled. The woman was not a little surprised to see hillocks of *cowris*, of pice, of eight-anna pieces, of rupees, and last of all a lofty hill of gold-mohurs. She saw also an exceedingly beautiful lady coming out of the palace hard by, and hastening towards her. The lady fell on the neck of the Brahman woman, wept tears of joy, and said, "Welcome, beloved sister! This is the happiest day of my life! I have seen the face of my dearest sister!" The party then entered the palace.

What with the stately mansion in which he was lodged, with the most delectable provisions which seemed to rise as if by enchantment, what with the caresses and endearments of his two wives, the one human and the other demoniac, who vied with each other in making him happy and comfortable, the Brahman had a jolly time of it. He was steeped as it were in an ocean of enjoyment. Some fifteen or sixteen years were spent by the Brahman in this state of Elysian pleasure, during which period his two wives presented him with two sons. The Rakshasi's son, who was the elder, and who looked more like a god than a human being, was named Sahasra Dal, literally the Thousand-Branched; and the son of the Brahman woman, who was a year younger, was named Champa Dal, that is, branch of a *champaka* tree. The two boys loved each other dearly. They were both sent to a school which was several miles distant, to which they used every day to go riding on two little ponies of extraordinary fleetness.

The Brahman woman had all along suspected from a thousand little circumstances that her sister-in-law was not a human being but a Rakshasi; but her suspicion had not yet ripened into certainty, for the Rakshasi exercised great self-restraint on herself, and never did anything which human beings did not do. But the demoniac nature, like murder, will out. The Brahman having nothing to do, in order to pass his time had recourse to hunting. The first day he returned from the hunt, he had bagged an antelope. The antelope was laid in the courtyard of the palace. At the sight of the antelope the mouth of the raw-eating Rakshasi began to water. Before the animal was dressed for the kitchen, she took it away into a room, and began devouring it. The Brahman woman, who was watching the whole scene from a secret place, saw her Rakshasi sister tear off a leg of the antelope, and opening her tremendous jaws, which seemed to her imagination to extend from earth to heaven, swallow it up. In this manner the body and other limbs of the antelope were devoured, till only a little bit of the meat was kept for the kitchen. The second day another antelope was bagged, and the third day another; and the Rakshasi, unable to restrain her appetite for raw flesh, devoured these two as she had devoured the first. On the third day the Brahman woman expressed to the Rakshasi her surprise at the disappearance of nearly the whole of the antelope with the exception of a little bit. The Rakshasi looked fierce and said, "Do I eat raw flesh?" To which the Brahman woman replied—"Perhaps you do, for aught I know to the contrary." The Rakshasi, knowing herself to be discovered, looked fiercer than before, and vowed revenge. The Brahman woman concluded in her mind that the doom of herself, of her husband and of her son, was sealed. She spent a miserable night, believing that next day she would be killed and eaten up, and that her husband and son would share the same fate. Early next morning before her son Champa Dal went to school, she gave him in a small golden vessel a little quantity of her own breast milk, and told him to be constantly watching its colour. "Should you," she said, "see the milk get a little red, then conclude that your father has been killed; and should you see it grow still redder, then conclude that I am killed; when you see this, gallop away for your life as fast as your horse can carry you, for if you do not, you also will be devoured."

The Rakshasi on getting up from bed—and she had prevented the Brahman overnight from having any communication with his wife—proposed that she and the Brahman should go to bathe in the river which was at some distance. She would take no denial, the Brahman had therefore to follow her as meekly as a lamb. The Brahman woman at once saw from the proposal that ruin was impending, but it was beyond her power to avert the catastrophe. The Rakshasi, on the river-side, assuming her own proper gigantic dimensions, took hold of the ill-fated Brahman, tore him limb by limb, and devoured him up. She then ran to her house, and seized the Brahman woman, and put her into her capacious stomach, clothes, hair and all. Young Champa Dal, who, agreeably to his mother's instructions, was diligently watching the milk in the small golden vessel, was horror-struck to find the milk redden a little. He set up a cry and said that his father was killed; a few minutes after finding the milk become completely red, he cried yet louder, and rushing to his pony mounted it. His half-brother, Sahasra Dal, surprised at Champa Dal's conduct, said, "Where are you going, Champa? Why are you crying? Let me accompany you." "Oh! Do not come to me. Your mother has devoured my father and mother, don't you come and devour me?" "I will not devour you; I'll save you." Scarcely had he uttered these words and galloped away after Champa Dal, when he saw his mother in her own Rakshasi form appearing at a distance, and demanding that Champa Dal should come to her. He said, "I will come to you, not Champa." So saying he went to his mother, and with his sword, which he always wore as a young prince, cut off her head.

Champa Dal had, in the meantime, galloped off a good distance, as he was running for his life; but Sahasra Dal, by pricking his horse repeatedly, soon overtook him, and told him that his mother was no more. This was small consolation to Champa

Dal, as the Rakshasi, before being killed, had devoured both his father and mother; still he could not but feel that Sahasra Dal's friendship was sincere. They both rode fast, and as their horses were of the breed of *pakshirajes* (literally, kings of birds), they travelled over hundreds of miles. An hour or two before sundown they descried a village, to which they made up, and became guests in the house of one of its most respectable inhabitants. The two friends found the members of that respectable family in deep gloom. Evidently there was something agitating them very much. Some of them held private consultations, and others were weeping. The eldest lady of the house, the mother of its head, said aloud, "Let me go, as I am the eldest. I have lived long enough; at the utmost my life would be cut short only by a year or two." The youngest member of the house, who was a little girl, said, "Let me go, as I am young and useless to the family; if I die, I shall not be missed." The head of the house, the son of the old lady, said, "I am the head and representative of the family, it is but reasonable that I should give up my life." His younger brother said, "You are the main prop and pillar of the family; if you go the whole family is ruined. It is not reasonable that you should go; let me go, as I shall not be much missed." The two strangers listened to all this conversation with no little curiosity. They wondered what it all meant. Sahasra

Dal at last, at the risk of being thought meddlesome, ventured to ask the head of the house the subject of their consultations, and the reason of the deep misery but too visible in their countenances and words. The head of the house gave the following answer: "Know then, worthy guests, that this part of the country is infested by a terrible Rakshasi, who has depopulated all the regions round. This town, too, would have been depopulated, but that our king became a suppliant before the Rakshasi, and begged her to show mercy to us his subjects. The Rakshasi replied, 'I will consent to show mercy to you and to your subjects only on this condition, that you every night put a human being, either male or female, in a certain temple for me to feast upon. If I get a human being every night I will rest satisfied, and not commit any further depredations on your subjects.' Our king had no other alternative than to agree to this condition, for what human beings can ever hope to contend against a Rakshasi? From that day the king made it a rule that every family in the town should in its turn send one of its members to the temple as a victim to appease the wrath and to satisfy the hunger of the terrible Rakshasi. All the families in this neighbourhood have had their turn, and this night it is the turn for one of us to devote himself to destruction. We are therefore discussing who should go. You must now perceive the cause of our distress." The two friends consulted together for a few minutes, and at the conclusion

223

of their consultations, Sahasra Dal who was the spokesman of the party, said, "Most worthy host, do not any longer be sad: as you have been very kind to us, we have resolved to requite your hospitality by ourselves going to the temple and becoming the food of the Rakshasi. We go as your representatives." The whole family protested against the proposal. They declared that guests were like gods, and that it was the duty of the host to endure all sorts of privation for the comfort of the guest, and not the duty of the guest to suffer for the host. But the two strangers insisted on standing proxy to the family, who, after a great deal of yea and nay, at last consented to the arrangement.

Immediately after candle-light, Sahasra Dal and Champa Dal, with their two horses, installed themselves in the temple, and shut the door. Sahasra told his brother to go to sleep, as he himself was determined to sit up the whole night and watch against the coming of the terrible Rakshasi. Champa was soon in a fine sleep, while Sahasra lay awake. Nothing happened during the early hours of the night, but no sooner had the gong of the king's palace announced the dead hour of midnight than Sahasra heard the sound as of a rushing tempest, and immediately concluded, from his knowledge of Rakshasas, that the Rakshasi was nigh. A thundering knock was heard at the door, accompanied with the following words:—

"How, mow, khow!
A human being I smell;
Who watches inside?"

To this question Sahasra Dal made the following reply:—

"Sahasra Dal watcheth,
Champa Dal watcheth,
Two winged horses watch."

On hearing this answer the Rakshasi turned away with a groan, knowing that Sahasra Dal had Rakshasa blood in his veins. An hour after, the Rakshasi returned, thundered at the door, and called out—

"How, mow, khow!
A human being I smell;
Who watcheth inside?"

Sahasra Dal again replied—

"Sahasra Dal watcheth,
Champa Dal watcheth,

Two winged horses watch."

The Rakshasi again groaned and went away. At two o'clock and at three o'clock the Rakshasi again and again made her appearance, and made the usual inquiry, and obtaining the same answer, went away with a groan. After three o'clock, however, Sahasra Dal felt very sleepy: he could not any longer keep awake. He therefore roused Champa, told him to watch, and strictly enjoined upon him, in reply to the query of the Rakshasi, to mention Sahasra's name first. With these instructions he went to sleep. At four o'clock the Rakshasi again made her appearance, thundered at the door, and said—

"How, mow, khow!
A human being I smell;
Who watches inside?"

As Champa Dal was in a terrible fright, he forgot the instructions of his brother for the moment, and answered—

"Champa Dal watcheth,
Sahasra Dal watcheth,

Two winged horses watch."

On hearing this reply the Rakshasi uttered a shout of exultation, laughed such a laugh as only demons can, and with a dreadful noise broke open the door. The noise roused Sahasra, who in a moment sprung to his feet, and with his sword, which was as supple as a palm-leaf, cut off the head of the Rakshasi. The huge mountain of a body fell to the ground, making a great noise, and lay covering many an acre. Sahasra Dal kept the severed head of the Rakshasi near him, and went to sleep. Early in the morning some wood-cutters, who were passing near the temple, saw the huge body on the ground. They could not from a distance make out what it was, but on coming near they knew that it was the carcase of the terrible Rakshasi, who had by her voracity nearly depopulated the country. Remembering the promise made by the king that the killer of the Rakshasi should be rewarded by the hand of his daughter and with a share of the kingdom, each of the wood-cutters, seeing no claimant at hand, thought of obtaining the reward. Accordingly each of them cut off a part of a limb of the huge carcase, went to the king, and represented himself to be the destroyer of the great raw-eater, and claimed the reward. The king, in order to find out the real hero and deliverer, inquired of his minister the name of the family whose turn it was on the preceding night to offer a victim to the Rakshasi. The head of that family, on being brought before the king, related how two youthful travellers, who were guests in his house, volunteered to go into the temple in the room of a member of his family. The door of the temple was broken open; Sahasra Dal and Champa Dal and their horses were found all safe; and the head of the Rakshasi, which was with them, proved beyond the shadow of a doubt that they had killed the monster. The king kept his word. He gave his daughter in marriage to Sahasra Dal and the sovereignty of half his dominions. Champa Dal remained with his friend in the king's palace, and rejoiced in his prosperity.

Sahasra Dal and Champa Dal lived together happily for some time, when a misunderstanding arose between them in this wise. There was in the service of the queen-mother a certain maid-servant who was the most useful domestic in the palace. There was nothing which she could not put her hands to and perform. She had uncommon strength for a woman, neither was her intelligence of a mean order. She was a woman of immense activity and energy; and if she were absent one day from the palace, the affairs of the zenana would be in perfect disorder. Hence her services were highly valued by the queen-mother and all the ladies of the palace. But this woman was not a woman; she was a Rakshasi, who had put on the appearance of a woman to serve some purposes of her own, and then taken service in the royal household. At night, when everyone in the palace was asleep, she used to assume her own real form, and go about in quest of food, for the quantity of food that is sufficient for either man or woman was not sufficient for a Rakshasi. Now Champa Dal having no wife, was in the habit of sleeping outside the zenana, and not far from the outer gate of the palace. He had noticed her going about on the premises and devouring sundry goats and sheep, horses and elephants. The maid-servant, finding that Champa Dal was in the way of her supper, determined to get rid of him. She accordingly went one day to the queen-mother, and said, "Queen-mother! I am unable any longer to work in the palace." "Why? What is the matter, *Dasi*[①]? How can I get on without you? Tell me your reasons. What ails you?" "Why," said the woman, "nowadays it is impossible for a poor woman like me to preserve my honour in the palace. There is that Champa Dal, the friend of your son-in-law; he always cracks indecent jokes with me. It is better for me to beg for my rice than to lose my honour. If Champa Dal remains in the palace, I must go away." As the maid-servant was an absolute necessity in the palace, the queen-mother resolved to sacrifice Champa Dal to her. She therefore told Sahasra Dal that Champa Dal was a bad man, that his character was loose, and that therefore he must leave the palace. Sahasra Dal earnestly pleaded on behalf of his friend, but in vain; the queen-mother had made up her mind

---

① *Dasi* is a general name for all maid-servants.

to drive him out of the palace. Sahasra Dal had not the courage to speak personally to his friend on the subject; he therefore wrote a letter to him, in which he simply said that for certain reasons Champa must leave the palace immediately. The letter was put in his room after he had gone to bathe. On reading the letter Champa Dal, exceedingly grieved, mounted his fleet horse and left the palace.

As Champa's horse was uncommonly fleet, in a few hours he traversed thousands of miles, and at last found himself at the gateway of what seemed a magnificent palace. Dismounting from his horse, he entered the house, where he did not meet with a single creature. He went from apartment to apartment, but though they were all richly furnished he did not see a single human being. At last, in one of the side rooms, he found a young lady of heavenly beauty lying down on a splendid bedstead. She was asleep. Champa Dal looked upon the sleeping beauty with rapture—he had not seen any woman so beautiful. Upon the bed, near the head of the young lady, were two sticks, one of silver and the other of gold. Champa took the silver stick into his hand, and touched with it the body of the lady, but no change was perceptible. He then took up the gold stick and laid it upon the lady, when in a trice she woke up, sat in her bed, and eying the stranger, inquired who he was. Champa Dal briefly told his story. The young lady, or rather princess—for she was nothing less—said, "Unhappy man! Why have you come here? This is the country of Rakshasas, and in this house and roundabout there live no less than seven hundred Rakshasas. They all go away to the other side of the ocean every morning in search of provisions; and they all return every evening before dusk. My father was formerly king in these regions, and had millions of subjects, who lived in flourishing towns and cities. But some years ago the invasion of the Rakshasas took place, and they devoured all his subjects, and himself and my mother, and my brothers and sisters. They devoured also all the cattle of the country. There is no living human being in these regions excepting myself; and I too should long ago have been devoured had not an old Rakshasi, conceiving strange affection for me, prevented the other Rakshasas from eating me up. You see those sticks of silver and gold; the old Rakshasi, when she goes away in the morning, kills me with the silver stick, and on her return in the evening re-animates me with the gold stick. I do not know how to advise you, if the Rakshasas see you, you are a dead man." Then they both talked to each other in a very affectionate manner, and laid their heads together to devise if possible some means of escape from the hands of the Rakshasas. The hour of the return of the seven hundred raw-eaters was fast approaching; and Keshavati—for that was the name of the princess, so called from the abundance of her hair—told Champa to hide himself in the heaps of the sacred trefoil which were lying in the temple of Siva in the central part of the palace. Before Champa went to his place of concealment, he touched Keshavati with the silver stick, on which she instantly died.

Shortly after sunset Champa Dal heard from beneath the heaps of the sacred trefoil the sound as of a mighty rushing wind. Presently he heard terrible noises in the palace. The Rakshasas had come home from cruising, after having filled their stomachs, each one, with sundry goats, sheep, cows, horses, buffaloes, and elephants. The old Rakshasi, of whom we have already spoken, came to Keshavati's room, roused her by touching her body with the gold stick, and said—

"Hye, mye, khye!
A human being I smell."

On which Keshavati said, "I am the only human being here; eat me if you like." To which the raw-eater replied, "Let me eat up your enemies; why should I eat you?" She laid herself down on the ground, as long and as high as the Vindhya Hills, and presently fell asleep. The other Rakshasas and Rakshasis also soon fell asleep, being all tired out on account of their gigantic labours in the day. Keshavati also composed herself to sleep; while Champa, not daring to come out of the heaps of leaves, tried his best to court the god of repose. At daybreak all the raw-eaters, seven hundred in number, got up and went as usual to their hunting and predatory excursions, and along with them went the old Rakshasi, after touching Keshavati with the silver stick. When Champa Dal saw that the coast was clear, he came out of the temple, walked into Keshavati's room, and touched her with the gold stick, on which she woke up. They sauntered about in the gardens, enjoying the cool breeze of the morning; they bathed in a lucid tank which was in the grounds; they ate and drank, and spent the day in sweet converse. They concocted a plan for their deliverance. They settled that Keshavati should ask the old Rakshasi on what the life of a Rakshasa depended, and when the secret should be made known they would adopt measures accordingly. As on the preceding evening, Champa, after touching his fair friend with the silver stick, took refuge in the temple beneath the heaps of the sacred trefoil. At dusk the Rakshasas as usual came home; and the old Rakshasi, rousing her pet, said—

"Hye, mye, khye!
A human being I smell."

Keshavati answered, "What other human being is here excepting myself? Eat me up, if you like." "Why should I eat you, my darling? Let me eat up all your enemies." Then she laid down on the ground her huge body, which looked like a part of the Himalaya Mountains. Keshavati, with a phial of heated mustard oil, went towards the feet of the Rakshasi, and said, "Mother, your feet are sore with walking, let me rub them with oil." So saying, she began to rub with oil the Rakshasi's feet; and while she was in the act of doing so, a few tear-drops from her eyes fell on the monster's leg. The Rakshasi smacked the tear-drops with her lips, and finding the taste briny, said, "Why are you weeping, darling? What aileth thee?" To which the princess replied, "Mother, I am weeping because you are old, and when you die, I shall certainly be devoured by one of the Rakshasas." "When I die! Know, foolish girl, which we Rakshasas never die. We are not naturally immortal, but our life depends on a secret which no human being can unravel. Let me tell you what it is that you may be comforted. You know yonder tank; there is in the middle of it a *Sphatika—sthambha*[①], on the top of which in deep waters are two bees. If any human being can dive into the waters, and bring up to land the two bees from the pillar in one breath, and destroy them so that not a drop of their blood falls to the ground, then we Rakshasas shall certainly die; but

① *Sphatika* is crystal, and *sthambha* pillar.

if a single drop of blood falls to the ground, then from it will start up a thousand Rakshasas. But what human being will find out this secret, or, finding it, will be able to achieve the feat? You need not, therefore, darling, be sad; I am practically immortal." Keshavati treasured up the secret in her memory, and went to sleep.

Early next morning the Rakshasas as usual went away; Champa came out of his hiding place, roused Keshavati, and fell a-talking. The princess told him the secret she had learnt from the Rakshasi. Champa immediately made preparations for accomplishing the mighty deed. He brought to the side of the tank a knife and a quantity of ashes. He disrobed himself, put a drop or two of mustard oil into each of his ears to prevent water from entering in, and dived into the waters. In a moment he got to the top of the crystal pillar in the middle of the tank, caught hold of the two bees he found there, and came up in one breath. Taking the knife he cut up the bees over the ashes, a drop or two of the blood fell, not on the ground, but on the ashes. When Champa caught hold of the bees, a terrible scream was heard at a distance. This was the wailing of the Rakshasas, who were all running home to prevent the bees from being killed; but before they could reach the palace, the bees had perished. The moment the bees were killed, all the Rakshasas died, and their carcases fell on the very spot on which they were standing. Champa and the princess afterwards found that the gateway of the palace was blocked up by the huge carcases of the Rakshasas,—some of them having nearly succeeded in getting to the palace. In this manner was effected the destruction of the seven hundred Rakshasas.

After the destruction of the seven hundred raw-eating monsters, Champa Dal and Keshavati got married together by the exchange of garlands of flowers. The princess, who had never been out of the house, naturally expressed a desire to see the outer world. They used every day to take long walks both morning and evening; and as a large river was hard by Keshavati wished to bathe in it. The first day they went to bathe, one of Keshavati's hairs came off, and as it is the custom with women never to throw away a hair unaccompanied with something else, she tied the hair to a shell which was floating on the water; after which they returned home. In the meantime the shell with the hair tied to it floated down the stream, and in course of time reached that $ghat^{①}$ at which Sahasra Dal and his companions were in the habit of performing their ablutions. The shell passed by when Sahasra Dal and his friends were bathing; and he seeing it at some distance said to them, "Whoever succeeds in catching hold of yonder shell shall be rewarded with a hundred rupees." They all swam towards it, and Sahasra Dal being the fleetest swimmer, got it. On examining it he found a hair tied to it. But such hair! He had never seen so long a hair. It was exactly seven cubits long. "The owner of this hair must

---

① Bathing-place, either in a tank or on the bank of a river, generally furnished with flights of steps.

be a remarkable woman, and I must see her,"—such was the resolution of Sahasra Dal. He went home from the river in a pensive mood, and instead of proceeding to the zenana for breakfast, remained in the outer part of the palace. The queen-mother, on hearing that Sahasra Dal was looking melancholy and had not come to breakfast, went to him and asked the reason. He showed her the hair, and said he must see the woman whose head it had adorned. The queen-mother said, "Very well, you shall have that lady in the palace as soon as possible. I promise you to bring her here." The queen-mother told her favourite maid-servant, whom she knew to be full of resources—the same who was a Rakshasi in disguise—that she must, as soon as possible, bring to the palace that lady who was the owner of the hair seven cubits long. The maid-servant said she would be quite able to fetch her. By her directions a boat was built of *Hajol* wood, the oars of which were of *Mon Paban* wood. The boat was launched on the stream, and she went on board of it with some baskets of wicker-work of curious workmanship; she also took with her some sweetmeats into which some poison had been mixed. She snapped her fingers thrice, and uttered the following charm:—

"Boat of Hajol!
Oars of Mon Paban!
Take me to the Ghat!

In which Keshavati bathes."

No sooner had the words been uttered than the boat flew like lightning over the waters. It went on and on, leaving behind many a town and city. At last it stopped at a bathing place, which the Rakshasi maid-servant concluded was the bathing *ghat* of Keshavati. She landed with the sweetmeats in her hand. She went to the gate of the palace, and cried aloud, "O Keshavati! Keshavati! I am your aunt, your mother's sister. I am come to see you, my darling, after so many years. Are you in, Keshavati?" The princess on hearing these words came out of her room, and making no doubt that she was her aunt, embraced and kissed her. They both wept rivers of joy—at least the Rakshasi maid-servant did, and Keshavati followed suit through sympathy. Champa Dal also thought that she was the aunt of his newly married wife. They all ate and drank and took rest in the middle of the day. Champa Dal, as was his habit, went to sleep after breakfast. Towards afternoon, the supposed aunt said to Keshavati, "Let us both go to the river and wash ourselves." Keshavati replied, "How can we go now? My husband is sleeping." "Never mind," said the aunt, "let him sleep on; let me put these sweetmeats that I have brought, near his bedside, that he may eat them when he gets up." They then went to the river side close to the spot where the boat was. Keshavati, when she saw from some distance the baskets of wicker work in the boat, said, "Aunt, what beautiful things are those! I wish I could get some of them." "Come, my child, come and look at them, and you can have as many as you like." Keshavati at first refused to go into the boat, but on being pressed by her aunt, she went. The moment they two were on board, the aunt snapped her fingers thrice and said:—

"Boat of Hajol!
Oars of Mon Paban!
Take me to the *Ghat*,
In which Sahasra Dal bathes."

As soon as these magical words were uttered the boat moved and flew like an arrow over the waters. Keshavati was frightened and began to cry, but the boat went on and on, leaving behind many towns and cities, and in a trice reached the *ghat* where Sahasra Dal was in the habit of bathing. Keshavati was taken to the palace; Sahasra Dal admired her beauty and the length of her hair; and the ladies of the palace tried their best to comfort her. But she set up a loud cry, and wanted to be taken back to her husband. At last when she saw that she was a captive, she told the ladies of the palace that she had taken a vow that she would not see the face of any strange man for six months. She was then lodged apart from the rest in a small house, the window of which overlooked the road; there she spent the livelong day and also the livelong night—for she had very little sleep—in sighing and weeping.

In the meantime when Champa Dal awoke from sleep, he was distracted with grief at not finding his wife. He now thought that the woman, who pretended to be his wife's aunt, was a cheat and an impostor, and that she must have carried away Keshavati. He did not eat the sweetmeats, suspecting they might be poisoned. He threw one of them to a crow which, the moment it ate it, dropped down Dead. He was now the more confirmed in his unfavourable opinion of the pretended aunt. Maddened with grief, he rushed out of the house, and determined to go whithersoever his eyes might lead him. Like a madman, always blubbering "O Keshavati! O Keshavati!" He travelled on foot day after day, not knowing whither he went. Six months were spent in this wearisome travelling when, at the end of that period, he reached the capital of Sahasra Dal. He was passing by the palace-gate when the sighs and wailings of a woman sitting at the window of a house, on the road-side, attracted his attention. One moment's look, and they recognized each other.

They continued to hold secret communications. Champa Dal heard everything, including the story of her vow, the period of which was to terminate the following day. It is customary, on the fulfilment of a vow, for some learned Brahman to make public recitations of events connected with the vow and the person who makes it. It was settled that Champa Dal should take upon himself the functions of the reciter. Accordingly, next morning, when it was proclaimed by beat of drum that the king wanted a learned Brahman who could recite the story of Keshavati on the fulfilment of her vow, Champa Dal touched the drum and said that he would make the recitation. Next morning, a gorgeous assembly was held in the courtyard of the palace under a huge canopy of silk. The old king, Sahasra Dal, all the courtiers and the learned Brahmans of the country, were present there. Keshavati was also there behind a screen that she might not be exposed to the rude gaze of the people. Champa Dal, the reciter, sitting on a dais, began the story of Keshavati, as we have related it, from the beginning, commencing with the words—"There was a poor and half-witted Brahman, &c." As he was going on with the story, the reciter every now and then asked Keshavati behind the screen whether the story was correct; to which question she as often replied, "Quite correct, and go on, Brahman." During the recitation of the story the Rakshasi maid-servant grew pale, as she perceived that her real character was discovered; and Sahasra Dal was astonished at the knowledge of the reciter regarding the history of his own life. The moment the story was finished, Sahasra Dal jumped up from his seat, and embracing the reciter said, "You can be none other than my brother Champa Dal." Then the prince, inflamed with rage, ordered the maid-servant into her presence. A large hole, as deep as the height of a man was dug in the ground; the maid-servant was put into it in a standing posture; prickly thorn was heaped around her up to the crown of her head: in this wise was the maid-servant buried alive. After this, Sahasra Dal and his princess, and Champa Dal and Keshavati, lived happily together many years.

Thus my story endeth,
The Natiya-thorn withereth, &c.

# CHAPTER V
## THE STORY OF SWET–BASANTA

There was a rich merchant who had an only son whom he loved passionately. He gave to his son whatever he wanted. His son wanted a beautiful house in the midst of a large garden. The house was built for him, and the grounds were laid out into a fine garden. One day as the merchant's son was walking in his garden, he put his hand into the nest of a small bird called *toontooni*, and found in it an egg, which he took and put in an almirah which was dug into the wall of his house. He closed the door of the almirah, and thought no more of the egg.

Though the merchant's son had a house of his own, he had no separate establishment; at any rate he kept no cook, for his mother used to send him regularly his breakfast and dinner every day. The egg which he deposited in the wall-almirah one day burst, and out of it came a beautiful infant, a girl. But the merchant's son knew nothing about it. He had forgotten everything about the egg, and the door of the wall-almirah had been kept closed, though not locked, ever since the day the egg was put there. The child grew up within the wall-almirah without the knowledge of the merchant's son or of anyone else. When the child could walk, it had the curiosity one day to open the door; and seeing some food on the floor (the breakfast of the merchant's son sent by his mother), it came out, and ate a little of it, and returned to its cell in the wall-almirah. As the mother of the merchant's son sent him always more than he could himself eat, he perceived no diminution in the quantity. The girl of the wall-almirah used every day to come out and eat a part of the food, and after eating used to return to her place in the almirah. But as the girl got older and older, she began to eat more and more; hence the merchant's son began to perceive a diminution in the quantity of his food. Not dreaming of the existence of the wall-almirah girl, he wondered that his mother should send him such a small quantity of food. He sent word to his mother, complaining of the insufficiency of his meals, and of the slovenly manner in which the food was served up in the dish; for the girl of the wall-almirah used to finger the rice, curry, and other articles of food, and as she always went in a hurry back into the almirah that she might not be perceived by any one, she had no time to put the rice and the other things into proper order after she had eaten part of them. The mother was astonished at her son's complaint, for she gave always a much larger quantity than she knew her son could consume, and the food was served up on a silver plate neatly by her own hand. But as her son repeated the same complaint day after day, she began to suspect foul play. She told her son to watch and see whether any one ate part of it unperceived. Accordingly, one day when the servant brought the breakfast and laid it in a clean place on the floor, the merchant's son, instead of going to bathe as it had hitherto been his custom, hid himself in a secret place and began to watch. In a few minutes he saw the door of the wall-almirah open; a beautiful damsel of sweet sixteen stepped out of it, sat on the carpet spread before the breakfast, and began to eat. The merchant's son came out of his hiding-place, and the damsel could not escape. "Who are you, beautiful creature? You do not seem to be earth-born. Are you one of the daughters of the gods?" asked the merchant's son. The girl replied, "I do not know who I am. This I know, that one day I found myself in yonder almirah, and have been ever since living in it." The merchant's son thought it strange. He now remembered that sixteen years before he had put in the almirah an egg he had found in the nest of a *toontooni* bird. The uncommon beauty of the wall-almirah girl made a deep impression on the mind of the merchant's son, and he resolved in his mind to marry her. The girl no more went into the almirah, but lived in one of the rooms of the spacious house of the merchant's son.

The next day the merchant's son sent word to his mother to the effect that he would like to get married. His mother reproached herself for not having long before thought of her son's marriage, and sent a message to her son to the effect that she and his father would the next day send *ghataks*[①] to different countries to seek for a suitable bride. The merchant's son sent word that he had secured for himself a most lovable young lady, and that if his parents had no objections he would produce her before them. Accordingly the young lady of the wall-almirah was taken to the merchant's house; and the merchant and his wife were so struck with the matchless beauty, grace, and loveliness of the stranger, that, without asking any questions as to her birth, the nuptials were celebrated.

In course of time the merchant's son had two sons; the elder he named Swet and the younger Basanta. The old merchant died and so did his wife. Swet and Basanta grew up fine lads, and the elder was in due time married. Sometime after Swet's marriage his mother, the wall-almirah lady, also died, and the widower lost no time in marrying a young and beautiful wife. As Swet's wife was older than his step-mother, she became the mistress of the house. The stepmother, like all stepmothers, hated Swet and Basanta

---

① Professional match-makers.

with a perfect hatred; and the two ladies were naturally often at loggerheads with each other.

It so happened one day that a fisherman brought to the merchant (we shall no longer call him the merchant's son, as his father had died) a fish of singular beauty. It was unlike any other fish that had been seen. The fish had marvellous qualities ascribed to it by the fisherman. If anyone eats it, said he, when he laughs, *maniks*[①] will drop from his mouth, and when he weeps pearls will drop from his eyes, the merchant hearing of the wonderful properties of the fish bought it at one thousand rupees, and put it into the hands of Swet's wife, who was the mistress of the house, strictly enjoining on her to cook it well and to give it to him alone to eat. The mistress, or house-mother, who had over-heard the conversation between her father-in-law and the fisherman, secretly resolved in her mind to give the cooked fish to her husband and to his brother to eat, and to give to her father-in-law instead a frog daintily cooked. When she had finished cooking both the fish and the frog, she heard the noise of a squabble between her stepmother-in-law and her husband's brother. It appears that Basanta, who was but a lad yet, was passionately fond of pigeons, which he tamed. One of these pigeons had flown into the room of his stepmother,

---

① *Manik*, or rather *manikya*, is a fabulous precious stone of incredible value. It is found on the head of some species of snakes, and is equal in value to the wealth of seven kings.

who had secreted it in her clothes. Basanta rushed into the room, and loudly demanded the pigeon. His stepmother denied any knowledge of the pigeon, on which the elder brother, Swet, forcibly took out the bird from her clothes and gave it to his brother. The stepmother cursed and swore, and added, "Wait, when the head of the house comes home I will make him shed the blood of you both before I give him water to drink." Swet's wife called her husband and said to him, "My dearest lord, that woman is a most wicked woman, and has boundless influence over my father-in-law. She will make him do what she has threatened. Our life is in imminent danger. Let us first eat a little, and let us all three run away from this place." Swet forthwith called Basanta to him, and told him what he had heard from his wife. They resolved to run away before nightfall. The woman placed before her husband and his brother-in-law the fish of wonderful properties, and they ate of it heartily. The woman packed up all her jewels in a box. As there was only one horse, and it was of uncommon fleetness, the three sat upon it; Swet held the reins, the woman sat in the middle with the jewel-box in her lap, and Basanta brought up the rear.

The horse galloped with the utmost swiftness. They passed through many a plain and many a noted town, till after midnight they found themselves in a forest not far from the bank of a river.

Here the most un-toward event took place. Swet's wife began to feel the pains of child-birth. They dismounted, and in an hour or two Swet's wife gave birth to a son. What were the two brothers to do in this forest? A fire must be kindled to give heat both to the mother and the new-born baby. But where was the fire to be got? There were no human habitations visible. Still fire must be procured—and it was the month of December—or else both the mother and the baby would certainly perish. Swet told Basanta to sit beside his wife, while he set out in the darkness of the night in search of fire.

Swet walked many a mile in darkness. Still he saw no human habitations. At last the genial light of *Sukra*[①] somewhat illumined his path, and he saw at a distance what seemed a large city. He was congratulating himself on his journey's end and on his being able to obtain fire for the benefit of his poor wife lying cold in the forest with the new-born babe, when on a sudden an elephant, gorgeously caparisoned, shot across his path, and gently taking him up by his trunk, placed him on the rich *howdah*[②] on its back. It then walked rapidly towards the city. Swet was quite taken aback. He did not understand the meaning of the elephant's action, and wondered what was in store for him. A crown was in store for

---

① Venus, the Morning Star.
② The seat on the back of an elephant.

him. In that kingdom, the chief city of which he was approaching, every morning a king was elected, for the king of the previous day was always found dead in the morning in the room of the queen. What caused the death of the king no one knew, neither did the queen herself (for every successive king took her to wife) know the cause. And the elephant who took hold of Swet was the king-maker. Early in the morning it went about, sometimes to distant places, and whosoever was brought on its back was acknowledged king by the people. The elephant majestically marched through the crowded streets of the city, amid the acclamations of the people, the meaning of which Swet did not understand, entered the palace, and placed him on the throne. He was proclaimed king amid the rejoicings of some and the lamentations of others. In the course of the day he heard of the strange fatality which overtook every night the elected king of those realms, but being possessed of great discretion and courage he took every precaution to avert the dreadful catastrophe. Yet he hardly knew what expedients to adopt, as he was unacquainted with the nature of the danger. He resolved, however, upon two things, and these were, to go armed into the queen's bedchamber, and to sit up awake the whole night. The queen was young and of exquisite beauty, and so guileless and benevolent was the expression of her face that it was impossible from looking at her to suppose that she could use any foul means of taking away the life of her nightly consort. In the queen's chamber Swet spent a very agreeable evening; as the night advanced, the queen fell asleep, but Swet kept awake, and was on the alert, looking at every creek and corner of the room, and expecting every minute to be murdered. In the dead of night he perceived something like a thread coming out of the left nostril of the queen. The thread was so thin that it was almost invisible. As he watched it he found it several yards long, and yet it was coming out. When the whole of it had come out, it began to grow thick, and in a few minutes it assumed the form of a huge serpent. In a moment Swet cut off the head of the serpent, the body of which wriggled violently. He sat quiet in the room, expecting other adventures. But nothing else happened. The queen slept longer than usual as she had been relieved of the huge snake which had made her stomach its den. Early next morning the ministers came expecting as usual to hear of the king's death; but when the ladies of the bedchamber knocked at the door of the queen they were astonished to see Swet come out. It was then known to all the people how that every night a terrible snake issued from the queen's nostrils, how it devoured the king every night, and how it had at last been killed by the fortunate Swet. The whole country rejoiced in the prospect of a permanent king. It is a strange thing, nevertheless it is true, that Swet did not remember his poor wife with the new born babe lying in the forest, nor his brother attending on her. With the possession of the throne he seemed to forget the whole of his past history.

Basanta, to whom his brother had entrusted his wife and child, sat watching for many a weary hour, expecting every moment to see Swet return with fire. The whole night passed away without his return. At sunrise he went to the bank of the river which was close by, and anxiously looked about for his brother, but in vain. Distressed beyond measure, he sat on the river side and wept. A boat was passing by in which a merchant was returning to his country. As the boat was not far from the shore the merchant saw Basanta weeping; and what struck the attention of the merchant was the heap of what looked like pearls, near the weeping man. At the request of the merchant the boatman took his vessel towards the bank; the merchant went to the weeping man, and found that the heap was a heap of real pearls of the finest luster; and what astonished him most of all was that the heap was increasing every second, for the tear-drops that were falling from his eyes fell to the ground not as tears but as pearls. The merchant stowed away the heap of pearls into his boat, and with the help of his servants caught hold of Basanta himself, put him on board the vessel, and tied him to a post. Basanta, of course resisted; but what could he do against so many? Thinking of his brother, his brother's wife and baby, and his own captivity, Basanta wept more bitterly than before, which mightily pleased the merchant, as the more tears his captive shed the richer he himself became. When the merchant reached his native town he confined Basanta in a room, and at stated hours every day scourged him in order to make him shed tears, every one of which was converted into a bright pearl. The merchant one day said to his servants, "As the fellow is making me rich by his weeping, let us see what he gives me by laughing." Accordingly he began to tickle his captive, on which Basanta laughed, and as he laughed a great many *maniks* dropped from his mouth. After this poor Basanta was alternately whipped and tickled all the day and far into the night; and the merchant, in consequence, became the wealthiest man in the land. Leaving Basanta subjected to the alternate processes of castigation and titillation, let us attend to the fortunes of the poor wife of Swet, alone in the forest, with a child just born.

Swet's wife, apparently deserted by her husband and her brother-in-law, was overwhelmed with grief. A woman, but a few hours since delivered of a child—and her first child, alone, and in a forest, far from the habitations of men,—her case was indeed pitiable. She wept rivers of tears. Excessive grief, however, brought her relief. She fell asleep with the new-born baby in her arms. It so happened that at that hour the Kotwal (prefect of the police) of the country was passing that way. He had been very unfortunate with regard to his offspring; every child his wife presented him with died shortly after birth, and he was now going to bury the last infant on the banks of the river. As he was going, he saw in the forest a woman sleeping with a baby in her arms. It was a lively and beautiful boy. The Kotwal coveted the lovely infant. He quietly took it up, put in its place his own dead child, and returning home, told his wife that the child had not really died and had revived. Swet's wife, unconscious of the deceit practised upon her by the Kotwal, on waking found her child dead. The distress of her mind may be imagined. The whole world became dark to her. She was distracted with grief, and in her distraction she formed the resolution of committing suicide. The river was not far from the spot, and she determined to drown herself in it. She took in her hand the bundle of jewels and proceeded to the river-side. An old Brahman was at no great distance, performing his morning ablutions. He noticed the woman going into the water, and naturally thought that she was going to bathe; but when he saw her going far into deep waters, some suspicion arose in his mind. Discontinuing his devotions, he bawled out and ordered the woman to come to him. Swet's wife seeing that it was an old man that was calling her, retraced her steps and came to him. On being asked what she was about to do, she said that she was going to make an end of herself, and that as she had some jewels with she would be obliged if he would accept them as a present. At the request of the old Brahman she related to him her whole story. The upshot was that she was prevented from drowning herself, and that she was received into the Brahman's family, where she was treated by the Brahman's wife as her own daughter.

Years passed on. The reputed son of the Kotwal grew up a vigorous, robust lad. As the house of the old Brahman was not far from the Kotwal's, the Kotwal's son used accidentally to meet the handsome strange woman who passed for the Brahman's daughter. The lad liked the woman, and wanted to marry her. He spoke to his father about the woman, and the father spoke to the Brahman. The Brahman's rage knew no bounds. What! The infidel Kotwal's son aspiring to the hand of a Brahman's daughter! A dwarf may as well aspire to catch hold of the moon! But the Kotwal's son determined to have her by force. With this wicked object he one day scaled the wall that encompassed the Brahman's house, and got upon the thatched roof of the Brahman's cow-house. While he was reconnoitering from that lofty position, he heard the following conversation between two calves in the cow-house:—

*First Calf.*—"Men accuse us of brutish ignorance and immorality, but in my opinion men are fifty times worse."

*Second Calf.* —"What makes you say so, brother? Have you witnessed today any instance of human depravity?"

*First Calf.*—"Who can be a greater monster of crime than the same lad who is at this moment standing on the thatched roof of this hut over our head?"

*Second Calf.*—"Why, I thought it was only the son of our Kotwal; and I never heard that he was exceptionally vicious."

*First Calf.*—"You never heard, but now you hear from me. This wicked lad is now wishing to get married to his own mother!"

The First Calf then related to the inquisitive Second Calf in full the story of Swet and Basanta; how they and Swet's wife fled from the vengeance of their stepmother; how Swet's wife was delivered of a child in the forest by the river-side; how Swet was made king by the elephant, and how he succeeded in killing the serpent which issued out of the queen's nostrils; how Basanta was carried away by the merchant, confined in a dungeon, and alternately flogged and tickled for pearls and maniks; how the Kotwal exchanged his dead child for the living one of Swet; how

256

Swet's wife was prevented from drowning herself in the river by the Brahman; how she was received into the Brahman's family and treated as his daughter; how the Kotwal's son grew up a hardy, lusty youth, and fell in love with her; and how at that very moment he was intent on accomplishing his brutal object. This entire story the Kotwal's son heard from the thatched roof of the cow-house, and was struck with horror. He forthwith got down from the thatch, went home and told his father that he must have an interview with the king. Notwithstanding his reputed father's protestations to the contrary, he had an interview with the king, to whom he repeated the whole story as he had overheard it from the thatch of the cow-house. The king now remembered his poor wife's case. She was brought from the house of the Brahman, whom he richly rewarded, and put her in her proper position as the queen of the kingdom; the reputed son of the Kotwal was acknowledged as his own son, and proclaimed the heir-apparent to the throne; Basanta was brought out of the dungeon, and the wicked merchant who had maltreated him was buried alive in the earth surrounded with thorns. After this, Swet, his wife and son, and Basanta, lived together happily for many years.

Now my story endeth,
The Natiya-thorn withereth, &c.

# CHAPTER VI
## THE EVIL EYE OF SANI

Once upon a time Sani, or Saturn, the god of bad luck, and Lakshmi, the goddess of good luck, fell out with each other in heaven. Sani said he was higher in rank than Lakshmi, and Lakshmi said she was higher in rank than Sani. As all the gods and goddesses of heaven were equally ranged on either side, the contending deities agreed to refer the matter to some human being who had a name for wisdom and justice. Now, there lived at that time upon earth a man of the name of *Sribatsa*[1], who was as wise and just as he was rich. Him, therefore, both the god and the goddess chose as the settler of their dispute. One day, accordingly, Sribatsa was told that Sani and Lakshmi were wishing to pay him a visit to get their dispute settled. Sribatsa was in a fix. If he said Sani was higher in rank than Lakshmi, she would be angry with him and forsake him. If he said Lakshmi was higher in rank than Sani, Sani would east his evil eye upon him. Hence he made up his mind

---

[1] *Sri* is another name of Lakshmi, and *batsa* means child, so that Sribatsa is literally the "child of fortune".

not to say anything directly, but to leave the god and the goddess to gather his opinion from his action. He got two stools made, the one of gold and the other of silver, and placed them beside him. When Sani and Lakshmi came to Sribatsa, he told Sani to sit upon the silver stool, and Lakshmi upon the gold stool. Sani became mad with rage, and said in an angry tone to Sribatsa, "Well, as you consider me lower in rank than Lakshmi, I will cast my eye on you for three years; and I should like to see how you fare at the end of that period." The god then went away in high dudgeon. Lakshimi, before going away, said to Sribatsa, "My child, do not fear. I'll befriend you." The god and the goddess then went away.

Sribatsa said to his wife, whose name was Chintamani, "Dearest, as the evil eye of Sani will be upon me at once, I had better go away from the house; for if I remain in the house with you, evil will befall you and me; but if I go away, it will overtake me only." Chintamani said, "That cannot be; wherever you go, I will go, your lot shall be my lot." The husband tried hard to persuade his wife to remain at home, but it was of no use. She would go with her husband. Sribatsa accordingly told his wife to make an opening in their mattress, and to stow away in it all the money and jewels they had. On the eve of leaving their house, Sribatsa invoked Lakshmi, who forthwith appeared. He then said to her, "Mother Lakshmi! As the evil eye of

Sani is upon us, we are going away into exile; but do thou befriend us, and take care of our house and property." The goddess of good luck answered, "Do not fear, I'll befriend you; all will be right at last." They then set out on their journey. Sribatsa rolled up the mattress and put it on his head. They had not gone many miles when they saw a river before them. It was not fordable; but there was a canoe there with a man sitting in it. The travellers requested the ferryman to take them across. The ferryman said, "I can take only one at a time, but you are three—yourself, your wife, and the mattress." Sribatsa proposed that first his wife and the mattress should be taken across, and then he, but the ferryman would not hear of it. "Only one at a time," repeated he, "first let me take across the mattress." When the canoe with the mattress was in the middle of the stream, a fierce gale arose, and carried away the mattress, the canoe, and the ferryman, no one knows whither. And it was strange the stream also disappeared, for the place, where they saw a few minutes since the rush of waters, had now become firm ground. Sribatsa then knew that this was nothing but the evil eye of Sani.

Sribatsa and his wife, without a pice in their pocket, went to a village which was hard by. It was dwelt in for the most part by wood-cutters, who used to go at sunrise to the forest to cut wood, which they sold in a town not far from the village. Sribatsa proposed to the wood-cutters that he should go along with them to cut wood. They agreed. So he began to fell trees as well as the best of them, but there was this difference between Sribatsa and the other wood-cutters, that whereas the latter cut any and every sort of wood, the former cut only precious wood like sandal-wood. The wood-cutters used to bring to market large loads of common wood, and Sribatsa only a few pieces of sandalwood, for which he got a great deal more money than the others. As this was going on day after day, the wood-cutters through envy plotted together, and drove away from the village Sribatsa and his wife.

The next place they went to was a village of weavers or rather cotton-spinners. Here Chintamani, the wife of Sribatsa, made herself useful by spinning cotton. And as she was an intelligent and skilful woman, she spun finer thread than the other women, and she got more money. This roused the envy of the native women of the village. But this was not all. Sribatsa in order to gain the good grace of the weavers asked them to a feast, the dishes of which were all cooked by his wife. As Chintamani excelled in cooking, the barbarous weavers of the village were quite charmed by the delicacies set before them When the men went to their homes, they reproached their wives for not being able to cook so well as the wife of Sribatsa, and called them good-for-nothing women. This thing made the women of the village hate Chintamani the more. One day, Chintamani went to the river side to bathe along with the other women of the village. A boat had been lying on the bank stranded on the sand for many days; they had tried to move it, but in vain. It so happened that as Chintamani by accident touched the boat, it moved off to the river. The boatmen, astonished at the event, thought that the woman had uncommon power, and might be useful on similar occasions in future. They therefore caught hold of her, put her in the boat and rowed off. The women of the village, who were present, did not offer any resistance as they hated Chintamani. When Sribatsa heard how his wife had been carried away by boatmen, he became mad with grief. He left the village, went to the river-side and resolved to follow the course of the stream till he should meet the boat where his wife was a prisoner. He travelled on and on, along the side of the river till it became dark. As there were no huts to be seen, he climbed into a tree for the night. Next morning as he got down from the tree he saw at the foot of it a cow called a Kapila-cow, which never calves, but which gives milk at all hours of the day whenever it is milked. Sribatsa milked the cow, and drank its milk to his heart's content. He was astonished to find that the cow-dung which lay on the ground was of a bright yellow colour; indeed, he found it was pure gold. While it was in a soft state he wrote his own name upon it, and when in the course of the day it became hardened, it looked like a brick of gold—and so it was. As the tree grew on the river side, and as the Kapila-cow came morning and evening to supply him with milk, Sribatsa resolved to stay there till he should meet the boat. In the meantime the gold-bricks were increasing in number every day, for the cow both morning and evening deposited there the precious article. He put the gold-bricks, upon all of which his name was engraved, one upon another in rows, so that from a distance they looked like a hillock of gold.

Leaving Sribatsa to arrange his gold-bricks under the tree on the river side, we must follow the fortunes of his wife. Chintamani was a woman of great beauty; and thinking that her beauty might be her ruin, she, when seized by the boatmen, offered to Lakshmi the following prayer—"O Mother Lakshmi! Have pity upon me. Thou hast made me beautiful, but now my beauty will undoubtedly prove my ruin by the loss of honour and chastity. I therefore beseech thee, gracious Mother, to make me ugly, and to cover my body with some loathsome disease, that the boatmen may not touch me." Lakshmi heard Chintamani's prayer, and in the twinkling of an eye, while she was in the arms of the boatmen, her naturally beautiful form was turned into a vile carcase. The boatmen on putting her down in the boat, found her body covered with loathsome sores which were giving out a disgusting stench. They therefore threw her into the hold of the boat amongst the cargo, where they used morning and evening to send her a little boiled rice and some water. In that hold Chintamani had a miserable life of it, but she greatly preferred that misery to the loss of chastity. The boatmen went to some port, sold the cargo, and were returning to their country when the sight of what seemed a hillock of gold, not far from the river side, attracted their attention. Sribatsa, whose eyes were ever directed towards the river, was delighted when he saw a boat turn towards the bank, as he fondly imagined his wife might be in it. The boatmen went to the hillock of gold, when Sribatsa said that the gold was his. They put all the gold-bricks on board their vessel, took Sribatsa prisoner, and put him into the hold not far from the woman covered with sores. They of course immediately recognized each other, in spite of the change Chintamani had undergone, but thought it prudent not to speak to each other. They communicated their ideas therefore by signs and gestures. Now, the boatmen were fond of playing at dice, and as Sribatsa appeared to them from his looks to be a respectable man, they always asked him to join in the game. As he was an expert player, he almost always won the game, on which the boatmen, envying his superior skill, threw him overboard. Chintamani had the presence of mind, at that moment, to throw into the water a pillow which she had for resting her head upon. Sribatsa took hold of the pillow, by means of which he floated down the stream till he was carried at nightfall to what seemed a garden on the water's edge. There he stuck among the trees, where he remained the whole night, wet and shivering. Now, the garden belonged to an old widow who was in former years the chief flower-supplier to the king of that country. Through some cause or other a blight seemed to have come over her garden, as almost all the trees and plants ceased flowering, she had therefore given up her place as the flower-supplier of the royal household. On the morning following the night on which Sribatsa had stuck among the trees, however, the old woman on getting up from her bed could scarcely believe her eyes when she saw the whole garden ablaze with flowers. There was not a single tree or plant which was not begemmed with flowers. Not understanding the cause of such a miraculous sight, she took a walk through the garden, and found on the river's brink, stuck among the trees, a man, shivering and almost dying with cold. She brought him to her cottage, lighted a fire to give him warmth, and showed him every attention, as she ascribed the wonderful flowering of her trees to his presence. After making him as comfortable as she could, she ran to the king's palace, and told his chief servants that she was again in a position to supply the palace with flowers, so she was restored to her former office as the flower-woman of the royal household. Sribatsa, who stopped a few days with the woman, requested her to recommend him to one of the king's ministers for a berth. He was accordingly sent for to the palace, and as he was at once found to be a man of intelligence, the king's minister asked him what post he would like to have. Agreeably to his wish he was appointed collector of tolls on the river. While discharging his duties as river toll-gatherer, in the course of a few days he saw the very boat in which his wife was a prisoner. He detained the boat, and charged the boatmen with the theft of gold-bricks which he claimed as his own. At the mention of gold-bricks the king himself came to the river side, and was astonished beyond measure to see bricks made of gold, every one of which had the inscription—SRIBATSA. At the same time Sribatsa rescued from the boatmen his wife, who, the moment she came out of the vessel, became as lovely as before. The king heard the story of Sribatsa's misfortunes from his lips, entertained him in a princely style for many days, and at last sent him and his wife to their own country with presents of horses and elephants. The evil eye of Sani was now turned away from Sribatsa, and he again became what he formerly was, the Child of Fortune.

Thus my story endeth,
The Natiya-thorn withereth, &c.

# CHAPTER VII
## THE BOY WHOM SEVEN MOTHERS SUCKLED

Once on a time there reigned a king who had seven queens. He was very sad, for the seven queens were all barren. A holy mendicant, however, one day told the king that in a certain forest there grew a tree, on a branch of which hung seven mangoes; if the king himself plucked those mangoes and gave one to each of the queens they would all become mothers. So the king went to the forest, plucked the seven mangoes that grew upon one branch, and gave a mango to each of the queens to eat. In a short time the king's heart was filled with joy, as he heard that the seven queens were all with child.

One day the king was out hunting, when he saw a young lady of peerless beauty cross his path. He fell in love with her, brought her to his palace, and married her. This lady was, however, not a human being, but a Rakshasi; but the king of course did not know it. The king became dotingly fond of her; he did whatever she told him. She said one day to the king, "You say that you love me more than anyone else. Let me see whether you really love me so. If you love me, make your seven other queens blind, and let them be killed." The king became very sad at the request of his best-beloved queen, the more so as the seven queens were all with child. But there was nothing for it but to comply with the Rakshasi-queen's request. The eyes of the seven queens were plucked out of their sockets, and the queens themselves were delivered up to the chief minister to be destroyed. But the chief minister was a merciful man. Instead of killing the seven queens he hid them in a cave which was on the side of a hill. In course of time the eldest of the seven queens gave birth to a child. "What shall I do with the child," said she, "now that we are blind and are dying for want of food? Let me kill the child, and let us all eat of its flesh." So saying she killed the infant, and gave to each of her sister-queens a part of the child to eat. The six ate their portion, but the seventh or youngest queen did not eat her share, but laid it beside her. In a few days the second queen also was delivered of a child, and she did with it as her eldest sister had done with hers. So did the third, the fourth, the fifth, and the sixth queen. At last the seventh queen gave birth to a son; but she, instead of following the example of her sister-queens, resolved to nurse the child. The other queens demanded their portions of the newly-born babe. She gave each of them the portion she had got of the six children which had been killed, and which she had not eaten but laid aside. The other queens at once perceived that their portions were dry, and could not therefore be the parts of the child just born. The seventh queen told them that she had made up her mind not to kill the child but to nurse it. The others were glad to hear this, and they all said that they would help her in nursing the child. So the child was suckled by seven mothers, and it became after some years the hardiest and strongest boy that ever lived.

In the meantime the Rakshasi wife of the king was doing infinite mischief to the royal household and to the capital. What she ate at the royal table did not fill her capacious stomach. She therefore, in the darkness of night, gradually ate up all the members of the royal family, all the king's servants and attendants, all his horses, elephants, and cattle; till none remained in the palace except she herself and her royal consort. After that she used to go out in the evenings into the city and eat up a stray human being here and there. The king was left unattended by servants; there was no person left to cook for him, for no one would take his service. At last the boy who had been suckled by seven mothers, and who had now grown up to a stalwart youth, volunteered his services. He attended on the king, and took every care to prevent the queen from swallowing him up, for he went away home long before nightfall, and the Rakshasi-queen never seized her victims except at night. Hence the queen determined in some other way to get rid of the boy. As the boy always boasted that he was equal to any work, however hard, the queen told him that she was suffering from some disease which could be cured only by eating a certain species of melon, which was twelve cubits long, but the stone of which was thirteen cubits long, and that that fruit could be had only from her mother, who lived on the other side of the ocean. She gave him a letter of introduction to her mother, in which she requested her to devour the boy the moment he put the letter into her hands. The boy, suspecting foul play, tore up the letter and proceeded on his journey. The dauntless youth passed through many lands, and at last stood on the shore of the ocean, on the other side of which was the country of the Rakshasis. He then bawled as loud as he could, and said "Granny! Granny! Come and save your daughter; she is dangerously ill." An old Rakshasi on the other side of the ocean heard t he words, crossed the ocean, came to the boy, and on hearing the message took the boy on her back and re-crossed the ocean. So the boy was in the country of the Rakshasis. The twelve-cubit melon with its thirteen-cubit stone was given to the boy at once, and he was told to perform the journey back. But the boy pleaded fatigue, and begged to be allowed to rest one day. To this the old Rakshasi consented. Observing a stout club and a rope hanging in the Rakshasi's room, the boy inquired what they were there for. She replied, "Child, by that club and rope I cross the ocean. If any one takes the club and the rope in his hands, and addresses them in the following magical words: 'O stout club! O strong rope! Take me at once to the other side,' then immediately the club and rope will take him to the other side of the ocean." Observing a bird in a cage hanging in one corner of the room, the boy inquired what it was. The old Rakshasi replied, "It contains a secret, child, which must not be disclosed to mortals, and yet how can I hide it from my own grandchild? That bird, child, contains the life of your mother. If the bird is killed, your mother will at once die." Armed with these secrets, the boy went to bed that night. Next morning the old Rakshasi, together with all the other Rakshasis, went to distant countries for forage. The boy took down the cage from the ceiling, as well as the club and rope. Having well secured the bird, he addressed the club and rope thus—

"O stout club! O strong rope!

Take me at once to the other side."

In the twinkling of an eye the boy was put on this side the ocean. He then retraced his steps, came to the queen, and gave her, to her astonishment, the twelve-cubit melon with its thirteen-cubit stone; but the cage with the bird in it he kept carefully concealed.

In the course of time the people of the city came to the king and said, "A monstrous bird comes out apparently from the palace every evening, and seizes the passengers in the streets and swallows them up. This has been going on for so long a time that the city has become almost desolate." The king could not make out what this monstrous bird was. The king's servant, the boy, replied that he knew the monstrous bird, and that he would kill it provided the queen stood beside the king. By royal command the queen was made to stand beside the king. The boy then took the bird from the cage which he had brought from the other side of the ocean, on seeing which she fell into a fainting fit. Turning to the king, the boy said, "Sire, you will soon perceive who the monstrous bird is that devours your subjects every evening. As I tear off each limb of this bird, the corresponding limb of the man-devourer will fall off." The boy then tore off one leg of the bird in his hand; immediately, to the astonishment of the whole assembly, for the citizens were all present, one of the legs of the queen fell off. And when the boy squeezed the throat of the bird, the queen gave up the ghost. The boy then related his own history and that of his mother and his stepmothers. The seven queens, whose eyesight was miraculously restored, were brought back to the palace; and the boy that was suckled by seven mothers was recognized by the king as his rightful heir. So they lived together happily.

Thus my story endeth,
The Natiya-thorn withereth, &c.

272

# CHAPTER VIII
## THE STORY OF PRINCE SOBUR

Once upon a time there lived a certain merchant who had seven daughters. One day the merchant put to his daughters the question: "By whose fortune do you get your living?" The eldest daughter answered —"Papa, I get my living by your fortune." The same answer was given by the second daughter, the third, the fourth, the fifth, and the sixth; but his youngest daughter said—"I get my living by my own fortune." The merchant got very angry with the youngest daughter, and said to her— "As you are so ungrateful as to say that you get your living by your own fortune, let me see how you fare alone. This very day you shall leave my house without a pice in your pocket." He forthwith called his palki-bearers, and ordered them to take away the girl and leave her in the midst of a forest. The girl begged hard to be allowed to take with her work-box containing her needles and threads. She was allowed to do so. She then got into the palki, which the bearers lifted on their shoulders. The bearers had not gone many hundred yards to the tune of "Hoon! Hoon! Hoon! Hoon! Hoon! Hoon!" when an old woman bawled out to them and bid them stop. On coming up to the palki, she said, "Where are you taking away my daughter?" For she was the nurse of the merchant's youngest child. The bearers replied, "The merchant has ordered us to take her away and leave her in the midst of a forest; and we are going to do his bidding." "I must go with her," said the old woman. "How will you be able to keep pace with us, as we must run?" said the bearers. "Anyhow I must go where my daughter goes," rejoined the old woman. The upshot was that, at the entreaty of the merchant's youngest daughter, the old woman was put inside the palki along with her. In the afternoon the palki-bearers reached a dense forest. They went far into it; and towards sunset they put down the girl and the old woman at the foot of a large tree, and retraced their steps homewards.

The case of the merchant's youngest daughter was truly pitiable. She was scarcely fourteen years old, she had been bred in the lap of luxury; and she was now here at sundown in the heart of what seemed an interminable forest, with not a penny in her pocket, and with no other protection than what could be given her by an old, decrepit, imbecile woman. The very trees of the forest looked upon her with pity. The gigantic tree, at whose foot she was mingling her tears with those of the old woman, said to her (for trees could speak in those days)—"Unhappy girl! I much pity you. In a short time the wild beasts of the forest will come out of their lairs and roam about for their prey; and they are sure to devour you and your companion. But I can help you; I will make an opening for you in my trunk. When you see the opening go into it, I will then close it up, and you will remain safe inside, nor can the wild beasts touch you." In a moment the trunk of the tree was split into two. The merchant's daughter and the old woman went inside the hollow, on which the tree resumed its natural shape. When the shades of night darkened the forest the wild beasts came out of their lairs. The fierce tiger was there; the wild bear was there; the hard-skinned rhinoceros was there; the bushy bear was there; the musty elephant was there; and the horned buffalo was there. They all growled round about the tree, for they got the scent of human blood. The merchant's daughter and the old woman heard from within the tree the growl of the beasts. The beasts came dashing against the tree; they broke its branches; they pierced its trunk with their horns; they scratched its bark with their claws: but in vain. The merchant's daughter and her old nurse were safe within. Towards dawn the wild beasts went away. After sunrise the good tree said to her two inmates, "Unhappy women, the wild beasts have gone into their lairs after greatly tormenting me. The sun is up, you can now come out." So saying the tree split itself into two, and the merchant's daughter and the old woman came out. They saw the extent of the mischief done by the wild beasts to the tree. Many of its branches had been broken down; in many places the trunk had been pierced; and in other places the bark had been stripped off. The merchant's daughter said to the tree, "Good mother, you are truly good to give us shelter at such a fearful cost. You must be in great pain from the torture to which the wild beasts subjected you last night." So saying she went to the tank which was near the tree, and bringing thence a quantity of mud, she besmeared the trunk with it, especially those parts which had been pierced and scratched. After she had done this, the tree said, "Thank you, my good girl, I am now greatly relieved of my pain. I am, however, concerned not so much about myself as about you both. You must be hungry, not having eaten the whole of yesterday. And what can I give you? I have no fruit of my own to give you. Give to the old woman whatever money you have, and let her go into the city hard by and buy some food." They said they had no money. On searching, however, in the work-box she found five *cowries*[①]. The tree then told the old woman to go with the *cowries* to the city and buy some *khai*[②]. The old woman went to the city, which was not far, and said to one confectioner, "Please give me five *cowries*' worth of *khai*." The confectioner laughed at her and said, "Be off, you old hag, do you think *khai* can be had for five *cowries*?" She tried another shop, and the shop-keeper, thinking

---

① Shells used as money, one hundred and sixty of which could have been got a few years ago for one pice.
② Fried paddy.

the woman to be in great distress, compassionately gave her a large quantity of *khai* for the five *cowries*.

When the old woman returned with the *khai*, the tree said to the merchant's daughter, "Each of you eat a little of the *khai*, lay by more than half, and strew the rest on the embankments of the tank all round." They did as they were bidden, though they did not understand the reason why they were told to scatter the *khai* on the sides of the tank. They spent the day in bewailing their fate, and at night they were housed inside the trunk of the tree as on the previous night. The wild beasts came as before, further mutilated the tree, and tortured it as in the preceding night. But during the night a scene was being enacted on the embankments of the tank of which the two women saw the outcome only on the following morning. Hundreds of peacocks of gorgeous plumes came to the embankments to eat the *khai* which had been strewed on them; and as they strove with each other for the tempting food many of their plumes fell off their bodies. Early in the morning the tree told the two women to gather the plumes together, out of which the merchant's daughter made a beautiful fan. This fan was taken into the city to the palace, where the son of the king admired it greatly and paid for it a large sum of money. As each morning a quantity of plumes was collected, every day one fan was made and sold. So that in a short time the two women got rich. The tree then advised them to employ men in building a house for them to live in. Accordingly bricks were burnt, trees were cut down for beams and rafters, bricks were reduced to powder, lime was manufactured, and in a few months a stately, palace-like house was built for the merchant's daughter and her old nurse. It was thought advisable to lay out the adjoining grounds as a garden, and to dig a tank for supplying them with water.

In the meantime the merchant himself with his wife and six daughters had been frowned upon by the goddess of wealth. By a sudden stroke of misfortune he lost all his money, his house and property were sold, and he, his wife, and six daughters, were turned adrift penniless into the world. It so happened that they lived in a village not far from the place where the two strange women had built a palace and were digging a tank. As the once rich merchant was now supporting his family by the pittance which he obtained every day for his manual labour, he bethought himself of employing himself as a day labourer in digging the tank of the strange lady on the skirts of the forest. His wife said she would also go to dig the tank with him. So one day while the strange lady was amusing herself from the window of her palace with looking at the labourers digging her tank, to her utter surprise she saw her father and mother coming towards the palace, apparently to engage themselves as day labourers. Tears ran down her cheeks as she looked at them, for they were clothed in rags. She immediately sent servants to bring them inside the house. The poor man and woman were frightened beyond measure. They saw that the tank was all ready; and as it was customary in those days to offer a human sacrifice when the digging was over, they thought that they were called inside in order to be sacrificed. Their fears increased when they were told to throw away their rags and to put on fine clothes which were given to them. The strange lady of the palace, however, soon dispelled their fears, for she told them that she was their daughter, fell on their necks and wept. The rich daughter related her adventures, and the father felt she was right when she said that she lived upon her own fortune and not on that of her father. She gave her father a large fortune, which enabled him to go to the city in which he formerly lived, and to set himself up again as a merchant.

The merchant now bethought himself of going in his ship to distant countries for purposes of trade. All was ready. He got on board, ready to start, but, strange to say, the ship would not move. The merchant was at a loss what to make of this. At last the idea occurred to him that he had asked each of his six daughters, who were living with him, what thing she wished he should bring for her; but he had not asked that question of his seventh daughter who had made him rich. He therefore immediately despatched a messenger to his youngest daughter, asking her what she wished her father to bring for her on his return from his mercantile travels. When the messenger arrived she was engaged in her devotions, and hearing that a messenger had arrived from her father she said to him "Sobur", meaning "wait". The messenger understood that she wanted her father to bring for her something called *Sobur*. He returned to the merchant and told him that she wanted him to bring for her *Sobur*. The ship now moved of itself, and the merchant started on his travels. He visited many ports, and by selling his goods obtained immense profit. The things his six daughters wanted him to bring for them he easily got, but *Sobur*, the thing which he understood his youngest daughter wished to have, he could get nowhere. He asked at every port whether *Sobur* could be had there, but the merchants all told him that they had never heard of such an article of commerce. At the last port he went through the streets bawling out—"Wanted *Sobur*! Wanted *Sobur*!" The cry attracted the notice of the son of the king of that country whose name was Sobur. The prince, hearing from the merchant that his daughter wanted *Sobur*, said that he had the article in question, and bringing out a small box of wood containing a magical fan with a looking-glass in it, said—"This is *Sobur* which your daughter wishes to have." The merchant having obtained the long-wished-for *Sobur* weighed anchor, and sailed for his native land. On his arrival he sent to his youngest daughter the said wonderful box. The daughter, thinking it to be a common wooden box, laid it aside. Some days after when she was at leisure she bethought herself of opening the box which her father had sent her. When she opened it she saw in it a beautiful fan, and in it a looking-glass. As she shook the fan, in a moment the Prince Sobur stood before her, and said—"You called me, here I am. What's your wish?" The merchant's daughter, astonished at the sudden appearance of a prince of such exquisite beauty, asked who he was, and how he had made his appearance there. The prince told her of the circumstances under which he gave the box to her father, and informed her of the secret that whenever the fan would be shaken he would make his appearance. The prince lived for a day or two in the house of the merchant's daughter, who entertained him hospitably. The upshot was, that they fell in love with each other, and vowed to each other to be husband and wife. The prince returned to his royal father and told him that he had selected a wife for himself. The day for the wedding was fixed. The merchant and his six daughters were invited. The nuptial knot was tied. But there was death in the marriage-bed. The six daughters of the merchant, envying the happy lot of their youngest sister, had determined to put an end to the life of her newly-wedded husband. They broke several bottles, reduced the broken pieces into fine powder, and scattered it profusely on the bed. The prince, suspecting no danger, laid himself down in the bed; but he had scarcely been there two minutes when he felt acute pain through his whole system, for the fine bottle- powder had gone through every pore of his body. As the prince became restless through pain, and was shrieking aloud, his attendants hastily took him away to his own country.

The king and queen, the parents of Prince Sobur, consulted all the physicians and surgeons of the kingdom, but in vain. The young prince was day and night screaming with pain, and no one could ascertain the disease, far less give him relief. The grief of the merchant's daughter may be imagined. The marriage knot had been scarcely tied when her husband was attacked, as she thought, by a terrible disease and carried away many hundreds of miles off. Though she had never seen her husband's country she determined to go there and nurse him. She put on the garb of a Sannyasi, and with a dagger in her hand set out on her journey. Of tender years, and unaccustomed to make long journeys on foot, she soon got weary and sat under a tree to rest. On the top of the tree was the nest of the divine bird Bihangama and his mate Bihangami. They were not in their nest at the time, but two of their young ones were in it. Suddenly the young ones on the top of the tree gave a scream which roused the half-drowsy merchant's daughter whom we shall now call the young Sannyasi. He saw near him a huge serpent raising its hood and about to climb into the tree. In a moment he cut the serpent into two, on which the young birds left off screaming. Shortly after the Bihangama and Bihangami came sailing through the air; and the latter said to the former—"I suppose our offspring as usual have been devoured by our great enemy the serpent. Ah me! I do not hear the cries of my young ones." On nearing the nest, however, they were agreeably surprised to find their offspring alive. The young ones told their dams how the young Sannyasi under the tree had destroyed the serpent. And sure enough the snake was lying there cut into two.

The Bihangami then said to her mate—"The young Sannyasi has saved our offspring from death, I wish we could do him some service in return." The Bihangama replied, "We shall presently do her service, for the person under the tree is not a man but a woman. She got married only last night to Prince Sobur, who, a few hours after, when jumping into his bed, had every pore of his body pierced with fine particles of ground bottles which had been spread over his bed by his envious sisters-in-law. He is still suffering pain in his native land, and, indeed, is at the point of death. And his heroic bride taking the garb of a Sannyasi is going to nurse him." "But," asked the Bihangami, "is there no cure for the prince?" "Yes, there is," replied the Bihangama: "if our dung which is lying on the ground round about, and which is hardened, be reduced to powder, and applied by means of a brush to the body of the prince after bathing him seven times with seven jars of water and seven jars of milk, Prince Sobur will undoubtedly get well." "But," asked the Bihangami, "how can the poor daughter of the merchant walk such a distance? It must take her many days, by which time the poor prince will have died." "I can," replied the Bihangama, "take the young lady on my back, and put her in the capital of Prince Sobur, and bring her back, provided she does not take any presents there." The merchant's daughter, in the garb of a Sannyasi, heard this conversation between the two birds, and begged the Bihangama to take her on his back. To this the bird readily consented. Before mounting on her aerial car she gathered a quantity of birds' dung and reduced it to fine powder. Armed with this potent drug she got up on the back of the kind bird, and sailing through the air with the rapidity of lightning, soon reached the capital of Prince Sobur. The young Sannyasi went up to the gate of the palace, and sent word to the king that he was acquainted with potent drugs and would cure the prince in a few hours. The king, who had tried all the best doctors in the kingdom without success, looked upon the Sannyasi as a mere pretender, but on the advice of his councillors agreed to give him a trial. The Sannyasi ordered seven jars of water and seven jars of milk to be brought to him. He poured the contents of all the jars on the body of the prince. He then applied, by means of a feather, the dung-powder he had already prepared to every pore of the prince's body. Thereafter seven jars of water and seven jars of milk were again six times poured upon him. When the prince's body was wiped, he felt perfectly well. The king ordered that the richest treasures he had should be presented to the wonderful doctor, but the Sannyasi refused to take any. He only wanted a ring from the prince's finger to preserve as a memorial. The ring was readily given him. The merchant's daughter hastened to the sea-shore where the Bihangama was awaiting her. In a moment they reached the tree of the divine birds. Hence the young bride walked to her house on the skirts of the forest. The following day she shook the magical fan, and forthwith Prince Sobur appeared before her. When the lady showed him the ring, he learnt with infinite surprise that his own wife was the doctor that cured him. The prince took away his bride to his palace in his far-off kingdom, forgave his sisters-in-law, lived happily for scores of years, and was blessed with children, grand-children, and great-grand-children.

Thus my story endeth,
The Natiya-thorn withereth, &c.

# CHAPTER IX
## THE ORIGIN OF OPIUM[①]

Once on a time there lived on the banks of the holy Ganga a Rishi[②], who spent his days and nights in the performance of religious rites and in meditation upon God. From sunrise to sunset he sat on the river bank engaged in devotion, and at night he took shelter in a hut of palm-leaves which his own hand had raised in a bush hard by. There were no men and women for miles round. In the hut however, there was a mouse, which used to live upon the leavings of the Rishi's supper. As it was not in the nature of the sage to hurt any living thing, our mouse never ran away from him, but, on the contrary, went to him, touched his feet, and played with him. The Rishi, partly in kindness to the little brute, and partly to have someone by to talk to at times, gave the mouse the power of speech. One night the mouse, standing on its hind-legs and joining together its fore-legs reverently, said to the Rishi, "Holy sage, you

---

① This story is not my own. It was recited to me by a story-teller of the other sex who rejoices in the *nom de plume* "An Inmate of the Calcutta Lunatic Asylum."

② A holy sage.

have been so kind as to give me the power to speak like men. If it will not displease your reverence, I have one more boon to ask." "What is it?" said the Rishi. "What is it, little mousie? Say what you want." The mouse answered—"When your reverence goes in the day to the river side for devotion, a cat comes to the hut to catch me. And had it not been for fear of your reverence, the cat would have eaten me up long ago; and I fear it will eat me some day. My prayer is that I may be changed into a cat that I may prove a match for my foe." The Rishi became propitious to the mouse, and threw some holy water on its body, and it was at once changed into a cat.

Some nights after, the Rishi asked his pet, "Well, little puss, how do you like your present life?" "Not much, your reverence," answered the cat. "Why not?" demanded the sage. "Are you not strong enough to hold your own against all the cats in the world?" "Yes," rejoined the cat. "Your reverence has made me a strong cat, able to cope with all the cats in the world. But I do not now fear cats; I have got a new foe. Whenever your reverence goes to the river side, a pack of dogs comes to the hut, and sets up such a loud barking that I am frightened out of my life. If your reverence will not be displeased with me, I beg you to change me into a dog." The Rishi said, "Be turned into a dog," and the cat forthwith became a dog.

Some days passed, when one night the dog said thus to the Rishi: "I cannot thank your reverence enough for your kindness to me. I was but a poor mouse, and you not only gave me speech but turned me into a cat; and again you were kind enough to change me into a dog. As a dog, however, I suffer a great deal of trouble; I do not get enough food: my only food is the leavings of your supper, but that is not sufficient to fill the maw of such a large beast as you have made me. O how I envy those apes who jump about from tree to tree, and eat all sorts of delicious fruits! If your reverence will not get angry with me, I pray that I be changed into an ape." The kind-hearted sage readily granted his pet's wish, and the dog became an ape.

Our ape was at first wild with joy. He leaped from one tree to another, and sucked every luscious fruit he could find. But his joy was short-lived. Summer came on with its drought. As a monkey he found it hard to drink water out of a river or of a pool; and he saw the wild boars splashing in the water all the day long. He envied their lot, and exclaimed, "O how happy those boars are! All day their bodies are cooled and refreshed by water. I wish I were a boar." Accordingly at night he recounted to the Rishi the troubles of the life of an ape and the pleasures of that of a boar, and begged of him to change him into a boar. The sage, whose kindness knew no bounds, complied with his pet's request, and turned him into a wild boar. For two whole days our boar kept his body soaking wet, and on the third day, as he was splashing about in his favourite element, whom should he see but the king of the country riding on a richly caparisoned elephant. The king was out hunting, and it was only by a lucky chance that our boar escaped being bagged. He dwelt in his own mind on the dangers attending the life of a wild boar, and envied the lot of the stately elephant who was so fortunate as to carry about the king of the country on his back. He longed to be an elephant, and at night besought the Rishi to make him one.

Our elephant was roaming about in the wilderness, when he saw the king out hunting. The elephant went towards the king's suite with the view of being caught. The king, seeing the elephant at a distance, admired it on account of its beauty, and gave orders that it should be caught and tamed. Our elephant was easily caught, and taken into the royal stables, and was soon tamed. It so chanced that the queen expressed a wish to bathe in the waters of the holy Ganga. The king, who wished to accompany his royal consort, ordered that the newly-caught elephant should be brought to him. The king and queen mounted on his back. One would suppose that the elephant had now got his wishes, as the king had mounted on his back. But no. There was a fly in the ointment. The elephant, which looked upon himself as a lordly beast, could not brook the idea that a woman, though a queen, should ride on his back. He thought himself degraded. He jumped up so violently that both the king and queen fell to the ground. The king carefully picked up the queen, took her in his arms, asked her whether she had been much hurt, wiped off the dust from her clothes with his handkerchief, and tenderly kissed her a hundred times. Our elephant, after witnessing the king's caresses, scampered off to the woods as fast as his legs could carry him. As he ran he thought within himself thus: "After all, I see that a queen is the happiest of all creatures. Of what infinite regard is she the object! The king lifted her up, took her in his arms, made many tender inquiries, wiped off the dust from her clothes with his own royal hands, and kissed her a hundred times! O the happiness of being a queen! I must tell the Rishi to make me a queen!" So saying the elephant, after traversing the woods, went at sunset to the Rishi's hut, and fell prostrate on the ground at the feet of the holy sage. The Rishi said, "Well, what's the news? Why have you left the king's stud?" "What shall I say to your reverence? You have been very kind to me; you have granted every wish of mine. I have one more boon to ask, and it will be the last. By becoming an elephant I have got only my bulk increased, but not my happiness. I see that of all creatures a queen is the happiest in the world. Do, holy father, make me a queen." "Silly child," answered the Rishi, "how can I make you a queen? Where can I get a kingdom for you, and a royal husband to boot? All I can do is to change you into an exquisitely beautiful girl, possessed of charms to captivate the heart of a prince, if ever the gods grant you an interview with some great prince!" Our elephant agreed to the change; and in a moment the sagacious beast was transformed into a beautiful young lady, to whom the holy sage gave the name of Postomani, or the poppy-seed lady.

Postomani lived in the Rishi's hut, and spent her time in tending the flowers and watering the plants. One day, as she was sitting at the door of the hut during the Rishi's absence, she saw a man dressed in a very rich garb come towards the cottage. She stood up and asked the stranger who he was, and what he had come there for. The stranger answered that he had come a-hunting in those parts, that he had been chasing in vain a deer, that he felt thirsty, and that he came to the hut of the hermit for refreshment.

*Postomani.*—"Stranger, look upon this cot as your own house. I'll do everything I can to make you comfortable; I am only sorry we are too poor suitably to entertain a man of your rank, for if I mistake not you are the king of this country."

The king smiled. Postomani then brought out a water-pot, and made as if she would wash the feet of her royal guest with her own hands, when the king said, "Holy maid, do not touch my feet, for I am only a Kshatriya, and you are the daughter of a holy sage."

*Postomani.*—"Noble sir, I am not the daughter of the Rishi, neither am I a Brahmani girl; so there can be no harm in my touching your feet. Besides, you are my guest, and I am bound to wash your feet."

*King.*—"Forgive my impertinence. What caste do you belong to?"

*Postomani.*—"I have heard from the sage that my parents were Kshatriyas."

*King.*—"May I ask you whether your father was a king, for your uncommon beauty and your stately demeanour show that you are a born princess."

Postomani, without answering the question, went inside the hut, brought out a tray of the most delicious fruits, and set it before the king. The king, however, would not touch the fruits till the maid had answered his questions. When pressed hard Postomani gave the following answer: "The holy sage says that my father was a king. Having been overcome in battle, he, along with my mother, fled into the woods. My poor father was eaten up by a tiger, and my mother at that time was brought to bed of me, and she closed her eyes as I opened mine. Strange to say, there was a bee-hive on the tree at the foot of which I lay; drops of honey fell into my mouth and kept alive the spark of life till the kind Rishi found me and brought me into his hut. This is the simple story of the wretched girl who now stands before the king."

*King.*—"Call not yourself wretched. You are the loveliest and most beautiful of women. You would adorn the palace of the mightiest sovereign."

The upshot was, that the king made love to the girl and they were joined in marriage by the Rishi. Postomani was treated as the favourite queen, and the former queen was in disgrace. Postomani's happiness, however, was short-lived. One day as she was standing by a well, she became giddy, fell into the water, and died. The Rishi then appeared before the king and said: "O king, grieve not over the past. What is fixed by fate must come to pass. The queen, who has just been drowned, was not of royal blood. She was born a rat; I then changed her successively, according to her own wish, into a cat, a dog, a boar, an elephant, and a beautiful girl. Now that she is gone, do you again take into favour your former queen. As for my reputed daughter, through the favour of the gods I'll make her name immortal. Let her body remain in the well; fill the well up with earth. Out of her flesh and bones will grow a tree which shall be called after her Posto, that is, the Poppy tree. From this tree will be obtained a drug called opium, which will be celebrated as a powerful medicine through all ages, and which will always be either swallowed or smoked as a wonderful narcotic to the end of time. The opium swallower or smoker will have one quality of each of the animals to which Postomani was transformed. He will be mischievous like a rat, fond of milk like a cat, quarrelsome like a dog, filthy like an ape, savage like a boar, and high-tempered like a queen."

Thus my story endeth,
The Natiya-thorn withereth, &c.